THE HOUSE OF

THE MADNESS

S.B. DE'VILE

S.B. De'Vile

The House of Death The Madness is a work of fiction. Names, characters and incidents are the product of the author's imagination or are used fictitiously. Any resemblance to actual persons, living or dead is entirely coincidental.

Paperback ISBN: 979-8-9887905-0-1

Ebook ISBN: 979-8-9887905-1-8

Book design by Shae Whitmore "Stala Designs" @stala.designs

To everyone who believed in me and in this story.

CONTENT WARNING

This story you're about to read contains adult themes and triggering content that might be troubling to some readers including, but not limited to, graphic or explicit violence, flashbacks to sexual violence and kidnapping, cannibalism, murder and gore. This series will feature relationships that are toxic. As the author, I personally recommend that the reader should be over 18 years old and not susceptible to triggering content. Reader discretion is advised

THE HOUSE OF DEATH

THE MADNESS

S.B. DE'VILE

LORCAN

1

Something is in there.

Something is *supposed* to be in there; a decaying mold of what once was a host to a soul. In other words, a body. The meaning of a graveyard implies for death to be inside of that grave, but as I inhale there's this illustrious vibrancy in the warm air that my tastebuds recognize immediately.

Life.

Death surrounds me here, as it very well should in a cemetery. To hear life is a conundrum considering where my feet are planted at this precise moment. The graves are supposed to be houses for the dead. However, the headstones are marked for the living, not the corpses under the earth. It can be argued that they're labeled for the deceased except why would they care? The dead do not need to keep a census.

All of this grandeur is for the sake of those still living to have a tangible place for mourning. For whatever reason, the living feel more connected to their departed ones when they have a place of symbolism.

These tombs, that are filled with bone and ash, do not grieve the loss of what once was. Life dwells here, walking amongst these headstones, ultimately to mourn the loss of another. They do not stick around for long. Often, they stop in for a moment to remember and pay respects. After that, they're gone for weeks and sometimes even months or years. Nothing dwells here in the graveyard, apart from the remains of a life once lived.

Despite it almost being spring, it is relatively warm in the city of New Orleans. That's nothing new for southern Louisiana. Still, I wear one of my finest suits, since the weather doesn't entirely have the same effect on me as it would on a mortal. I press my ear to the mausoleum wall. The coolness of the marble feels like a mirror of my face, cold and firm. Unbreakable. Beyond the layer of the wall, there is a soft thumping sound that no ordinary creature would normally be able to hear. It is faint and only apparent if you are looking for it, that is, if you know *what* to look for.

I am intimately familiar with the sound, but it does not belong here in the land of the deceased. A heart's steady, rhythmic beat sings its way to my ear drum, caressing it seductively. As a vampire lurking on the streets of New Orleans, I know just what to listen for.

Apart from myself, and the lull of an ominous heartbeat belonging to a creature unknown, there are a few other hearts thumping along to their own rhythm. A few rows over, a couple of tourists are paying a visit to the resting place of a beloved local author. Their hushed voices are crystal clear to my own ears as they speak of her wonderful work and the way she inspired them when she was alive.

A strange energy radiates from within the tomb. The warmth of it is much like the body heat similar to the living humans in this cemetery. There's a tangible taste to the air when the deceased are among it and inside this tomb is quite the opposite.. Whatever is residing in there is not dead by any means. If a creature like myself was placed in a grave, it would make more sense. I'm living but I'm not alive. Vampires are walking enigmas.

This particular mausoleum is unlike the others in the graveyard. It isn't unusual for a tomb to go unmarked, still a structure of this grandeur not bearing a name is… suspicious. It's such a simple structure compared to most of the other tombs. In New Orleans, many of the graves are raised above the ground due to the rising flood waters and the city being extremely under sea level.

No one else has paid any mind to it, and that also doesn't sit right with me. The mortals who walk by don't even seem to pay any attention to this one, as if it repels any ordinary living thing. I am no ordinary living thing. It must be warded by powerful magic. If that is the case, it only makes this puzzle even more curious. There should not be anything alive in this tomb, so why is there something inside it with a beating heart? What secrets does this grave have to harbor? What's the reason this creature is being kept from the world? My cold, dead heart would've flipped at the thought of another monster like myself in there *if* my heart would have been beating in the first place.

Someone is in there.

Life is in there.

My name is Lorcan Mortem. As a vampire prowling on the streets of New Orleans for many years, I'm not surprised by anything that happens here in this city. The unexpected is what's to be expected at every corner, yet this is something surprising indeed.

Up my sleeve is my infamous knife that has ended its fair share of lives. I unearth it to tap its tip against the marble stone. With my lips just a whisper from the tomb's walls, I ask, "Can you hear me?"

There's no verbal reply from whatever it is. The slight increase in the tempo of its heartbeat tells me that it definitely hears me. The corners of my cracked, blood-stained lips lift upward slowly to reveal razor sharp fangs. I came here tonight, just as a simple shortcut to the city nightlife for my next meal. However, this little puzzle caught my attention and grasped it firmly.

And I am going to be the one to solve it.

"You have to get closer, Lorcan. I can't see it."

On my iPhone screen, Wisteria squints and pushes her glasses up the bridge of her nose. The *it* she is referring to is the mausoleum I recently stumbled upon. It's harboring something that someone does not want out in this world.

Naturally, my curiosity got the better of me. After many failed attempts at trying to pry open the door, I realize that it is not sealed by any mortal. A strong ward was placed by a powerful witch or something of the sort to keep anyone from opening it.

"A powerful creature locked up whatever is in there," Wisteria says. A friend of many years, Wisteria De'Vile is one of the few people I trust. Being a witch herself is the main reason I called upon her first. Surely she could help me on this little quest.

"Well, I certainly can't open it," I reply, "and you know damn well I am not weak." No vampire is fragile.

My eyes scan over the marble wall's gray surface, studying for the hundredth time for something I might've missed previously. There's nothing. Hours have already been poured into this, that I will not let go to waste.

"Why do you want to bother with it?" she sighs. "Whatever is in there was placed there on purpose, so no one would disturb it, Lorcan. It's probably best to leave it be."

My hand holding the phone falls to my side. I'm hardly paying attention any longer. "Can't you hear it?"

In response to my question, Wisteria's voice silences as she probably tries to listen for herself. "No, Lorcan. I don't hear anything," she says softly from the phone's speaker.

Of course, she can't hear it for many reasons, apart from the phone not being close enough. Often what I *hear* is simply in my mind. No one else can detect or understand those voices. What I hear *now* is far too alive to just be in my head.

"Something in there needs me to get it out." Whatever it is, I hear a challenge. And I do so love a good challenge.

"Lorcan." My name momentarily brings me back to her.

"I'm in Egypt. I can't just drop what I'm doing to free some possibly dangerous monster. Surely, it's locked up for a reason. This could be insanely reckless." That's never stopped her before.

The witch is, of course, more than likely correct, though admitting that I'm wrong is not easy for me to do. If I work on other projects this one will creep up to break my focus. Once my mind is set on something, pulling away to focus on anything else is a damn near impossible task to achieve.

"I was locked up as well, for some time, if you jog your memory,"

I remind her. A long time ago in my human years, I was locked in one of the first asylums ever created. "It took the help of someone just as sinister as myself to get me out of there." That also could be warranted as reckless too.

The memory of my stay in the insane asylum rushes in, as if it only happened yesterday. It was Barcelona, in the year 1677. The darkness was thick and dense like fog. I barely made out the small pebbles on the dirt ridden floor. They left no candle lit for me. I assume it was the fear of me possibly knocking it over and burning the whole place to the ground, including them. I could still see the stones on the floor, though barely. At the time, I was only a human with simple human abilities. Supernatural hearing was not needed there; the walls of the room they placed me in were thin. I heard every word coming from the next, no matter how soft they whispered.

"Doctor, we need to purge her."

Somehow, however, they managed to create the walls strong enough to keep me inside. My arms were bound inside a white cloth or a jacket of some sort. Four hundred and seven hours. I was in that room for almost seventeen days. Dust, blood, and dirt coated the floors and, with no protection on my feet, I was covered in the filth as well. There was no reason to clean the place. The people in the institution were not worthy of such an act. Besides, many didn't live through the treatments anyway.

"Find the instruments."

The only other object they'd left in the little room, besides myself and the filth, was a cross that hung above the door. They tried to keep the demons out as best they could. It was a pity they didn't realize it was they who were the demonic ones.

Counting the filthy little pebbles on the floor was the only reprieve

I had. It became an obsession, muffling the screams of other patients who were receiving the treatments. The sound of wood creaking would usually signify if the person was conscious or not. Silence could also mean death. My nose was constantly filled with the scent of burning flesh. It was their way to keep track of the treatments, they marked each one of us accordingly. I suppose it was to see how many tries it would take to make us normal. There'd been no interaction between myself and the other patients there. I would think they did not want us to conspire against them. Smart.

When the door to my room opened, the doctor walked in. He wore a mask out of fear he would catch my insanity. I remember in his hands a large, rusting needle and a hot poker. If one wasn't deranged when they arrived, surely they would be by the time the treatments were over.

The vampire who changed me came there looking for food. It was an easy meal, we were all on the brink of death anyway and none could fight back. Except, for whatever reason, my case was different. The vampire who took my humanity did not stick around after the fact. He left me hungry and desolate in that asylum, though I wasn't starved for long. No one was alive by the time I escaped.

Pulling myself from the memory, I slide my free hand over the marble as the soft beating of its heart increases. It knows I'm out here. It can hear me. *Never fear… I'm coming for you.*

"Whatever is waiting in the tomb," Wisteria says, breaking the silent communication between myself and the tomb, "probably has been there a awfully long time. It can wait another week until I return."

The amount of patience I have depends on the situation. I could stalk a victim for weeks, months even, just to play with my food. With this, I feel an urgency like no other.

"It cannot wait, Wisteria."

My patience is far too thin. I do hate pestering, but there is another person who I need to ask for help now. After hanging up the call with Wisteria, I dial the one creature that can do anything with a simple snap of her finger.

"Hello, Mistress Divine."

ERASMUS

2

er er noget derude.

Something is out there. Perhaps not something, however some*one*. It is not common for wanderers to remain in the cemetery. For the fifth time in a row, he returns. I can not tell if it's a different day or not. Judging by the span of silence between his rummaging around, I believe it's safe to say at least a day passed between each of his visits.

I hear the same dark, sinister voice through the thick marble and stone. It's been so quiet apart from the visitors of other tombs. The man became a familiarity to me, a constant in this ever changing world.

Initially, I would try to get the outsiders' attention and quickly found they could not hear me. For whatever reason, this man does. I do not know why nor do I care. That's a problem to figure out later.

This man always comes by unattended. Tonight's visit, he has someone else with him. They speak cheerfully to one another, as old friends might. Together, they laugh in unison at something the male spoke, in the same charismatic tone always has. Often, he would come here and speak to me through the wall of this grave, and also to himself. He talks to himself a great deal while trying to formulate many ways to get in my tomb. I wonder briefly if this is his wife accompanying him.

"Divine," the man begins with a shock, "I hear your heartbeat, the creature in the tomb, and there's an undeniably light, soft one amongst us."

There is silence between the two and then I hear the smile in his voice when he asks, "Are you pregnant?"

Unless she answers it without speaking, she seemingly ignores the question and instead dodges it with a question of her own. "Tell me, Lorcan, what reason have you lured me out into this garden of bones?" The woman's voice is much more feminine, though no less powerful than his. A witch, perhaps? She's more than that. I can hear the crackling of ethereal magic just in her presence alone.

Lorcan and Divine they call each other.

"You hear it," Lorcan sings out the words to her. It does not really answer the question she asked at all. "It's in there for a reason, Divine. Someone does not want this monster unleashed."

Oh, how right you are.

"But I do," Lorcan continues. "I am so curious about what's inside. It's kept me up the last few nights. I can't concentrate on anything else."

What type of man is this? Why is he even bothering with me if he suspects that I'm a monster?

"I do have to admit," Lorcan begins, "I did call Wisteria for help first. Oh, don't look at me like that, I hate to bother you with my trivial little games."

"Your games are never trivial, Lorcan. If you don't understand by now that I'd do anything for you, then you're clearly more insane than I thought." Her words are stern, still they have an air of play in them. This conversation going on between the two carries on for a while and the voices shift as they walk around my prison.

"Well," he says curtly, "luckily for you, she was busy in Egypt. She's always there lately, though I'm not entirely positive what she's chasing this time."

"Wisteria is a studious witch," Divine replies carelessly. I can tell her attention is elsewhere—scrutinizing the walls of my tomb no doubt. The word witch has me frozen. Those creatures I do not trust at all. Then again, I don't trust anyone.

"He's been in there a long time," Divine says, and I instantly become rigid. She distinctively said *he*. How does she know this when my regular visitor does not? This tomb has been warded against all others. Have these two somehow broken that spell?

What the fuck *are* they?

Silence permeates the air to the point I think they vanished. There's no sound to indicate they walked away. There are no sounds to prove they are even *breathing*. After being here for so long, I've become quite attuned to listening to the outside world. What else is there to do?

The tomb I reside in is big enough for me to stretch out, even sit up, but I'm not able to stand to my full height. The witch that sealed me here made certain I would not be comfortable for the rest of my existence or the end of the world, whichever comes first. Seeing as I am immortal, it'll be the latter. There is nothing here except myself and darkness. At first the pitch black was the maddening part of it, then it was the isolation. In the beginning, I spent the majority of my time trying to escape. It was foolish to attempt. The witch made absolutely certain there is no way out. Over time, it became much easier to adapt to this solitude when I learned how to strengthen my hearing to listen as the world changed outside. I kept myself entertained the best way I could, with memories and plots of revenge, even though I knew the situation was hopeless.

Just then, the walls that encase me begin to shiver. It soon turns into full shaking within seconds. The magic sealing these marble walls are no match whatever force is at work. Executed perfectly, the walls separate from each other to hover above the ground and break apart at the corners.

When I do not move from my spot, the woman closes her palms into a fist, and the hovering walls crumble to dust in a blink. With her hands still raised, she lowers one in a silent invitation to me. I'm watching her cautiously. Devoid of any and all emotion, I share nothing to let them on to what I'm thinking. Trust only happens when I understand their intentions. Nevertheless, I slip my larger hand into her much smaller one and come to stand before her. The heel of my barefoot touches the soft earth and slowly lowers until my toes are secure to the ground, making sure I am positively free. The grass feels faint and unfamiliar, considering I've been living in stone for an eternity.

Standing before me are my two saviors. Confidence radiates from the woman and with every reason for it. Deadly, voluptuous curves are framed with a white dress that fits like a second skin. Fire-red hair cascades down her back and shoulders.

Lorcan is tall and skinny, with a head full of dark black hair and matching charcoal eyes. I cannot tell the iris from the pupil. With his ghostly pale skin, it could easily be assumed he's the one who belongs in this tomb. The smile on his face, if that is what you'd call it, is sinister beyond comparison. That part is hard to look away from. His mouth thins and stretches so far upward it almost appears as if he has no lips at all. Fangs gleam in the soft moonlight, and the blood staining them gives warning of a predator. Though he says only two words next, the tone of his voice is nothing short of ominous.

"Welcome home."

What you see isn't always what you get. I have meticulously constructed this illusion of myself as a well mannered, moral being. This man, this Lorcan, as he calls himself, has somehow seen right through my visage. It is highly impressive, considering he has never set eyes upon me before today.

Lorcan has not stopped talking since Justice gave me my freedom. What a fitting name for someone to provide me with the fairness of liberty. Depending on who you ask, I do not rightfully deserve it.

"What is your name?" Lorcan asks through a broad, manic smile.

"Erasmus Rasmussen."

After all these years, I did not think it possible I would ever see the outside world again. I have already made peace with it, yet here I am, feeling the lush grass beneath my feet. It has been far too many years. The scenery has changed drastically. There were only a few tombs in this cemetery and those are now hidden amongst endless rows of headstones. The city itself has been modified dramatically. More houses and less trees. It's truly a sight to behold.

After assessing I am indeed a person, not an illusion, Lorcan begs Justice to bring us to his house and she somehow transports us through space and time to a grand mansion. The sensation is overwhelming and my stomach heaves despite not having anything in it.

"This is where I'll leave you, Lorcan," she says to the rambling man, before turning to me. I am too overcome with the understanding that I'm out of the confines of those walls to pay attention fully. "I'll be seeing you again," she says, and disappears, leaving me alone with him.

We stare at one another for a long while. I am sure his mind is filled with questions, yet none are being asked. He is smiling, still, like he's been since I first saw him.

"This is my home." Lorcan gestures around. I do not bother to look. "You'll be staying here with me." He says it as a command, not a question as to if I want to stay here with him. Where else would I go anyway?

He gapes up at me, the lights in the room reflect off the darkness of his eyes like glass. "It is truly an honor to meet a like-minded person."

My head cants to the side at his comment, mimicking the curiosity of a mortal. "How are you so sure that we are?"

I thought his smile couldn't get any wider, he proves me wrong. It stretches further, like a grotesque parody of joy, revealing stained teeth with residue of last night's victims. His lips split like an overripe fruit, exposing a dark, abyssal void within.

"One monster always senses the presence of another," he answers softly. "Come." He motions for me to follow him down a massive hallway and, out of curiosity, I do.

Lorcan opens the door to a room and I feel like my eyes are play-ing tricks on me. The bed slides into place, the curtains magically pull themselves up to the window, and the walls adjust to a new length to create a fireplace that wasn't there a moment earlier. All of this should shock me. On the other hand, seeing as a witch previously imprisoned me, nothing surprises me anymore.

"Your room is here." Lorcan gestures around. "The washroom is right through the door. The house has taken the liberty to light the fireplace for you. Alert me if you need anything or can't figure out this decade's new gadgets."

In the light of the fire, I register the sharpness of his teeth again. Those fangs could tear skin right off the bone if they want to and the dried blood staining them collude my thoughts about how it got there to begin with.

He's a *vampyr*.

The legend of this creature goes back many centuries in history. It is understood their main food source is blood which is pulled from the vein by piercing flesh with its sharp teeth. Stories were told about the lure of their appearances too. It is said most vampires are beautiful to look at. While this man is surely a sight to behold, he is also tremendously strange looking indeed. Vampires are supposed to be pale and he is remarkably so. They're storied to have chiseled features and, while his fall precisely in that description, there is something more disturbing about him. The attraction to the vampire is their predominant temptation. Lorcan is quite the opposite. Nothing apart from danger rolls off of him. One would think this repels the humans away from him.

As Lorcan walks off, I slip into the room and close the door. No sense locking it; he can easily peel the wall apart if he truly wants to get in here. At this moment, I need to plan how to peel the skin off of *him*. Ja, he may have just saved me from an eternity in the tomb but I've been bored and itching for something wicked.

"Godnat, Lorcan. Behagelige drømme." I know my own dreams will be anything but pleasant, if I sleep at all.

LORCAN

3

There's someone else in the house.

I left Audelia here some time ago, explaining there was business for me to attend. She understands by now it does no good to ask why or where I go. I rarely give answers. I do often leave her alone in the house. She calls it 'a museum of historical artifacts'. There is an unspoken trust that will not make a complete mess of my things, however she's still learning what makes me tick. I'm thankful she never leaves a soda can on the coffee table without a coaster. It's been said I'm obsessive and compulsive with my home and I must agree, I do hold it highly. This house is not *just* a house, it is a living and breathing entity that allows me to call it my own. In taking care of the house, it rewards me by taking care of me in return.

I found Audelia in the middle of Bourbon Street one night, her teeth were gnawing away at the shoulder of a tourist. I guessed she was in her early twenties or so. The poor thing was running around with no clue who she was or how she even got there. All she could remember was feeling this overbearing hunger to eat but not your typical food... she wanted blood. She had no recollection of the transformation from human to vampire. She didn't even remember her name. We just decided later on to give her a new one.

People were screaming when they saw her. Who wouldn't? A deranged looking girl, barefoot, in tattered clothing, chewing the skin off of another person. I felt a strong urge to intervene, so I clapped my hands and yelled, "What a show!"

They were fooled into thinking it was just a part of the allure of New Orleans. It's always been a city full of legends, of vampires and other creatures, so why not allow them to think it was another tourist attraction?

"New Orleans is full of the unordinary and supernatural," I told the 'audience.' "What else will you find tonight?" They were in awe of how realistic her act was. Audelia almost hadn't come with me, until she understood I was just like her: a vampire. I could help her; teach her the ways and keep her safe from the humans—as well as the many other monsters out there.

After Audelia decided it was me or the world, I scooped up her little dinner and carried the corpse happily with us. It was eleven months ago and she has come a long way from the lost girl I found in the streets. My darling girl is still immensely afraid in general. A single, gentle poke can unleash a force capable of shattering the thickest stone, if she isn't cautious, especially when handling one of my prized sculptures. Her senses are still fairly fresh and new. She'll ask about the music blaring a few streets down. Of course, to her it sounds like it's coming from right within the house.

"Is someone else here?" she asks.

The soft thumping of Erasmus' heartbeat gave it away that upstairs we have a guest. Typically, there is only one other person who lives here: Clouden. He is currently still a human and my prodigy. This heart beat is different from his. This one is much more steady and consistent. It's soft whereas Clouden's is often erratic pulses, in return it makes Audelia go into a blood lust.

When I don't answer right away, curiosity gets the best of her and she goes in search of the newcomer. Even though they're upstairs, I don't need to move from my chair to hear their conversation perfectly.

"It's rude to sneak up on people." Erasmus' tone is serious with her.

There is silence between them and I imagine the two are having a staring contest. Audelia is headstrong, and she will not give in easily. I'm eager to hear how this conversation is going to go.

"It's rude to be unannounced in someone's home," Audelia replies finally.

"Your home?" Erasmus asks. "I thought this is my home now."

More silence stretches before I hear Audelia speak again. "I suppose we'll have to share it. What's your name?"

"Erasmus."

He doesn't ask for hers. She gives it anyway. "Lorcan calls me Audelia."

"Godaften, Audelia. It's a pleasure to meet you." The tone of his voice does not sound like he is highly pleased to meet her at all. I take note as well that he mixed English with another language. Is it Swedish? Norwegian? No. Possibly Danish. Just how did this Dane arrive in the United States and come to be imprisoned in a tomb?

"You're not human," she says. Good girl. Audelia is not rushing in to tear at his neck, like she did when I introduced her to Clouden. Erasmus is *not* human though, obviously living as long as he did without food or water. What is he then? More answers I'll have to find out.

"Nej, I should hope not," he says to her. "But neither are you."

The smile on her lips is heard in her words. "No, I should hope not."

Shuffling of feet indicated they went their separate ways. I wanted to introduce them to one another myself, though this turned out just fine. They both are aware of each other and now it's only Clouden I need Erasmus to meet at some point... as soon as the boy arrives back from his latest task.

The obnoxious sound of my cell phone alerting me to an incoming call pulls me from my thoughts. Surprisingly, it's Blaze, my adopted son, who is currently touring England with his friends. I quickly fill him in on the current events.

"For someone who doesn't trust others easily, you sure are opening your home to many strangers," Blaze says.

Just because I bring them home does not mean I trust them thoroughly. I refrain from telling him this little part, though.

Blaze doesn't live here any longer. He decided to leave the nest and make the rest of the world his home. After his departure, I began to feel very lonely here in this house. He already knew of Clouden before he left and I suppose he assumed it would stay just the two of us. I found Audelia on a whim and now Erasmus. That brings my housemates to only three.

"They are monsters, Blaze. They're homeless and they need my help."

Truth be told, I felt empty nest syndrome tremendously. Many years ago, I kidnapped the little vampire, Blaze. I have a daughter as well, Blair. She is not living here anymore. Prior to them, I relished in my loneliness. Though was I ever truly alone? The voices in my head who counsel me have always been here with me and this house is a creature of its own kind. I loved being by myself, however, as the year progressed it became quite dull to have no one to talk to on those lonely days. After Blaze left the house in search of his own adventures, I realized just how boring it was to be alone. I do love my own company, but there is something wonderful about having others around.

"That's right." I can hear my son's tone take a sarcastic turn. "Lorcan the Savior."

I am much more of the opposite, especially to the delicious humans I hunt almost nightly.

"The world needs more of us monsters, Blaze. We are a dying breed." I'm exaggerating a bit. I love to be dramatic.

"You do know all of this can and will go wrong, at some point, right?"

I roll my eyes. Blaze can't see me through the phone.

"And don't roll your eyes at me like that."

I've become far too predictable. "Ever optimistic, aren't we, son?"

His response is a soft laugh.

"Well, have fun in England, Blaze. I'll be here teaching our newest resident all about the new world."

"I wager he'll go insane in a week."

We end the call and I sit there for a moment longer. "Tsk," I say to no one, "it'll be longer than a week."

ERASMUS

4

She is suspicious of me.

Even though Audelia seemed to be welcoming at first, she doesn't trust me. I've caught her multiple times lurking in the shadows of this house watching my every move, when I'm not in the room Lorcan designated for me. The room is strange. I can not perceive how he caught the essence of me so well. Everything about the space feels like it was created precisely for me.

Outside of the room is a dilemma. As pleasant as this place is, it feels off. The windows I look out of feel like they're trapping me in. Yesterday, I tried to leave, but the front door wouldn't budge. I've gone from one prison to another. At least this one I can walk around and inspect.

Every step I take from the hallway, Audelia follows me. Whether

or not she realizes she's not hidden so well is the question. I don't
acknowledge her and let her believe her presence is concealed, all
the while I'm forming a plan. Lorcan released me from the tomb for
some reason and quickly stows me away here in this mansion. Just
as much as Audelia does not trust me, I do not trust Lorcan either.
I waited until Audelia left to initiate my little scheme. It's not going
as I thought.

During my time of isolation I mastered the art of being calm, and,
in doing so, I have mastered the art of being myself. When something like this has been conquered, it might be easy to think, *'Is there
anything else worth living for?'* Simply because something is conquered
does not mean there's no room for advancing elsewhere. I have to
master the mind of Lorcan. I may have thought to outwit him, to
beat him, and possibly kill him, except he has not survived this long
to be an easy target.

It's impossible. I give nothing away. Not breathing hard, my heartbeat remains a steady thumping, yet he still knows I am up to something. His voice is melodic and cool when the tip of my knife is just
a centimeter from his side.

"A knife? Are you flirting with me, Erasmus?"

He's caught me. When I lower my knife, I assume he thinks I've
given up. Once more, he knows better than that. This time I move
swiftly, swiping right across the back of his neck with my blade... or
so I think. He moves as if he is a beam of light; rapid and thorough.
The knife in my hand never even connects with his flesh.

"Are we playing a game?" The sound of Lorcan's voice is a completely different tone from a moment ago. Lorcan is illuminated like
the electricity I learned in this house; a switch on the wall can be
turned on to fill a room with light. My plot has given him enter-

tainment. He is vampyre and stronger than I thought. How this paper-thin-looking man holds all of this power in his tiny frame is not fathomable. It proves we can't judge anyone by the way they look.

The knife in my hand disappears before I can catch where it goes. The sharp pain in the front of my neck makes it obvious where it went. Lorcan stole it from me and is trying to attack me with it. Being whatever I am cursed to be, the wound heals almost right away. This doesn't seem to deter Lorcan in the slightest. He's already moving on to sawing the same knife into the bone of my shoulder and the pain is excruciating.

"Say when!" Lorcan's voice is rapid and far too thrilled.

When I say I'm immortal and heal rapidly it does not mean I do not feel the pain that goes along with injury. Oh, I feel every bit of it. In the way he cuts, it almost feels so deeply inside of me I become the very knife itself. You can't tell where the blade begins and I end.

He quickly changes course. The knife is not digging any longer. It's sliding gracefully as if cutting a slice of ham for a nice, delicious dinner after a long day. There is no breaking loose from his grasp. It doesn't do any good to even think of escaping it. He is already calculating your next move. Out of the corner of my eye, I see him slurping the layers of my skin he carved off of me. His lips move slowly and he's chewing carefully, as if to savor each bite. As my skin slowly reappears after the assault, Lorcan's laughter echoes through the room. It's a cold, mirthless sound that sends shivers down my spine.

"You," Lorcan says, "are the never-ending feast I was always meant to have!"

He angers me. For whatever reason he assumes I'm here just for his entertainment. "I'm not one of the children you can just adopt as your own!" I say to him finally. The hacking away at my flesh ceases in an instant. "Nor am I a pet you can leash."

"If you leave you'll have no one. Where will you go? This world isn't the same one you were in before." Lorcan's laughter through the words is almost comical. "You owe me a debt, Erasmus."

"Is it a debt or do you just wish to not be alone?" I heard his previous conversation with the tiny box in his hand. He spoke to it like it was alive. It even replied, calling itself Blaze.

"I am not alone. I collect monsters, Erasmus, and you are one of us. I can also have you put back in the tomb. Hm, but where is the fun in that?" Lorcan moves to shove the tip of the knife into my arm once more and I'm able to free myself from his grasp, or perhaps he lets me go. I can't be certain. This man's mind does not work in the same fashion as many. The chase, I am sure, is part of his play. He is far too overjoyed, rather than shocked, that I tried to kill him.

"Kræft æde mig." I force the old words out. May the power devour me. It's a term we use in Danish meaning the gods just need to take me and end it now.

"*English!*" he yells in return.

"So, you freed me," I say, "and now what? I will spend eternity in this house, *with you*?"

His smile is wide and fearless. "You make it sound like it's such a chore."

We stare at one another for what feels like hours. It doesn't matter though. Whatever I choose to do next, he is two paces ahead of me and gives me no indication that he is well aware of my next move.

"Are we going to continue this little game you started," he asks, "or did I win?"

The way he smiles is unlike anything I'd seen before in a person.

His lips become so narrow and he bares every single one of his teeth at me. The most frightening part of the whole thing is how much raw emotion is in that smile, but his eyes are completely devoid of anything. Whether he learned this, or was simply born this way, is a mystery to me.

After I walk off, Lorcan's laughter echoes hysterically behind me. He is conceited with the knowledge that he just triumphed in a game I didn't mean to set in motion. I head back to my room where I should plan the next scheme, only this time I will make certain to come more prepared. Now I have more of an idea of what I'm up against.

I am not alone for long. As if I haven't been annoyed enough at this moment, another man pokes his head in the door of my room.

"I heard noises," he says.

I say nothing in reply, hoping he will get the hint that talking is not of my interest right now.

He does not.

"Audelia mentioned there is another member added to this family." He's almost as tall as the door frame he's leaning easily on. There's something different setting him apart from the other two in this house. He's not a vampire. This one has a heartbeat similar to mine.

"I am not your family," I say.

"You will be," the man says, as if he is absolutely positive of what the future holds. "I'm Clouden."

He's not granted a reply from me. If Audelia told him about me, then she certainly would have told him my name and everything else.

"Oh, and careful" —he pauses to look around the walls as he adds— "the house, it's… well, let's just say it's different."

LORCAN

5

The shovel tip slams into the ground, disturbing the grassy earth and all of its tiny inhabitants below. In this yard, there's at least a few decades worth of evidence from my work. For the most part, there's never anything left to bury. I do tend to use as much of each and every piece of the victim. Sometimes, I like to be a bit theatrical and put a part of them in the ground. A few times, I even cultivated a little funeral of my own right here in the yard for them. It just depends on the scenario. Their death is like a broadway for me. Giving them the ending they deserve is just part of the act.

"New Orleans," I say to the unmoving air, "you are not supposed to be this humid!"

This hole could've been emptied a lot faster, if I just used all of my strength. I do like to slow it down a bit; savor the process. Plus it gives the neighbors something to talk about if they're peeking through the windows. It's not like they can do anything about their little speculations. I have the sheriff under my thumb and, apart from that, the house would protect me. If they came snooping in, the house would take action. It's alive in a sense. Once or twice, I'd forgotten where I buried a few parts, dug up the whole backyard only to find the house was being cheeky and consumed the remains. I'm still not sure why it did and I don't really question it.

When the circle becomes deep enough, I place the bag with the fingers and toes down into the dirt and stare longingly down at it. This one was a fairly easy kill. He didn't put up a fight, which typically makes me upset, but this man was someone I wanted to end quickly anyway. Stalking him was such a bore, he talked entirely too much and that laugh of his was horrendous. All full of screeching. With enhanced hearing, the shrill sound just sliced right into my eardrum. I didn't kill him because of his laugh though, not this one. He tended to poke at people for little to no reason; emotionally and physically. His wife was not happy and I witnessed more than once how he treated her at gala events and such. It was in private, when I began thoroughly stalking him, that I found he was much more deviant.

Most of my victims are rich snobs who aren't the most pleasant of people. Is 'victim' even the correct term? Most of them get what's coming to them after all. None of them are good little humans. I suppose I could say I'm karma in a way. Hm, there are times I kill periodically just for fun or to secure my means of life for the future. Before they're truly gone, I devise a scheme to have their funds sent to me somehow. I always have a cover up, buying them a plane ticket to South America or somewhere far from where they're from. No one bats an eye. The majority of the rich travel for leisure quite often anyway. It's fun to slip into their lives and pretend to be them for a moment, just to keep up their appearance for a bit. Then their private jet is nowhere to be found, or a bit of clothing belonging to them is spotted in the ocean where the sharks are ruthless. Poor little rich dearies. And then there's a nice fat check donated to one of the charities I created. No one suspects a thing. Though, depending on what the victim did, I always share my profits with a real charity they would despise.

As I begin covering the package with soil, my phone rings. Smiling at the name on the screen, I answer by singing a nice long, "Helllll-loooooooooo, darling Justice Divine."

There's only two people who ever call me and they are the lovely goddess, Justice Divine, and the wonderful witch, Wisteria De'Vile. Blaze did surprise me with a call instead of a text yesterday. It was a shock indeed.

"How's the new roommate?" she asks.

"Well, he tried to kill me." Cradling the phone between my cheek and shoulder, I smile out the next words. "Key word, *tried*"

Justice laughs. "Excuse me, tell the other Mister Deadly Psycho I'm the only one who can do that."

We both laugh in unison. There once was a time, when I first met the goddess, that I thought I could beat her at her own game. I was foolish in my younger years to ever assume such. I had no idea what I tried to put myself up against. After a long fight between us, resulting in buildings being demolished to mere dust, we became the greatest of friends. She is someone who is extremely dear to me and always will be. Over the years, I learned just how powerful she truly is. With just a flick of her wrist she took out substantial amounts of armies. An ancient goddess who walks this Earth to have her fill of any pleasures she desires. She doesn't often mingle in the affairs of mortals. It is their free will to do as they wish anyway, and she will only step in if one of her children, or myself, asks her to.

Her power isn't why I keep her friendship. Justice Divine is the only person to accept me fully as insane as I am. She makes no attempt to change me, instead relishes in the creature who is Lorcan Mortem. We share an affinity for the darkness and all that dwells in it.

"Yes, and I do hope you don't plan to off me any time soon, Divine." With one more shovel of dirt, the hole was back to being concealed, this time with a new treasure hidden beneath.

"Never." This one word seals it. It was already agreed that she won't ever kill me off. Even if she decides to end the entire world, she would take me and mine elsewhere before doing so.

"Good." I look up to the house where Erasmus' form stood in a window on the third floor watching me. "Well should you ever change your decision, just keep in mind there's still much for me to accomplish before I meet my end."

"The house of yours wouldn't allow you to go before your time," she says. "I'm shocked it didn't intervene when Erasmus tried to kill you."

I laugh heartily, so much my chest shakes. "I think the house knew I could take him, and that I probably need a little entertainment anyway."

I end the call with her shortly afterward and take my shoes off before trudging back inside. I'm particular about the cleanliness of my home. There is a specific standard I keep here. This house has been my companion for years and its reward for keeping me safe is that I respect it in all ways possible. Even if it means filling my house with strangers to also find comfort here.

Erasmus is standing on the stairs when I close the door behind me. "Are you finished with your ploy to kill me?" Before I even let him answer, I add, "It won't be an easy thing to achieve, if that is your goal. I haven't lived this long to die by the hands of just anyone."

Golden eyes stare back at me, though I cannot read the emotions swirling in them. They seem to hold a thousand secrets.

"Many have tried and all have failed." With the exception of Justice Divine. The day we fought and nearly desecrated a whole town, she did have me on the thread of death, however the goddess felt it's worth keeping me alive. "What makes you think that you will accomplish what others couldn't?"

"Jeg er mig," he replies quickly.

My response is an eye roll and placing my hands on my hips to show my obvious annoyance. Erasmus smirks. I can only imagine he thinks he has the upper hand here. I'm an old vampire but one thing I did not take the time to do is to learn all of the languages in the world. I stick to what I can comprehend: French and English.

"Vous savez que je ne peux pas comprendre cela. Vous l'avez fait exprès." I essentially tell him in French that I can't understand him. I say he deliberately made sure I could not comprehend what he was saying by speaking in his own language.

His expression is full of annoyance as well. "We speak in English so we can understand one another." I command.

He closes the space between us. He's almost a full head taller, and I have to lift my chin to look up at him.

"I am me," he says. "That is why I will win."

Half excited, I snarl up a smile at him. "If you think you've got what it takes, then be my guest."

Erasmus turns slowly to end this conversation. Before he is out of earshot I make sure to add, "Do make it entertaining at least. Honestly, being in that tomb for years, and all you could come up with was to sneak up on me with a knife? Tsk. Get creative, Erasmus."

The only reply from him is a low grunt.

"Come." I wave for him to follow me. "Until you can figure this out, let me prepare us all dinner. I can introduce you to my favorite dish. Tell me, Erasmus, have you ever tasted human meat before?"

For a moment he simply gawks at me just like anyone who was asked that question would.

I speak through a smile, "Don't knock it until you try it."

He follows me to the kitchen. I begin gathering the ingredients, including the bag of human substance from the fridge that I have marinating in a decadent honey sauce. Erasmus says nothing as he slips onto a stool at the island. He appears appalled yet curious at the same time.

"Can I make an assumption that before you were imprisoned you hunted for your food?" I ask. While I'm busying myself with the dinner preparations, Erasmus' gaze follows me flitting about the kitchen.

He nods.

I say, "I too am a hunter."

"I thought *vampyres* only drink blood." His accent grows thick around the word vampires, yet it also forms a hidden question.

"We only need blood as our sustenance but tell me… do you need food to live? No. I'm quite certain you'd devour it anyway. The taste of food is the desire." I begin to pan sear the meat in a nice olive oil coated pan. "Low heat," I tell him. "We cook this portion of the body slower to release the bold flavors."

It becomes nicely charred from the heat, so I pour in just a drizzle of what looks like wine to help scrape the bottom of the pan, where the seasoning browns nicely. Serving up the finished product on my finest dish, I slide it in front of him.

"I can assure you, your taste buds will thank me."

Erasmus hesitates but decides to give it a go after a tad bit of mulling it over. The fork slices through the slab of meat cleanly. When he places it in his mouth, I'm absolutely full of delight by the way his pupils dilate.

"Meget god," he says.

With my elbows resting on the counter and cheeks placed gently in my palms I watch him lick the plate clean. "What is that language? It sounds Scandinavian. Norwegian? I suspect Danish, perhaps?"

"Danish," he says, after also licking the fork.

"Ah, I thought so." I answer and take the dish from him to wash. "I'm glad you like it."

"Will there be more?"

My back is to him while I clean up and I smile so he doesn't see. "If you want it… Every day of your immortal life, Erasmus."

SEVEN

6

My brother is in there.

Clouden has been missing for some months. Almost a year, to be exact. The last I saw him, he said he was going for a run. That evening... he didn't come back. All of his things are still in his room, untouched. It's no secret my brother can't be without his laptop for long. It's been undisturbed, in its case, on his bed.

The police filed a missing persons report and unfortunately they haven't had any such luck in finding him. My parents think he's dead. I should probably come to accept this as a possibility but I just can't. My baby brother is not dead. There's no way.

So, I have taken the situation into my own hands. The police have not found any link to any kidnapping, and they resolve to believe he ran off on his own. *Men don't get kidnapped. Didn't you know?* False.

The media wants you to believe they don't. We can't see men as weak as they like to portray women. How preposterous. Sarcasm, by the way.

Clouden is not *very* adventurous. Maybe a bit more than I am, for me it's none. Clouden is level-headed. I do not believe he just decided one day to disappear and not come home. No. Something has happened.

My thoughts go to the worst of the worst. He's being held prisoner somewhere, being forced to eat his own shit for dinner. He's been bound and raped repeatedly. Someone is injecting him with poison or drugs for kicks, to see how long he lasts before his body caves.

Some might assume I have a wild imagination. The things mentioned are not things I just happened to make up out of thin air. For me, they were real and a nightmare I relive every time I close my eyes. I find it astonishing how my parents refuse to consider the likelihood of Clouden facing the same situation I once did.

My brother is not as weak as I am. He would have killed himself before he let any of it happen to him. I don't believe Clouden is dead. If he was indeed kidnapped, I plan to find him. Or at least find out what transpired. What I lived through will not happen to anyone else, if I have anything to say about it. Not that I am even anything to begin with.

Before I was abducted, I wasn't a courageous or adventurous person in any way. Having lived through such traumatic events, I have no interest in ever being courageous or adventurous at all. I remind myself this is my little brother. I have to push past any fear. I might have to save him, before it's too late. What's frightening is, after many weeks of research, I think I'm on to something. Typically, I would've turned off the computer, unplugged it, and thrown it in the trash if it was leading me to danger. Clouden missing has triggered something in me that has never been sparked before.

This overwhelming determination has consumed my mind. It's transformed into what I believe is an obsession. The thing is, I am aware this is taking over my life. Finding Clouden is giving me purpose, not just for saving him... but for saving me as well.

The sun is blistering as I stand on the sidewalk across the street from the large, white mansion on Canal Street. The modern style finish of this house doesn't fool me one bit. There's a strong, unpleasant impression I get from it. People appear to be going in and out all morning. What I find odd is the front door has not opened once since I've been here, and I've been here for three days.

In the windows of the house, lights go on and off, signaling someone is home. The newspaper was on the porch one second and gone in another. No one comes out to check the mailbox, unless, like the newspaper, it just disappears as well. The trash can is on the street and then vanishes in the blink of an eye, too. I have come to the conclusion whatever is in the house is not human. Everything in me says Clouden is in there and I'm about to find out.

ERASMUS

7

"Where is Clouden? I know he's here."

An unfamiliar voice bellows through the halls. There is a sudden commotion at the front door. At first, I paid no mind to the shouting and simply turned the page of my newspaper to finish reading the article on the latest homicide. The noise is becoming quite excessive, so I roll the paper up and go to witness the fuss. Whoever this man is raising his voice at Audelia is ignorant of what he has stepped into.

"You might wish to get your blood pressure checked," I say calmly as I stalk behind him to close the door. Since I arrived here a few months ago, Lorcan has taught me quite a great deal about human anatomy.

"What?" he seethes through gritted teeth. "Where's my brother? I'm here for Clouden!"

As I thought. The details of who he is would unfold easily through his anger. Similar features are there to signify his relation to Clouden, without a verbal contribution. He's older than Clouden, no doubt, or terribly unfortunate in the aging process.

"Jeg er imponeret," I say, sharing with Audelia that I'm impressed with her. Both her hands are clenched tightly into fists. She is resisting quite well in her blood lust. Impressive indeed. I shift my focus back to our guest to acknowledge him again. "Clouden is preoccupied at the moment."

"Who the hell are you people and why are you holding my little brother hostage." See? He's older. Even after all this time away from society I still remember how to read people. They tend to answer our questions, without us even asking them. All it takes is patience, and I have ample amounts of it.

Audelia snorts at the man's remark.

"Hostage?" I laugh. "We are doing nothing of the sort. Won't you come in and wait for him to come home?"

That last word sets him off. "*Home*?"

He is rambling, going off with questions and more shouting, threatening to call the police. I simply turn and walk towards the living room, where I sat moments before.

When the man does not get his way, he tries to unlock the door to leave. Of course, it doesn't work. The house locked itself. "You might as well come and have a seat. You won't be leaving any time soon."

At that, his face turns a startling shade of white. I gesture to the chair opposite me, while the situation slowly begins to wash over him. He comes over and sits.

"What is your name?" I ask. The male barely even looks at me. It's a pity, because *he* is very easy to look at. Wide blue eyes overwhelm his innocent face and on top of his head is a pile of short, dark curls. Sweat glistens on the surface of his skin. I wonder if it's a response to the cruel summer heat or perhaps we just make him utterly uncomfortable. From the way he avoids looking at any of us, I have to wonder if it's our presence making him uneasy or just society in general. My gaze flicks to his fingers. They're fidgeting nervously in his lap. There's an urge taking over me to clamp my teeth around his pinky and bite it off but, like Audelia, I refrain from making any sudden move.

He smells a little like Clouden. Deep inside, there's something different about him. There's a subtle yet unmistakable distinction setting him apart from his brother. It's as if the same notes of their shared fragrance have been rearranged. I can't quite put my finger on it, but it's there, a whisper of something new and unexplored. Everything about his demeanor intrigues me; the way he never quite lingers his gaze for more than a second on you...

"Seven," he finally answers.

My brow pops up. "How illustrious."

He rolls his eyes. "Our parents are quite eccentric."

This *Seven* still won't even glance my way, though I can taste his curiosity permeating the air. Unabashed, I stare at him.

"What do we have here?" Lorcan's melodic voice sings through the room, diluting the scent of the human in the house, as he steps in the living room with us.

"His name is Seven," I say. "Clouden's brother."

"Clouden's... brother?" Lorcan spaces apart the two words yet somehow mingles them together in the same sense. "I had no idea he had a brother!"

"Where is he?" Seven asks. His heart begins to race more after seeing Lorcan, and, when I glance up at the vampire, I can see why. He's damn near covered in crimson. When he's not prancing around the house, Lorcan can be found dragging a corpse through the hallway and down to his basement. He tells me often how this is one of the only houses in this city that has a basement. It floods easily with storms but this house is special. It's 'protected' and that's all he says about it.

"He'll be home soon." Lorcan reiterates the word *home* and I can vividly see Seven about to lose it again. I am getting quite desperate to see him snap again. "Would you like something to drink while you wait?"

Audelia pipes in. "I do!" She's been staring at our guest intently.

Seven's nostrils flare and Lorcan smiles out a response. "Now, now, Audelia, have some manners."

"I'm fine," Seven replies. "I just want to see my brother."

He thinks we killed him. It's obvious in the way he's acting and he thinks he's going to be next. He's trying to play it cool, hoping to get out of here, while he can. Seven will not be leaving. Not if I have anything to do with the fate of this little human.

"You're trembling," I say as I watch his leg bounce incessantly. A nervous tick, I assume. His heart rate is out of this world. Honestly, I am shocked he's still sitting upright. The amount of sweat draining from his pores is enough to fill a gallon, I'm sure. Oddly enough, I feel I would happily drink it up.

"I'm afraid," he admits to me, and I'm shocked he did it so easily. Full of surprises.

"Of what?" He's piqued my curiosity for sure.

Seven does not look at me while he talks. He has not held any of our eye contact longer than a simple second. A clear sign that he is seriously lacking confidence. Why? What makes him so unlike Clouden?

"Everything," he answers, and it's so soft and defeated that it makes my heart ache.

I'm ready to hear more from this man. We're interrupted before I can continue. As if we conjured his brother out of our minds, the front door opens and Clouden comes in. He stops short when his gaze lands on Seven.

"Seven? What are you doing here?" Clouden's eyes widen as he glances quickly from each of us back to his brother. He probably assumes we brought the man here to play with him. It would be easy enough to dangle him in front of Clouden before we kill him.

"I came to bring you home! I've looked everywhere for you! The police looked everywhere for you! Everyone thinks you're—" Seven is standing, staring slightly up at his brother, jaw locked as he did not finish the sentence. "Why won't you come home?"

"I am home," Clouden says.

Oh, this is the best drama I've heard in decades. "Clouden. You look... Why do you look different?" Seven glances back at Lorcan and the rest of us, then Clouden again as he puts two and two together. "You're one of them, aren't you?"

The truth that vampires exist doesn't seem to bother Seven in the least. He's more angry than anything. The majority of the people in this city are well aware of the types of creatures that are running around. After our little tiff, Lorcan and I slowly became acquaintances. He damn near gave me the entire history of this strange little city we live in called New Orleans. He was proud of it, to say the least. I have spent some time playing tourist with him. I am still not impressed.

"I am not," Clouden replies gently. "Yet."

"Nej! One of what?" I intervene. It doesn't matter truly as they ignore me for the moment. "I'm not a *vampyre.*" I'm still indeed one member of the household and part of the group of *them* Seven is talking about.

"Clouden… What the fuck?" It's all Seven manages to say.

"They're my family, Seven. They're—

Seven interrupts him with a shout. "You have a family! And you left us for these—"

He almost said *monsters*. I can see the word begging to release from his tongue and here I am imagining that same tongue on my dinner plate. For whatever reason this man has me instantly craving for him. Maybe the reason behind it is how Lorcan only cooks up humans for dinner. It could play a part in my sudden hunger. I do not need to eat to sustain my life but, after that first taste of the food Lorcan cooked, I am hooked. The flavor of his dishes are like nothing I've ever tasted before. Saliva is damn near pooling in the corners of my mouth, while the desire to taste him builds it up. I want Seven Wilbrate on the table for me to feast on.

Lorcan's hand is immediately on Seven's shoulder and the male's jaw locks. "Why don't you stay for dinner? Get acquainted with us a little more."

"I can't," Seven says as he shakes Lorcan's hand from his shoulder. "I have to…"

"I already told you." My voice drops to a menacing whisper. "You're not leaving any time soon."

All of them look my way. We haven't killed every single person to stumble upon this lair of ours. Maybe they think I do wish to kill Seven. Perhaps I will. First, I'm going to enjoy chewing each morsel of him. All of us, apart from the new human here, understands how the house works. If it doesn't allow you to leave, you don't. Seven can turn the knob until his fingers blister, until the skin cracks and blood seeps out. He will never be free unless the house itself allows him to go. I can bet it won't.

LORCAN

8

After the whole charade between the two brothers, Seven tried to leave and the doors wouldn't budge. He kept yelling at us, screaming we're tricking him. Clouden managed to calm the raging lunatic, and he led his brother to an empty room for the time being. Since the house won't allow him to leave, I suspect it's for a reason. I can hardly say why it does the things it does. Perhaps the other Wilbrate is just as much in need of us as Clouden is.

While everyone else is busy, I occupy myself with cooking up a delicious, savory souffle. Of course my recipe is a bit out of the ordinary. In place of your typical flour, I use finely ground bone. For the milk, it's substituted with chilled cerebrospinal fluid to make it creamier.

I'm in here cooking and without notice there's chaos. The madness in the house is currently from Audelia and Clouden arguing, about god only knows what this time. They bicker worse than children. Audelia, my darling girl, tends to be more needy than Clouden. Not in the sense she requires things constantly but she does seek out my attention more than he does. When I do accidentally seem to grace Clouden with my presence, just a little more than her, Audelia becomes restless. She then will poke at Clouden to rile him up on purpose. I can guess she thinks if she can get him angry enough, he will eventually leave.

This time, the war between them surrounds the new human who arrived: Seven. Clouden's brother who seemingly appeared out of thin air and is adamant on taking Clouden back home.

"Why don't you just go with him?" Audelia asks, loudly. She never is one to hold her temper. Clouden typically shields his irritability. He did not today.

"Because my place is here… with Lorcan."

With my name being said, I can read Audelia's expression perfectly. The jealousy rages inside of her, reaching her eyes all too quickly. If there is one thing I have tried to instill in them, it's to not be quick to allow others to see your emotions. They can easily be used against you. These two, separately, seem to do that well, but when butting heads against one another, all my teaching goes out the window.

"You have a family," Audelia says angrily. "They care about you. They love you enough to come to *this* house and you refuse them?" The way Audelia spat the word regarding the house, explains without detail just how dangerous this place is. Humans can feel it and most are repulsed by it. Unless the house warmly invites them over to play in my little game of *will this one live or survive?*. Either Seven disregarded the unease or the house dropped its walls to him. Both are curious situations indeed.

Pretending to be preoccupied with stirring the pot, I listen in while they continue to go at it.

"I did not refuse Seven. I would hope we could allow him to stay here too." Clouden's voice is raised a tad bit at the last part as if he is trying hard to get me involved in the conversation by doing so. I won't intervene. I would like nothing more than to see them play this one out alone.

Peeking up from cooking, I can't truly read Audelia's face for that one. Will she mind the other brother being here? Perhaps she thinks Seven will occupy Clouden's time and leave my schedule more open for her.

"What is so special about you?" The question is not sincere from her and rather full of sarcasm.

Clouden appears to be too aghast to answer it. He's definitely no fool and is damn well aware she doesn't want an answer, still he indulges anyway very curtly. I can tell he's forcing back a smile. "I don't understand what you mean."

She scoffs at his response. "Of course you don't. *You* have someone who came looking for you."

With eyes blazing with such raw intensity, her jaw clenched in a scowl. Audelia looks as though she's more than ready to bust open Clouden's skull at any moment. Family is a touchy subject for her. She feels distant from the rest of us, at times, because of it. We all have memories of our past to hold on to. Audelia does not. We've tried to access them in the few ways we could. Wisteria pulled out her crystal ball but nothing appeared. It was just as dark for the witch as it was for my darling Delia. Wisteria also tried to tap into Audelia's mind. Even her magic failed. There's even limitations for the gods and Justice Divine could neither see nor hear Audelia's past. We're still working on it.

Additionally there is the matter, like she said, no one is searching for her. The news shared no story on the girl who mysteriously vanished. I checked the police station for the missing person reports and she fit none of them. We don't even have her name. One day I just decided to grant her one and she agreed.

Clouden just stares at Audelia again, understanding the meaning of her rant. She just wants to be found like he was. Instead of keeping this frustration to herself, Audelia finds it easier to take it out on Clouden, who accepts the burden perfectly.

"You're here now," Clouden tells her. "And if you go missing we will find you. No matter what."

This promise from him to her is heartwarming and touching. Whether or not Audelia takes the sincerity of it, I'm not sure. She walks off, leaving Clouden to turn and look my way. I smile and wave a spoon at him to show my appreciation.

"What do you think?" he asks me.

"Your question could mean a number of things. Narrow it down a bit more for me, yes?"

He sighs and glances away briefly, before regaining himself again. "Asking Seven to stay here."

I did not imagine another person in this house so soon. The many empty rooms can be filled as necessary as the house permits, it just feels rather soon to do so. Seven does not give off the notion he wants to stay anywhere else, apart from his own home, where he came from. His purpose is to take Clouden back with him.

"If you wish to do so, I have no objection." I do not state my concerns out loud for him because I'm sure he has considered noting Seven will not want to stay here. The way Clouden's heart has been racing since his brother arrived, is the tell tale sign of just how excited he is for him here. The house has made it so Seven can't leave, for some reason anyway. Once it allows him to exit, I wonder if the man will go screaming down the street, running as fast as his legs will carry him. I hope Clouden will explain to him what we are here and how we survive, before he offers the invitation to stay but it's not my concern how Clouden approaches this.

He nods and then says, "I can't wait to be like you and Audelia."

The permanent smile forged on my mouth widens. This was something we talked about many times over in the last few months. Clouden wants to be a vampire and I could not be happier for him. We are simply waiting for him to train just a bit more. He previously spoke about concerns of being immortal in a vessel that isn't ready, so in due time we will achieve this dream of his. If he were to ask me, I'd say he is more than ready. "Neither can I, dear boy."

We leave it at that, momentarily. I was already planning for his transformation soon. Perhaps, since his brother is here we can push it up a bit. I'm sure Clouden would like to have him for support as well.

The recipe I'm cooking calls for additional ingredients and, as I open the fridge this time, I take into account it's getting quite low. Time for a hunt soon. A familiar sensation creeps its way up my spine to the base of my skull. Someone is near the house; not a threat necessarily. I spot them out the window. It's the nosey neighbors across the street, who often pry into everything they possibly can. They have a feeling I'm not something natural in this world; however, they cannot prove anything. Today they're planting religious signs in the front of every lawn on the street, making sure to leave more in mine than the others.

"Clouden!" I yell. "The Catholics are in the yard again."

SEVEN

9

My life consists of nothing but one series of fucked up shit after the next.

It wasn't always like that. My childhood was good. I grew up in the warm, yellow fields of a honeybee farm surrounded by the sweet nothings of the bayou. The cypress trees were like sentinels of the swamp with tangled branches creating a canopy of hanging moss which swayed in the humid breeze. With every step in the lush grass it felt closer to a mythical realm I could never fully touch. That honey-coated life changed when my family decided to buy a house right smack in the middle of the busy city of New Orleans. At first, it was a nice change, a little too noisy but we adapted. I graduated high school and completed my first year of college. No big conundrum there.

The turn of events transpired during my second year of college. Who would have ever thought one small, seven minute walk could fuck things up so much. I often wonder how the hell I'm even still alive at this point? I should have opted out of dorm housing. Maybe my life would be entirely different today. I didn't need to stay in a dorm any longer, only freshmen were required to be on campus for housing, but I enjoyed my privacy away from my family. The convenience of using the library to study made the choice easy for me to pick the dorm again for my sophomore year at college.

The walk from the library to my dorm wasn't excruciating on a typical evening. My nose was shoved in books for the last nine hours, with small intervals of a break for the bathroom. So, naturally, my legs weren't too pleased with the amount of movement in this stabilized length of time. It was after this debilitating study session the course of my life was altered completely.

I can't tell you much about the kidnapping part. It happened as I was walking from the library to my dorm. Seven minutes. The irony of the time it takes to get from one place to another would be that of my name. Lucky fucking seven.

The back of my head was bashed with something to know me out. Whatever I was hit with felt so sharp I could swear to you my skull was split open. The physicians who tended to me many months after said it wasn't as bad as I guessed.

When I woke up, all I saw was darkness. As stupid as it sounds, I remember thinking *I must be dead*. My heart was beating, and I could feel my chest moving from my breathing, so I knew I was still alive. The pain throbbing in my skull should have been more than enough evidence to prove it too. I couldn't move, though. Ropes were tied so tightly around my ankles and wrists, securing me to poles cemented into the floor. They kept me from even an inch of leeway. I didn't ever think I would be kneeling on all fours like that for many months to come.

At first, I didn't realize I'd been kidnapped. It doesn't happen to grown men, does it? Nothing truly dawned on me when I woke up. Before he bound me, probably while I was still unconscious from the head blow, I am certain I was drugged after being knocked out. The way I reacted to being bound and in darkness was not how I typically would react. I didn't quite panic, you see. I just felt like… I was there. Nothing more. But, somehow the world around me had an edge to it. A bite I can't explain. My vision was warped, like I was tossed into a bad cartoon or something. The air even felt diluted.

When he fed me, I ate whatever it was. I never once saw his face. He always wore a mask of some sort, so I can't even tell you what he looked like. He smelled like shit though. Everything he fed me tasted like shit. The food even smelled like shit too and after a while, I realized it simply was. My stomach recoiled. Everything I vomited he spooned right back into my mouth over and over.

He let the drugs or whatever wear off of me for a while. I think he liked to watch me writhe in agony. The absolute worst was the with-drawals. My body ached in ways I never thought it could. I felt like someone could tear the muscle from my bone and I would be happy, ecstatic even, just to feel something other than the hollow, gnawing emptiness of withdrawal. The craving clawed at my soul. Just when I thought it couldn't get any worse, a different kind of pain crept in its place. My body became a battleground. The cold sweats came on. It made no sense since it felt like a thousand degrees in the room. I'm fairly certain it was an attic, though don't quote me on it.

And the next thing I felt was the assault of something tearing inside my rectum. There was so much pain. It was all too much—coming down from the high, being tied up, and whatever he shoved inside of me. I can't tell you which was worse. You'd think physically having something inside of your body would hurt far worse than something leaving your body. It is a comparison not many can comprehend. Nor should they ever have to.

I was never once unbound from the ropes. Trust me, I tried undoing them with my teeth at small intervals. It was hopeless. Not to mention how weak I'd grown from lack of proper nutrition and whatever poison he was constantly injecting into me. The restroom was just as you'd picture it, right there. Sometimes, I just tried to hold it all in. What was the point? What was there to be embarrassed about? It was just me and this fucking psychopath.

Either there were no windows in the room or he they were boarded up. No light. It was as if he blindfolded me. I knew I hadn't been. I could see him when he came back, never his face, just his form. He never spoke, no matter how many times I tried to get him to. When I did speak, I probably didn't make much sense anyway. And, when he touched me, it was always with latex gloves. I don't even know why he would touch me. I was not aroused in any way, always too tired, too much in pain for it to even be a slight thought. He tried anyway. At one point, after many many attempts, he succeeded and I remember it being the worst experience tied to an orgasm. He made it happen a few more times after, which literally took so long it left my skin raw, painful, and throbbing for a time after. I was so ashamed of myself.

I wasn't aware of it then, but the latex left residue on my skin the forensics found later. No fingerprints of his. No DNA. I only say 'his' because I try not to think women are capable of being so evil. That's not true. Everyone can be evil, no matter what they are.

How long did this go on? The police say my family began to question the school when I didn't show up for Thanksgiving. I hadn't seen them for a few weeks before, so the timing could be a bit off. I was enduring these assaults for at least eight months. It felt infinitely longer.

At some point, he grew tired. What doesn't make any sense is I'm alive to tell this tale. After he was through with me, he drugged me one more time. Maybe he did mean to kill me with the last dose because I can tell you it was the worst fucking dose. He didn't check to make sure I was dead before he dropped me off, filthy, bleeding, and naked, on my parents doorstep. It was my little brother Clouden —who at the time was fourteen—opened the door to find me there half dead the next morning. He knew where I lived. The psychopath knew where to leave me for them to find.

They knocked me out for any kind of doctor to examine me. I would lash out and fight everyone who tried to touch me. When I woke up with my wrists bound to the bed, of course it triggered something awful. I would start screaming, so loud and so much, I would induce a coughing fit that ended up being full of blood from irritating my throat so badly.

After much testing, the hospital found no evidence of another person anywhere near me. They would only find my fecal matter, semen, and blood in many areas of my body—places they shouldn't have been. He would feed me more than just my own shit at times it seemed.

I would then go on to try to live a normal life of daily panicking and medication. I started with weekly therapy for the first few years after the incident and ended up graduating from it to only needing the therapy every few months.

Everyday life is just a balance of *how can I keep from panicking today?* When Clouden or my parents left the house, I would start to panic and worry. I don't fear for myself as much as I fear they won't come home. Before we would go to bed, I'd lock the doors and windows. I wouldn't sleep much, just check on them over and over again. When I'd get up the next day, I would check them again to make sure they were still in the house.

The lights are on all of the time. I cannot be in darkness for a second. The electricity went out once for a storm and I feel so much regret for that fit I had. Clouden chased me in the yard. It was even darker out there than in the house, so I panicked more. When Clouden grabbed me, I unleashed a punch to his face so hard we thought I broke his jaw. I couldn't control it, just as I couldn't control being kidnapped and assaulted for all those months. I'm thirty-two, life shouldn't be like this. Afterwards, I worked desperately not to lose my temper and to keep my emotions in check.

Even after completing multiple rehabilitation sessions, I still feel this overwhelming craving for something I truly never wanted. In a masochistic way, I miss the edge of the drug he gave me, but I will never let myself indulge in drugs no matter how much my body tries to betray me. I will not allow myself to be trapped in a cycle of suffering. The list of what he injected in my body was so long and so sickening. I hate myself for even thinking of wanting it in me again.

I did not return to college, and I did not get another job. I rarely leave the house apart to check the mail, which is even a task in itself. I often let others do it instead. My relationship with my parents is strained. They do not look at me the same any longer. I see the sympathy, and they walk on eggshells around me. While I want to be thankful for this, I can't be. I can also forget about ever having sexual relations with anyone ever again. The thought alone of someone touching me intimately revolts me to the point of vomiting so extremely it induces more panic attacks. I can't even take a shit without the smell or feel of it completely making me want to hurl and then the process starts all over again.

Even though I typically only go to the mailbox, I never leave without a knife. It's in my hand as I sit here in this room Clouden left me in. I am on the verge of a huge panic attack, looming to erupt at any given second. Therapy must've worked a bit because I'm holding it together right now, barely. I imagine if I want to survive again I need to be smarter than I was before.

Clouden deposited me in this room, some time ago, while he and Lorcan talk about this situation. I have no idea what he means, and to be honest, I'm too exhausted from keeping myself from the brink of a panic attack to care. It's oddly nice in here. The room is different from the rest of the house. Everything outside of it feels gothic and dark. Here, it's warm and cozy. The walls are painted a soft green and there's a lamp pouring in light at each corner. It's not too big and not small at all. In the center there's a beautiful canopy bed covered with lush blankets and pillows. It's the perfect place to end a stressful day.

The door to the room slowly opens to reveal Erasmus staring at me from the doorway. The knife stops twirling between my shaking fingers. Something in his eyes angers me; the way he looks at me angers me. For a moment, I thought he was the man who kidnapped me. It's not true. Erasmus doesn't fit the profile. He's much taller and more masculine, and his eye color and shape are completely different. No. For a moment my thoughts went to the kidnapper, because panic was settling in once more, bringing that very traumatic experience to light again.

Erasmus takes one large step in the room closer to where I stand and I waste no time shoving the knife into the side of his neck.

ERASMUS

10

"Fuck!"

Well, to be honest, this is a surprise indeed. I half imagined Seven would be cowering in the corner quivering with the fear of being isolated but instead, he's there, defiantly staring back at me as I stand in the doorframe. I figured he would try to run. Once again, a surprise was in store. I don't even have to look at my neck where the sharp pain rose quickly to the surface to conceive that I was stabbed. Everyone's weapon of choice in this house is a fucking knife.

The throbbing in my neck continues long after I pull the blade out. The look of shock on his face when the wound begins to immediately seal up is a beautiful sight. Being a cursed immortal has many advantages.

Seven's eyes widen and the blue intensifies. The hottest of fires burn blue and his eyes are no exception. Somewhere deep in this man is a fire still lit. Whatever he's been through in this life has dimmed it. After being in my tomb for so long, I need a good challenge and, at first, I thought it was going to be Lorcan. It would seem Seven Wilbrate is going to be my challenge instead.

When I finally speak, it is with the same tone I give everyone in this house: calm and hiding any significant emotion. "I simply came in to see if you needed anything…"

As I take a few steps forward, Seven takes a few wobbly steps backward.

"I panicked!" he shouts.

"And stabbed me."

What does that say about him? That this is his first reaction to someone entering his room, yes his room—as I've said before he's not leaving any time soon. I am too utterly intrigued by this seemingly sensitive human to let him slip through my fingers so easily, and the house will not allow him to exit just yet anyway. Something must be special about the Wilbrates. More than one of us here has been easily drawn to them in one way or another.

"You lived!" he shouts again.

Seven's tone is getting louder and antsier with each step I take toward him. Since he doesn't have the knife any longer, he has no way of truly protecting himself, unless he uses his hands. I have a feeling he will not.

"How unlucky for you," I say softly as I lean in closer. I'm being careful not to touch him. I do this just to make the point how I can and will be in his personal space, if I choose to do so. "But it's my turn now."

"Seven?" Clouden appears in the doorway just as my palms press to Seven's chest, shoving him backward. He stumbles and tries to grasp at something to break his fall. He failed to catch anything. The look on his face as his body smashes the glass, and then falls backward out of the window, is priceless.

"Seven!" The brother is frantic, pushing past me to get to the shards of window glass hanging on by a thread. Never fear. I had a feeling Seven wasn't going to die. Before this whole charade, I could hear Lorcan prowling about in the garden below, probably digging another hole. Enhanced sight and smell do come in handy—no, I am no vampire. I was in the tomb long enough in complete darkness to teach myself how to strengthen my senses.

"Eraaaasmus," Lorcan's sing-song voice echoes out. "This is no way to treat a dinner guest."

As I lean over the windowsill next to a much calmer Clouden, I see Seven is passed out in Lorcan's arms, just as I expected. If Lorcan hadn't caught him... Well, I guess the hole Lorcan was digging would've come in handy.

LORCAN

11

've been a menace to this city for many years. The owner of the famous LeBeaux's restaurant on Decatur Street can absolutely vouch for that. He doesn't like to agree that we're friends, but we are. He says it's all in my head and I beg to differ. Can't imagine why he would think otherwise.

"Lorcan," Hunter says sternly. "You've got a lotta nerve comin' up in here." He's standing behind the bar in the middle of his restaurant. He opened LeBeaux's many years ago after leaving the southern bayou. The restaurant specializes in cajun cuisine and is said to have the best gumbo in the city. Pft. If they're making this assumption they haven't tasted mine.

"Do I?" I hold back a smile and, while twirling my knife in hand, I lean my hip casually against the counter. "I'm just stopping by to see an old friend."

"We are not friends," Hunter replies through gritted teeth. His fingers are gripping the counter so hard they're turning white.

I sigh and place my elbows on the opposite side of the counter from where he stands so we are face to face. Resting my chin on my palms, I let out a dramatic, audible sigh.

Hunter LeBeaux and I have history together, though not romantically at all. Hunter is a burly, large man filled with far too much muscle for my liking. His brown hair is a little longer than shoulder length currently. When we first met it was substantially shorter. There's another thing about Hunter LeBeaux that turns me off completely, he constantly smells like a wet dog who's been in the yard all day. Probably because he is one; a dog, I mean. A wolf shifter to be fair—that's neither here nor there.

Just then, Hunter's best friend, Marcus Trahan, walks in with hands full of utensils to set the tables.

"Leech," he says and I roll my eyes. It's such an outdated term for vampires. "You finally gonna get a bite to eat here?"

I grimace at him. "From *here*? Not a chance, Trahan."

Marcus resembles Hunter enough to be considered his brother however they aren't blood related. I should know, since I've tasted both of their blood before—they weren't very willing to share it. The taste was far too different and when you've been terrorizing this planet for as long as I have, you can distinguish little things like blood type easily. They both dress horribly. I don't think I've ever seen them in suits before, even on Hunter's wedding day. No, I wasn't invited but I wouldn't have missed it for the world. I blend in to places I need to be, though I wouldn't say seamlessly. Most do suspect something is different about me, aside from my killer fashion sense.

"Whatcha want, Lorcan?" Hunter is visibly over this little visit already.

"Come now, is that any way to treat an old friend?"

Hunter grunts in response and Marcus ignores us completely to go finish his duties.

"I'm just checking in. Making sure you're all still alive and well." The words come out like a tune and I smile at Hunter's scowl.

"What about your other friend?" I ask while I glance around the establishment. The building has grown over the years, he's remodeled quite a bit but there is one thing that hasn't changed. My eyes land on the old man who sits, day after day, at the bar counter at the far end, sipping a cold beer: Barry. He's been a consistent customer in this place forever. "The one with the tics. Jojo."

I smile.

Hunter growls.

It was partially my fault why Joseph Therrien is the way he is presently. The once suave man now secluded to his home for fear of his spasms being the focus of others too much. Joseph was once just like Hunter and Marcus; a wolf shifter. After my adopted daughter Blair bit him, there was a problem. Instead of transforming him into this supernatural entity that coexisted with both species, his body rejected the vampire venom. Joseph was Hunter's beta in their pack. After the incident he couldn't quite get in tune with his wolf again. The venom and wolf gene collide to fight each other for dominance resulting in the tremors he endures daily. This is also another reason why Hunter doesn't like to admit we're friends.

"Why?" Hunter asks. "So you can finally finish him off like you did the rest of the family?

There's more of the reason. I slaughtered his entire family. All of them. I had my reasons and they were very selfish. While I don't feel remorse for it, I can't understand why Hunter doesn't feel a connection with me, as I do with him. Of course, the connection is something of bitterness. There is a cord tethering us to one another, whether he likes it or not.

"No, no," I wave a dismissive hand at him. "Not today."

Hunter growls.

I smile.

We've played this little game for years. Hunter finally understands he can't dispose of me and so Erasmus will also come to this conclusion. With the new immortal I've acquired, our connection is quite different. He may want me dead as well. He needs to get in line behind the rest of them.

"For the last time," Hunter began, "Jojo ain't gonna live with you."

My lips purse at the response. "I can't imagine why." Oh, I really can.

Jojo would be a perfect addition to my house of monsters. He could've been the first. Regretfully, Hunter and Marcus are hell bent on keeping him away from me.

My response is the last straw for LeBeaux. With a large finger he points to the door. I take another glance around the little restaurant. "You know, I could sell you some good prime meat."

"Out!" Hunter yells. He's familiar with my choice of food and obviously still doesn't approve of it. I do love to play with him. He's a riot when he's angry.

"What?" I smile. "Most of them are rich, obnoxious, and given the chance they'd eat you first, in a heartbeat."

The finger of his pointing to the door never lowers.

"Well…" I tap my knife to the counter once. "I'll be at my usual haunt if you ever change your mind."

Unlikely. The LeBeaux pack has very poor taste indeed.

SEVEN

12

The thing about sleeping is sometimes I'm not aware I'm asleep. Everything playing in my head is so vivid and lifelike I truly cannot distinguish it's a dream. Even the scents of my dreams feel like reality. Many times it's just the memories of those months haunting me, as if I am not allowed a reprieve, even when my eyes close.

Most nights, I would wake to Clouden or my parents shaking me, ripping me away from one nightmare right into another. So, when my eyes open, I cannot register if I am still in the dream or if my entire life is just made to be nothing more than such. This time is no different. The darkness around me is so rich, I assume for a moment I'm still sleeping. Everything that transpired must have been from a previous nightmare, until I realize I'm not in my room at home.

Tangled in the sheets, I fumble off the bed and crawl until I reach a wall where my shaking hands slide up to flip a light switch. The light blares to life and I run down the hall to find the front door. I'm almost there, it's just within reach, when I feel the warmth of fingers around my wrist.

It's the small, stupid things like this I wish I could manage. I can't. Just the feel of his skin on mine, anyone's skin on mine, revolts me. I can not control what happens next. I feel it happening but I can't stop the bile that rises in my throat and then spews from my lips all over the front of Erasmus' shirt.

"Not on my carpet!" Lorcan shouts from not very far. No matter how loud he yells, there's no stopping it. More is shoving its way out of my body as if it's cleaning my insides on its own. It's happened pretty badly before and this feels like a repeat. I heaved up so much and so hard just now, I ended up passing out for the second time today.

This time, when I come to, I'm seated upright in a chair. Erasmus is sitting right in front of me, only a few inches away. I'm more startled at the closeness of him that I suck in too quick of a breath and am suddenly lightheaded from it. I try to stand and find I can't move my legs. I try my arms next and can't move them either.

When I look down at the ropes keeping my arms to the armrest of the chair, I completely lose it. I'm flooded instantly with the thought that it's happening again. I'm in my nightmare, reliving it. I start thrashing, enough that the chair scoots forward a bit. It doesn't help any.

"I am awfully observant. I can tell by your reactions something happened to you in the past," Erasmus says. "I don't know all of the details but I think I have the gist of it."

This man absolutely terrifies me. The way he watches me is so unnerving. His gaze is almost feral, and his eyes scrape over my body in ways other people never do.

"Let me fucking go." My words come out frantic and hurried. Erasmus does not move one inch to free me. "Let me go!"

"Calm yourself," he says, and I laugh so fucking hard I think I'll pass out or vomit. Maybe both.

Through my hysterics, I'm able to say, "Calm myself? I've been held captive, thrown out of a window, and then held captive again."

"You were in a fit after you passed out. Didn't want to take the chance you'd hurt yourself," Erasmus says.

"I'm fine," I reply through gritted teeth.

Erasmus says nothing to this. His eyes lock unnaturally to mine while I try not to flip the fuck out from this absolutely insane situation.

"Can we take the fucking ropes off?" I ask and it's getting harder to keep myself under control.

"Ja. Soon," he says slowly. "I have a question I want you to answer first."

"I can answer them out of this." I yank against the ropes knowing nothing will happen.

"How long ago was it?"

"How long ago was what?" I have a sneaking suspicion he meant the kidnapping. Clouden probably told him and when Erasmus doesn't answer it's pretty much confirmed.

I dare not look at him. "Why does this matter?" The way Erasmus stares at me is so unsettling. He never looks away, just keeps those light-brown, honeyed eyes on me at all times. I feel trapped by them.

"It doesn't," Erasmus replies a bit too calmly. "I am very curious about you."

I laugh again. He's curious about my trauma. The thought makes me laugh even more. "Why should I tell you? Why should I have to tell anyone anything?"

"You don't have to. But the sooner you tell me the sooner I'll take the ropes off."

"Years," I say. "It's been years. Almost thirteen."

With one long, purposeful stride Erasmus is standing in front of me. He simply nods and pulls a switchblade from his pocket. He begins to cut me free and I hold my breath as his fingers brush over my skin. I do not vomit this time.

"You said you're not a vampire, yet I stabbed you, and you lived." My fists are balled so tightly my nails are digging into my palms, "What are you then?"

"Cursed," he sits back in his chair that mirrors mine. "So they say. It feels more like a blessing."

I can run again. The door isn't far. How far will I get out the door before he binds me in ropes again?

"You won't make it," he says as if he's reading my mind. "Your heartbeat quickened when you glanced at the door. You gave yourself away."

"No getting past you, is there?"

Erasmus smiles.

"Come with me." He stands and I watch him for a second without moving before he says, "If you haven't observed, you're sitting in your underwear and a shirt. Your clothes were heavily saturated with vomit. Didn't think humans could hold that much liquid in them."

"Wait, you *undressed* me? While I was out? You... touched me?" I'm appalled at the thought.

"Ja," he replies, and then adds, "If you're asking if I removed your slimy clothing, the answer is yes. If you're asking if I violated you in any way, the answer is no. Unless you count being shoved out of a window."

Instantly, I'm standing. "By the way, you could've killed me!"

Erasmus grins, "Shame for you isn't it. You lived." Confidence oozes from him. Everything about him screams danger at me.

I blink at him. "You couldn't possibly have known I would live through that!"

"Nej," he says, smiling still. "It was simply a chance I wanted to take. You did stab me in the neck." He walks out of the room and I follow.

"It was a survival instinct." I say through another laugh of hysteria. "It was a basic instinct to protect me!"

"All I did was open the damn door," he opens another door for me to go inside.

"Are there more fucking ropes?"

"Not unless you're into that sort of thing."

My lips purse and I storm in. Internal alarms are going off, but it doesn't stop me from turning to tell him off again. "Oh fuck you!"

Outside the open bedroom door, I can see Clouden standing in the foyer watching the scene unfold, seemingly in shock.

Me too, Clouden. Me too.

ERASMUS

13

Dinner is delightful tonight.

"What? No ropes this time?" Seven asks as he stares up at me.

There's still a dimly lit fire behind those pristine blue eyes. Those eyes, though sparkling with warmth, hold a whispered promise of a storm yet to pass. A persistent shadow dances in the depths, like a testament to the agony he once lived through. Does he realize just how resilient he is? I have him right where I want him, on the table and bared for me to have my feast. Oddly enough he is welcoming me to that.

"Nej," I reply. "Do I truly need them?" The paradox of Seven Wilbrate is that he is full of anxious turmoil, yet the relaxed manner of his form signifies his acceptance. It's his eyes that give him away. There's so much vitality in them.

Without breaking eye contact, his whisper consists of one word: "No." A submissive little human but for how long will he be such? When will that fire burn so brightly that he, and everything in its path, will finally be consumed by it? I yearn to taste the ash of his flames.

I sit, staring down at him—and he stares back at me, and it is a victory of its own accord. He has yet to hold my gaze for more than a few seconds, or anyone in this house since his arrival. A knife is in one of my hands, a fork in the other. Which instrument will triumph over the other?

There is a sudden internal battle colliding inside of me that I find a tad difficult to choose sides on. Let's weigh them out, shall we?

On the fork's side of this, I am practically salivating to have a taste of every part of his body and then to ingest him completely. To carve him open and savor the flavors of Seven Wilbrate would be a beautiful act indeed. My mind is a treasure trove of creativity, a boundless expanse of ideas and every single one of them surrounds the thought of 'What does Seven taste like?'

On the knife's side, I am utterly intrigued by this man's mind and, I assume for that reason alone, I want to protect him at all costs. If I kill him I will never truly understand the inner workings of his intelligence, and I can guarantee Seven is clever. There's a deep desire to understand his perspective of the world and his outlook on life. I'm curious about the lens he sees reality through. What is he passionate about? I must know all of this. I would give up my immortality in return to connect with him on a deeper level.

This is a true dilemma. Seven's mind is a conundrum in itself that I want to unfold layer by layer. I watch as the knife in hand glides across his forehead seemingly like butter as blood pools quickly to the surface. If you close your eyes, the sound a human makes when in pain can often be confused with that of pleasure.

The bone there is difficult to break through. Somehow I manage. The sounds he makes are a little more hurried, more excited. It makes me wonder if we truly decipher the sounds of pain from ecstasy. His hands are gripping the side of the table, humans tend to do in both scenarios.

I leave my fork and knife on the table as I peel apart the layers of that pink, squishy brain of his with my bare hands. No utensils, I want to feel this part of him. I want to taste more than his physicality… I want to taste his thoughts and memories.

I blink and he's seated across from me cutting into the meal on his plate. I wish I could have stayed in the daydream. There is a solution to how I can have both sides collaborate as one. He simply has to agree to the terms. I can indeed just take what I want, but I will give Seven Wilbrate the decency of a choice.

My attention has momentarily diverted from slaughtering Lorcan to being consumed with Seven. At that moment, he peers up from his plate and meets my gaze, because I indeed have been staring unabashedly at him this entire time. His cheeks blush and he holds my stare briefly and there it is; a tiny spark of that full fledged fire that I wanted to witness. Since he arrived here, he's all I find myself thinking about. He probably isn't even aware that just the vibrancy of his presence fills up the room. I'm drowning in the depths of my own fascination and I do not wish for anyone to save me.

Seven simply picks up his glass of, what I'll call wine, and raises it to me in salute. I can take the move as a silent agreement to his option. He's still in the dark about the question, and therefore, he can't possibly know his choices. If he says no, I can't say the outcome of him will be anything but disastrous. I know what I want, and trust me I will have it.

LORCAN

14

"Do you realize what the mistake was?"

Clouden has been with me for almost a year. He understood and accepted the training process for him to become one of my own. With that said, he completely disregarded all the training the moment he stepped through the front door and laid eyes on his brother.

In response to my comment, Clouden says nothing. This was probably best, for fear that he would say the wrong thing. He doesn't even look at me. To anger me is a difficult task though not unheard of.

"You were rash," I say.

"He's my brother."

Up until these recent events, it was yet to be proven if Clouden has a weakness. So, it would seem I have finally found that. I will have to choose my words carefully and precisely for the duration of this conversation, otherwise it could possibly not end well.

"When you first came here, you said you had no one. Your parents gave up on you. Your brother gave up on himself. Do you recall that conversation?"

Once more, Clouden is silent. It's his story, his life. Truly, it does not matter to me where he came from. He could've been a part of a loving family, a safe home, and been loved by all who met him. He has potential that I haven't seen in anyone else for the hunt. I'd have accepted him into my home either way. I need to make sure this life is still what he wants. "What changed out of the blue to make him your brother once more?"

There's a pause while he gathers his words. Clouden is not stupid by any means. He's aware how every word he speaks out into the universe will inevitably be returned.

"He came for me," he says. "You don't understand how big of a step that is for him."

No. I do not, nor do I care honestly. The other Wilbrate brother does not mean anything to me. I am unfamiliar with him, and I don't have any interest in establishing a connection with him. Erasmus is drawn to him, for whatever reason, but it's not my business.

"You've come such a long way," I say. "Is he the only one you'll break your training for?"

Clouden's head nods slowly.

"How can we be so sure? Your parents, what if they come looking for you?"

"They won't. If they surprise me and they come, I'll let you do as you wish with them but Seven... he's off limits." The boy's face is a mask of determination, his features chiseled in stoic resolution.

"And if Seven interferes?"

"He won't," Clouden says, sternly. "I'll make certain of that."

"I did tell you for your transition into immortality to go smoothly you have to let go of all human things," I remind him.

Clouden speaks softly, yet directly. "He needs me now, more than ever." His entire demeanor radiates an aura of unshakable resolve, like a young pecan tree standing firm against the hurricane.

"Wrong," I say. "He needs us"

And with that, Clouden blinks at me, utter confusion lining that youthful face of his. His eyebrows, once straight, now furrow into a soft crescent, as if the weight of his puzzlement is too much to bear.

"You heard me correctly." I simply say this because I know I'll have to fight Erasmus over the other man if I send him away. While I can take Erasmus with one hand sliced off and placed on the table, I truly want to see how those two will play out. Besides, if the house doesn't unlock for him he can't leave anyway. I do believe the house wants just as much as I to see how this will unfold.

And then Clouden speaks again. "There are those *you* would give everything for, aren't there?"

Of course there is. I have my family, including himself—extending to the Divine clan of course who have been my family before I had anything at all—and any of these people I would give everything for and do anything to protect, without a second thought.

"Clouden, there is a way to have all of what you want, even within this training. Control. The main focus of your training is to be in control. If you *show* something is your weakness, the world will use it against you." I can tell he's soaking all of this in. Clouden is highly observant. No, I'm not angry at his moment of weakness. I want him to learn from it. "I could easily dangle Seven in front of you, make you crack just by slicing his pretty little cheek... hold fast and control yourself. Don't show the world what your weakness is right away. Am I understood?"

He nods my way and I shoo him away with my hand, leaving myself alone in my study. It's time to update my recipe cards. The previous one for the gumbo I make has changed, with a few added ingredients that enhance the spices perfectly to create a smoothe, flavorful roux.

This growing family of mine is all I need. There are creatures who are aware that this house is my weakness. Many also know not to fuck with any of it or suffer the dire consequences– like ending up in my next pot of gumbo.

SEVEN

15

I'm still rattled being here. I mean, in the short time since walking in, I was pushed out of a window, bound to a chair, and I've stabbed someone. I've never in my entire life stabbed anything! My family is full of fishermen, including myself when I was younger. Even then I couldn't even scale or filet the fish, and they were already dead by that point. It's been impossible to stop shaking. I feel like they're holding me hostage here like I thought they did with Clouden. He says they're not. I'm not so sure I believe him.

How can Clouden possibly feel safe in this house, especially with what these creatures are? Yes, this city is full of them and as citizens we try not to think about it and tend to avoid them, which was easy enough for me. I never left the house. The irony of it all astounds me. The one time I leave my safety bubble and I'm smack in the middle of danger.

I don't think the man who kidnapped me was something other-worldly. Maybe he was and that's why no one could find him. Perhaps he has magic to cover his tracks. It's scary to think that he's human because we don't like to think humans are capable of such disgusting things, but they are... and worse ones are out there.

My anxiety is through the roof. As nice as this room is that I've been pacing in, I can't stay in here. The quiet is so profound and heavy through the house. I guess they've all gone out. Since I'm here alone, I take my time looking around the hall. The room they placed me in is on the second floor. There's a wrap around balcony in the middle. I can look down to the living room area of the house from it. No one's sitting on any of the luxurious chairs or sofas. Glancing up, there's another floor and another circular balcony where you can look down from as well. From the floor above there is a large chandelier hanging. It's probably more for decorative purposes than lighting. Various portraits hang on the walls and peer at my every move.

The house feels endless. It stretches out like a labyrinth. Rooms and hallways unfold like a maze, with no discernable exit. From the outside, it did not seem this large at all. The second and third floor have so many doors, it feels impossible for that many rooms to be in this building. Sconces light the way down the second floor hall, casting eerie shadows across the walls and the silhouettes seem to move on their own accord. Each step reveals a new wonder. Time itself feels to bend and warp here. What is only minutes gives off the sense it's been hours. In this house, the laws of reality are just a rumor, no more than simple gossip.

Not far from the circular balcony is what appears to be a common area with two chairs each across from a coffee table. Two large bookshelves are filled to the brim with books, jars, and other objects. I take a glance at one of the jars and find it filled with pink tongues floating in some clear substance. Mentally, I try to tell myself they're just Halloween decorations even though we're still in summer.

There are so many doors. I don't know where to start, or even what I'm doing. I figure at this point I need something to occupy my time, and if they're going to kill me, they're going to do it whether I'm left cowering in the room or being nosey in the others. The room next to mine is open already, so I poke my head in. It's cold and dreary, completely opposite of mine with dark purple walls and absolutely no sign of being occupied anymore. I leave this one alone.

I stop in the hall again. 'Mine?' I called the room I'm staying in *mine*. It most certainly is not. Quickly releasing this thought, I continue on my hunt. I have no true goal apart from just wanting to view the area I'm in. Silence swallows my footsteps, making it seem as if I'm walking on air. The door across the balcony from mine is pulling me in like a magnet. When I push it open, the room feels warm and inviting. It's so strange how each room gives the impression that they belong in different houses, rather than share the same roof.

The one I'm standing in has visible signs that it's being lived in; clothes are tossed on an armchair, the bed is unmade, and other small items are strewn across the room. My pocket knife is on the small table by the window. I've been too preoccupied with my thoughts to notice I don't have it on me. It truly doesn't matter, I can't kill any of these creatures with it. The air in here is thick with mystery. This room must belong to Erasmus. Well, since he took the liberty of changing my clothes when I passed out and took my knife, he can't get angry at how I'm snooping through his shit for the hell of it. For reasons I can't explain, this room feels like it matches the man who lives in it. It's warm but threatening at the same time. I'm just opening the top drawer of his dresser when a voice creeps in.

"I don't trust him," Audelia says. She's unexpectedly standing right next to me, looking around the room before her eyes land on me. My heart is racing. I'm more afraid at how I didn't even hear her enter the room, let alone get to be in such close proximity to me. I have no doubt she means it's Erasmus she doesn't trust. "He tried to kill Lorcan once, you know."

I did not know that.

"Lorcan is always alert," she adds. "You can't get much over him. Erasmus had no chance. He's stupid and tried anyway." Audelia laughs and I can see the tips of her soft white fangs momentarily. "*And* he pushed you out of the window."

"He was upset. I did stab him." I have to look away. It's uncomfortable looking at her. She's gorgeous, blond and absolutely beautiful. That's not why I have to avert my eyes. It's the excuse I made for a man who tried to kill me. Of all the things to say, I chose to say this. I go back to snooping around the room since she doesn't seem to mind and doesn't seem to be here to kick me out of it.

She changes the subject. "Your brother's annoying," she says flatly. "Yes, he was here before me, but I don't care about seniority. He irks me."

I stop digging and turn to face her. "What about me?" I should ask why she thought Clouden is annoying. Somehow, I can already imagine it. He's very confident and often quiet when you don't want him to be. Sometimes you just need to talk and for him to talk back, instead of just listening. He was never much for conversation.

Audelia shrugs. "I like you. You have empathy."

That's a bit perplexing. Empathy is the understanding of another one's feelings. I understand no one here at all. She laughs and it's probably at the blatant look of stupidity on my face.

"You just basically pardoned Erasmus for trying to kill you." Her head cocks to the side as she speaks. "And your reasoning is because you stabbed him, despite not knowing he could live through such an event."

"Perhaps you're misusing empathy here for sympathy then."

She doesn't respond. From the way she looks at me, I believe she sees it as a mix of both of those things together. I should just let it be. Erasmus tried to kill me. Who cares why or why not. It's the fact he tried to kill me that should've mattered.

I go back to my quest and open another drawer. There's a couple of shirts and a tiny black box. Maybe I'm going too far, but I open that too. Inside is a compass the size of my palm. It fits perfectly and it's absolutely stunning, with a gold and bronze base and some kind of intricate design underneath.

"It must be broken," I whisper to myself. Audelia's head pops in just above my shoulder and thankfully does not touch it. "It's not pointing right. The compass should be at the north, it isn't."

Audelia shrugs. "Maybe it's just sentimental and he can't let it go."

She has a point. We all keep things that are broken and should have been discarded years ago. We just don't have the heart to throw them away. It is odd though. No matter what I do, the arrow only points back at me when it should be finding true north. Instead of placing the compass back in the drawer, I shove it in my pocket. If Erasmus could steal my shit, then I can do the same with him.

ERASMUS

16

The most profound turn of events often happens at the dinner table. Upon gathering at the table for a second time, per Lorcan's request, I take notice of the seating cards at the table and the seating arrangement changes.

Typically, two chairs went without bodies in them; one for Lorcan's daughter Blair and one for his son Blaze, but for the second evening in a row, Audelia's chair is empty as well. What is she up to?

Next to Audelia's chair is an extra one Lorcan pushed between hers and Blaze's. Instead of allowing Seven to seat himself in Audelia's chair, he has his own. One thing about Lorcan is, if you have a place at this table, you *always* have a place at this table. The evidence alone of Seven having his own chair and place card means, without Seven knowing, Lorcan is already adopting him as one of us.

"Sleep well?" Lorcan asks Seven as we all sit down.

"Uh, yeah sure."

No one believes him. Clouden knows better and between Lorcan and I, we can hear his erratic breathing. Then there was the tossing and turning and, though just once, a sharp bellowing in the night. The lights in his room were bright all night, indicating he either slept with them on like that, or he didn't sleep at all. Then again, when you're a human in a house full of monsters, would it truly be wise to close your eyes?

Changing the subject, Seven quickly says, "This is really good." Between chewing, he adds, "What's in it?"

The Adam's apple of Seven's throat—a delicacy of its own—bobs with each ingesting bite of his dinner. This man is oblivious to his delicious vessel of perfection. To lick the blood of the undeserving from his flesh would be the ultimate reward.

"Who," says Lorcan. "You mean 'who is in it?'"

Next to Lorcan, on the other side of me, Clouden's fork stops moving as he looks up. His brother is sitting across from us, conveniently by himself, with the empty chairs on each side of him. No distractions for me to keep my eyes on the prize. As if anything could make my focus pull away from him anyway. I am already becoming increasingly obsessed with this mortal.

"Who's in what?"

No one says a word to reply. Realization hits Seven at once and his chewing begins to slow. He's still for a solid moment before damn near hurdling himself across the table. Silverware and glasses are everywhere as Seven's hands go for his brother's neck. Lorcan and I are quick to move, though Lorcan is just a bit faster. He saves Clouden from the fight just in the nick of time by whispering something to

Seven that makes him evidently rethink the whole charade. Instead of continuing the assault, Seven's shoulders melt as he sits back down in his seat. I wonder briefly if Lorcan threatened him.

"Well," Seven says and swallows hard, "Can't say it's the worst thing I've ever ingested." He glances at Clouden who in return frowns his way. More of Seven's past just unfolded.

Seven's brows almost fuse together and the lines of his forehead deepen as he inhales a deep breath. "We can't stay here forever, Clouden." But Clouden ignores his brother. "You know our parents are worried sick."

Clouden sighs. "In case you haven't noticed, no one is worried sick. Just you are. We have released them from their burden."

Seven swallows quicker this time, causing his throat to bounce more dramatically. "Burden? Is that what you think?"

"They haven't slept a full night's sleep in years because you scream all hours of the night," Clouden replies, and it is a brutal choice of words. I'm sure they are true.

Seven sits there, simply staring at his brother with tired and remorseful eyes. "Is this why you left? Was it all because of me?"

Quickly Clouden shakes his head. "No, no I did this because of me. I'm not wired the same as everyone else in the family, Seven. I have needs and wants that go beyond what the mundane can offer me. They don't understand us."

"Us?" Seven says. "As in you and..." He examines us around the dinner table at the rest of the monsters that surround him there, listening while we eat.

"You and I, dear brother, are the same."

Both Wilbrate's stare at one another trying to decipher what each means by the words they shared.

"We aren't," Seven says. "We are nothing alike and you know it. We never have been."

Clouden leans over his plate, stretching himself as if doing so, he can reach Seven from where he sits. "We are *now*, Seven."

There is a silent form of communication happening between them, and I am extremely curious about what is said. I've seen many like Clouden before. Those people simply want a different life than what they think they were meant for. They want power over others. Seven is different. The older brother is typically the one in charge of others. It would seem the only person Seven wants control over is himself.

"I know you want to leave," I say to Seven, who doesn't glance my way. His whole body stiffens at the sound of my voice. "You should stay here at least to witness your brother's transition."

Without moving his head, *now* Seven's eyes shoot in my direction. "Transition?"

Lorcan pipes in. "Oh, it won't be long. I am quite excited to have him permanently join this family."

Seven's blue eyes darken with a cauldron of emotion bubbling in them. If his heart could break any more, this no doubt shattered it. "You're going to become one of them… like him?" Seven nodded at Lorcan.

Clouden sat back in his chair and answered, "Yes. Yes, I am."

"Why? What is the allure of being like him that makes being human not enough for you?"

Lorcan's smile never strays as he watches the two converse. He's thoroughly entertained by them both.

"I'll have power," Clouden says. "I'll be difficult to kill."

This time I can't tell what is going through Seven's mind at all. A momentary invisible shield covers his face. He doesn't respond but I wish he would; let me in his mind some more.

"You could stay too," Clouden says to Seven. "Be a part of something great. Lorcan said you can. Transition with me."

"Why can't I be simply me?" Seven asks.

"Because…" I start before anyone else can, "You are not simple."

"I meant human." He says this to me harshly. He isn't looking at me again. It's very obvious he holds some disdain towards me. Ripping apart inside of me is a war between wanting to spoon out his eye to keep it in my pocket, so that I control when he looks at me, and the sheer pressing reality that I want him to look at me of his own accord.

"You could…" Lorcan says "Except you'd be surrounded by higher beings all of the time. Who's to say we won't forget our strength, hm? Pop your little head like a bubble…" Lorcan takes a bite of dinner from his fork.

I'm only half paying attention, too lost in my thoughts to keep my focus. There is something I want to ask Seven right this instant, then again, maybe this little dinner conversation will help at least see where he stands. I will not pick fruit with this conversation, just simply plant a seed.

"Stay," Clouden says eagerly before I can speak again. "Stay for my transition."

Yes, I urge silently, *that's right. Stay. Stay because you have to. Stay because if you do leave, I'll kill you.*

LORCAN

17

All along the shelves of my home are the many artifacts of my past. Manuscripts and documents humans think are long lost from fires or other disasters, I keep as souvenirs from my travels. Statues I carved with old friends, who are sadly in graves somewhere, and art that was given to me as gifts, are set on the shelves for me to view at leisure.

Jars of my history are scattered throughout. Each one houses a time in my past I decided to keep to remember. Being a vampire, you get to live a long time. It doesn't always mean you remember every detail of your life. I check the first jar's name and date and snicker. This one is the first person to ever break my heart. Inside of the jar is a single eyeball floating in a case of liquid I'd acquired to keep it from turning into mush. My so-called lover acquired a wandering eye, so I felt inclined to keep it.

It wasn't easy to spoon out the eyes from its socket. I had to be careful and its owner was thrashing about so much I popped the first one. For the second one, I made sure it came out unscathed enough to be my trophy. When I sealed the jar, I was still feeling uneasy. That night I indulged in the rest of my ex by adding the rest of its body to my dinner. I'd already begun devouring humans prior to any of this, of course, but it didn't dawn on me right away to actually eat this one. I didn't want it completely gone, so I kept the eye and prepared myself a nice dinner with the rest.

The next jar holds a lip and is labeled again with a date and a name of one who loved to tell a great deal of lies and gossip. It gave me so much pleasure to peel the bottom lip from the mouth that tried to talk sweet nothings to me. Instead the words were all lies. I was never fond of the slice of it though, the line is too crooked. My victim wouldn't keep still, for some reason.

On the far right is a jar with just a finger in it. This is one who truly didn't do anything wrong to me. I was bored and bored is not something anyone ever wants me to be. I grew tired, tremendously, with this one. There was never any true reason to pardon them. None of them were creative or inspiring of any kind. I've yet to find anything that truly is, besides my knife, of course. I gave up looking for that.

It was the same fate for all of them on this shelf. There are four in total. Each one has a different body part or piece enclosed. The rest of the creature is gone, devoured, or buried long ago. I refuse to allow myself the company of anyone romantically again. I highly doubt I ever will. These four are enough heartache to last me the rest of my eternal life. The creatures of this earth are all the same. We look different, but everyone has an agenda to work toward. Mine is no longer involving intimacy of any kind, apart from murder.

Blaze, my son, has said it is a tad funny how I never mourned losing any of them. There was never some kind of longing after. They were gone, and by my own hand at that, yet it didn't bother me in the least. He said it's the dealings of a psychopath. Scientifically, do I fit the term? I don't think there's a word in any language capable of describing me.

The voices in my head are coaxing, toying with me in saying I dress to impress others. They tell me I'm still searching for the person I want to keep.

"Now, now," I say to myself. "I only dress this way to pleasure my own eyes."

I love my suits and the clean feeling of the crisp fabric right from the cleaners or directly from the store. They're as much a part of my identity as the knife I have stowed up my sleeve. My suits are for my own sake, not others. Of course, sometimes I have to admit, I do use how I look to lure my victims in. Don't get the wrong idea. It's not to flirt or anything. It's simply just to fill my freezer.

SEVEN

18

After tonight's dinner concluded, I corner my brother for a talk. Even though we are the only two in the kitchen, I can't fully believe our conversation will be private. With all the nosy supernatural creatures living here, I'm sure they're listening from wherever they are in this house. We need this chat no matter what.

"Clouden, you can't seriously be considering doing this?"

At first, all he does is pour the rest of the wine that could be remaining in the dinner glasses down the drain. "Absolutely."

"Why? What does this even mean," I ask, as I watch him add the dishes to the dishwasher. Big ass mansion and no maids? How strange.

"You know what it means. This life—this lifestyle is what I want."

"What's the price?" I ask. "Nothing is free. Everything comes with a price. Every. Damn. Thing.

"I just have to be loyal to Lorcan."

"What's that mean, hm? He asks you to kill me and you'll do it?" My hands ball into fists at the thought, the betrayal, of his loyalty shifting from our brotherhood. We were never 'best' friends. Our age gap didn't quite help that we found next to nothing in common. We still had each other.

"I don't know what Lorcan's intention with you is. It seems like you've been manipulated into joining a damn cult."

Clouden simply smiles and picks up a towel to wipe down the counter— it's already pretty damn clean to me. He's keeping busy so he doesn't have to focus on me and this conversation. I do the same shit.

I need to feel out how deep in this my brother is. "If he says to kill me… will you do it?"

"Seven." He stops wiping the counter to look at me. "To die by his command would be an art."

I need to remember at this moment which one of us went through a traumatic fiasco and which one of us should be falling into insanity, because right now it's the wrong brother. How am I the level-headed one here? "You sound pretty fucking insane, Clouden."

He quickly averts the subject. "Stay with me here, and you'll understand it all. You'll learn, just as I have."

"Learn what exactly? What are you even *doing*!"

"Living," is all he answers, and this one word is closure to me and that's it. He will not open up anymore on the subject, so I press on to something else.

"You were missing for almost a year," I say, after a pause.

He goes back to picking up the kitchen. "I'm not missing, Seven. I was never missing. I have been found."

"You didn't even call. Not one message! Just to tell me you're alive!" I can't tell what's going on between us at this moment because so many emotions flood inside of me at once that I can't decipher one from the other. I'm so angry with him but at the same time I'm proud of him. He's doing what he wants and doesn't care what anyone has to say about it.

"Don't you see?" Clouden says. "I was not alive. I was not living. I was… surviving."

I'm quite familiar with this. I know what surviving is. Day in and out… I fear everything. The lights can't go out and I need a weapon on me at all times, like I do right now; a little switchblade someone left behind on the coffee table. As if it will save me from these monsters anyway. I just feel better having it. My life has been completely altered and changed so drastically I'm not even the same person I was born as. It's not by my own choice that I changed.

"Still, a word would've been nice. I thought—" I do not want to admit I thought for some time the same abductor grabbed Clouden. Maybe he had an itch for Wilbrate that needed to be scratched again. Clouden is far too savage and brutal to have endured what I did for so long. If he were in my position, he would've probably freed himself the same night he was caught.

"What's going on with you and Erasmus?" Clouden asks.

I'm so taken aback by that question I'm unsure how to respond to it. "What? Don't change the subject!"

"You're more verbal around him than I've seen in a long time." He's talking about when he watched me follow Erasmus to his room for clean clothes, after I ridiculously covered mine in vomit.

"He was helping me. I had to at least try to be civil!" It's a lie. I didn't have to do anything.

"Like the time you were nice and punched me dead in the face? I was trying to corral you back in the house during the blackout because you were having a fit!"

I am confused as to what he means by all of this. I was rash and not entirely nice to Erasmus at all, like I am to most people. I mean, technically, I don't even respond when a lot of people talk to me but... that was before I arrived at this house.

"Listen, just stay with us. Stay with me here. Be a part of this family. You seem to like them and they seem to like you too."

Family. When did we become so broken beyond repair? Was it after my abduction? Was it before? We were a part of a decent, normal family and he's trading it in for something else. And I seem to like them? They are all strangers to me.

"Stay, Seven. I want you here."

I don't know how to answer that. I don't know what all of this even consists of.

"I'll stay for your transition," I say, because I'm at a loss for what else to do. I can at least give him this promise.

Clouden smiles at me and, behind it, I can see something calculating in his mind. I can't help but wonder what other secrets are hidden beneath that enigmatic grin.

ERASMUS

19

The compass is gone.

Immediately upon entering my room, I can smell the remnants of Seven being in here. His scent isn't strong, telling me he wasn't in here for a long time. It lingers just enough to notice. For whatever reason, he smells a bit like the woods. I can't say I understand it. He says he rarely goes outside and here he's locked in. So, the woodland scent in his blood is a mystery to me.

What was he doing snooping around in my room? The thought of him here, touching my things, makes my head spin. What else did he touch? My nose presses to the bed, hoping to find some kind of residue of him there, but the scent is all mine. He didn't go far in my room, just to the dresser where my compass is noticeably gone. The box is all wrong. I don't even have to open it to know it's missing. I check anyway.

Apart from my clothing, the compass was the only item I had with me in the tomb. It was a gift forged many years ago, by the same witch who imprisoned me. I begged her, did unthinkable things with her, just to have that compass, but it appeared to have been broken. It wasn't meant to show me the cardinal directions, instead to lead me on the right path of finding a person. Meandering aimlessly, the arrow spun in all directions unsure of where to go or which way to point. Either it was possessed or just incapable of being what I needed it to be. It was deemed a failure up until arriving here. I'm not entirely sure why I would even take the compass out at random—sentimental, I suppose—and that's when I noticed it wasn't spinning erratically any longer. It was ticking slowly toward the east until one day it stopped and hasn't moved since. That was the day Seven arrived at the front door. It's directing me to what it's created to do. Can it be mistaken?

The compass is pointing to Seven Wilbrate. Every tick of the compass' mechanical heartbeat echoes with an eerie synchronicity to him, as if the device was attuned to his existence and his alone. With this information, the boundaries between chance and destiny begin to blur. It's beginning to be clearer why I'm so obsessed with the human. This fixation with him is not just about intellectual curiosity. It's so much deeper than that.

His knife is still on my table near the window. If he was in here searching for it, he should have seen it. He came in here just to spy on me. I'm sure of that. Did the compass call to him? Or is he merely just curious about it? He should be. If he's who the compass is pointing to, he's exactly what I'm looking for.

"Erasmus," Lorcan's voice bellows like a song as he appears in the doorway. "I'm going out tonight, there's leftovers in the fridge for you and Seven. Clouden is off somewhere and Audelia is fuck only knows where." He rolls his eyes and fixes the cufflink on his suit.

"It is mind boggling how you can hunt in those suits," I say. I've been here with Lorcan for many months and I have yet to see him dress any other way.

Lorcan winks. "It's my uniform. Never feels right without it." Then he adds, "You look pensive."

I wave him off. "Det er ikke noget." My mind is a maelstrom of thoughts and I do not wish to speak with him about them tonight. It's easier to keep it all trapped in my head than to try to explain them in English to him.

He rolls his eyes even harder, "I have no idea what you're saying. Anyway," he says before I can translate, "I'll see you tomorrow. And do *not* leave the sink full of dishes again! You know how that irks me." In a blink, Lorcan is gone.

"Ja," I say to myself. "That's why I left them there."

Lorcan is terribly particular and fastidious about every corner of his home. Each item, from the tiniest knickknack to the elaborate furniture, all has its designated purpose and place here. Chaos and clutter are banished almost the instant it starts. Surely a house filled with magic in its walls can clean itself but Lorcan does not allow it. This home is a sanctuary, and he guards it fiercely.

My thoughts go back to the missing piece. If this compass is truly pointing to Seven then he is partially responsible for my imprisonment. It was my love for him in a past life that led to me betraying the witch. It's my fault for indulging in it, but it is his fault for making me love him so.

LORCAN
20

The rain does nothing to damper the smile on my face at seeing one of my oldest companions in New Orleans on my doorstep. Though, if you ask him, we are nothing of the sort. Much like Hunter LeBeaux, he says we are not friends, not acquaintances, nothing more than the hero and the villain. Or so he thinks.

The sheriff at the door is indeed looking every bit his age, and older, while I remain the same as I had when we first met. Awful to be a human at times like this, isn't it? I am quite certain, if he was immortal, he would've come for me multiple times over the many decades we've been rivals.

"I haven't been sloppy in years." I give nothing short of a dangerous smile to the elderly man at my door.

Sheriff Bernard Williams has been a man of his word over the years, as am I. You see, I don't have to bribe anyone to get what I want—I simply have to exist—what is the fun in killing everyone who crosses me? Life is a game and you don't always play fair, but to break *all* of the rules, *all* of the time, gets boring, when you're an immortal. At some point, you want to let them believe they're in charge. So, we made a deal. I would do as I wish, as long as I kept it covered, and don't go overboard. Fair, of course, for me. Not so much the citizens and tourists of this beloved city.

"Same kind of killings as before, all drained of blood," the Sheriff says in a huff.

Every conversation I've ever had with him was comical to me. This human once sought to end me. There's no contest about who the real winner is here. I can indeed kill off so easily. I won't. The sheriff has a little, lovely place in my heart... The simple truth is I have him in the palm of my hand.

"Am I the only vampire in the vicinity?" I ask even though I have an inkling what the answer will be.

"They're missing organs," he replies.

For the duration of this entire conversation, my smile did not falter. Instead, with this current comment of his, it widens. During our first few encounters, I removed my victim's internal organs and laid them as a little token of my appreciation for the new sheriff. He did not entirely believe that New Orleans was home to an array of supernatural killers. He was brand new and had just been inducted. What better way to pay tribute than to lead him on his first chase?

For years, I eluded the sheriff only to arrive in his kitchen in the middle of the night. I could've killed him and his entire family, but

I do love a good cat and mouse chase. It lasted a long time before I decided, and not a second sooner or later, that the time came to end our little charade. It was simply to show who the king of these shadows is. I have lived up to my word and did everything according to our plan.

The pictures the sheriff hands to me are different from my work, yet familiar in the very same sense. Oh, it's obvious exactly what is going on this time. Holding the photographs out for him to take once more, I meet his gaze as understanding washes over me.

"Rest your weary little head, Sheriff. I will take care of it."

SEVEN

21

"You know they found him in a tomb, right?" Audelia asks. She's following me down the hall and has been increasingly eager for my attention. It's all so strange to me. I don't have a sister, and I never wanted one. Audelia has me quickly wishing I grew up with one. "No one knows how he ended up there or why." For whatever reason, Audelia is droning on and on, filling me in on all the gossip about Erasmus. As much as she dislikes him, she does talk an awful lot about him.

"Probably because he was pushing people out of the windows." I'm being sarcastic but Audelia laughs, taking it as a serious joke.

"I think he's into you," Audelia says.

I stop walking. "How can you say that, Audelia. He *pushed* me out of a fucking window." Funny enough, I do kind of get the feeling Erasmus likes me a bit, though I can't imagine why he would.

"If he wasn't so grumpy he would actually be handsome," she says.

She's wrong about that. Erasmus isn't hard to look at all. If you're into men. Which I'm not. Dusty, light blond hair streaked with soft gray lines is almost always slicked back, never hiding the impressively chiseled cheek bones of his face. He has this old fashioned look about him that reminds me of Ancient Greece. Not only does he favor what I imagine a gladiator to look like, he acts like one too. He's a born leader, where I'm just the opposite. It's obvious he isn't from this era in time.

I pretend to ignore that part of her conversation and try for the front door again. "I feel like this is some kind of sick joke." It still won't budge. "You try it." I say.

She does and the door easily opens for her. The instant I set foot towards it, the heavy wooden slab thuds shut. The world out there beyond its threshold grows increasingly distant, as if it's trying to isolate me.

"This is getting so weird." Just the thought of being trapped in this house makes my heart race. Audelia must sense it. Her expression changes and she sniffs the air around my face.

"Stop being excited," she says. "It's making the blood rush to your cheeks. I can smell it there." She inhales deeply and adds, "It smells lovely."

I'm blushing even harder from her compliments. It's easy to forget she's a vampire. Her movements mimic so we match at a much slower speed than I'm sure she cares to go. Maybe she does it so I don't feel uncomfortable. As a supernatural creature, I get the idea she would like to use all of her powers all of the time.

"Come on." She pokes my arm playfully. "Let's go play Monopoly or something."

I begin to follow her, but I take a look back at the front door again. "I wish it would let me out of here."

Audelia sighs. "Are we really a terrible company?"

"No! No, nothing like that." My head shakes wildly. "It would just be nice to have the option to go outside, that's all."

A perfectly sculpted eyebrow pops up. "You don't want to go outside, do you?" I suppose it's obvious I'm not a super outdoorsy guy anymore.

"No," I say through an exhale. "Still. I would like to have the option." It's still a mystery as to why I can't leave. Clouden said the house is haunted or something. That should freak me out by itself. I'm more afraid of living people than ghosts. Speaking of Clouden, I'm actually shocked he isn't around a lot while I'm stuck here too. He's been popping in and out. I tried to follow him outside too, and the front door slammed closed before I got there and it wouldn't budge.

Audelia and I make it back to the room they call mine. She's busy digging around the closet looking for the board game, I guess it's stashed in there. I notice a box sitting neatly on my bed. It's just a plain cardboard box with a big messy bow on top. The bow is tied too loosely on one end and too tightly on the other, like a child wrapped it in haste to get it done. A small, torn piece of paper is left next to it and it reads:

Seven,

Med kærlighed,

Erasmus

I have no idea what it says or even means. I tear open the box and drop the whole thing to the floor immediately.

"What's wrong?" Audelia uses her inhuman speed to be at my side.

All I can do is point at the box and the grotesque, slimy thing half hanging out of it. The object is about the size of my inner hand, with a sickly red and dark brown color, and appears to be disturbingly damp. The wet, glistening sheen only increases the sense of unease I feel. "Please tell me that's not what I think it is," I say.

Audelia picks it up and in her bare hands confirms it's indeed what I assume: a human heart.

"Aw, it's a heart!" She's beaming happily and picks up the box to set it back inside before handing it back to me. "See? He likes you."

I stare down at it and anger fills me. Surprisingly, I'm not mad at Erasmus. I'm angry at myself for feeling like this is actually romantic, in a sense. It's insane to me. This dead heart in a box touches the living, beating one in my chest. This scares me more than anything.

Not a moment more is wasted before I stalk the hallway, banging on every door in the house, even though I know which one belongs to him. A few doors down, Erasmus pokes his head out, and that's when I lose it.

"What is this?" I shove the box toward him. Adrenaline surges through me and my heart is racing, not from the gift anymore. It's from seeing him. Knowing he means this as a sweet gesture should disturb me more than it does. When he doesn't answer, I steer the conversation and begin to yell things I don't mean…

"What am I supposed to do with this? Huh?" He opens his mouth but I stop him from answering. "*This* is gross, Erasmus!" I shake the box at him with all the anger bubbling inside of me. "It's unsanitary and it's going to smell! It's not what you give people as a present."

Erasmus is calm and, from the soft grin that momentarily washes across his face, he's pleased by my reaction. It doesn't last. He begins to yell at me in another language so fast, even if I could understand it, the speed alone throws me off.

"What are you saying?" I shout back at him.

"If you don't want it, give it back!" He spews the words at me.

I pull the box close. "No! You can't just take something back you gave away. It doesn't work like that."

A sadistic looking grin creases his mouth again. "Then stop complaining."

"I wasn't complaining!" I am and I *know* I am. I'm absolutely disgusted I find this gesture amorous in any way, but here we are.

Somehow, I manage to back away from him and head back to my room, where the door slams behind me on its own, as if the house agrees with me on this matter. The breath in my throat catches and I toss the box to the chair, before another wave of panic begins. Only, this time, I don't go running out like a lunatic, I seek to ground myself in the present moment.

He meant no harm. His intention was the opposite. The monsters— No, the *people* in this house are unorthodox. They show love and care in the strangest of ways. Their way is no less meaningful. The heart in the box is completely unhinged but amorous. Erasmus is just trying to show how he feels in the only way he knows how. It should not be comforting at all, yet the knot of panic is slowly untangling, if only for a second. My calm response to this wild gift creates an even bigger onset of anxiety. I cannot possibly be alright with this shit.

The door to my room opens and Clouden slips in. I let out a deep exhale and rush over to close the door behind him. I'm not taking any chances of Erasmus popping in too.

"I came to see if you need anything," he says.

"I *need* to get out of here." I say these words, but I don't know if I actually believe them. A part of me yearns to actually stay and I can't explain why. My heart and brain are conflicted with one another.

Clouden shifts from one foot to the other. "Seven, being here will all make sense one day."

"I wish you'd stop trying to be mysterious and tell me why."

He shakes his head. "I can't. I only know you need to be here. The house knows this. It's why you can't leave. You're here for a reason."

"Yea, I came here to bring you home."

"It's more now. You feel it, I know you do. You have to be patient."

He would say this. Clouden is one of the most patient people I know and it's partially because of me. Growing up with an older brother who needs extra care shapes your outlook on life.

"Just give it time. I hate to say it, but relax." Clouden laughs softly. He knows I can't fucking relax. I haven't been able to in years.

I don't argue with him. I just glance at the box containing the heart and imagine Erasmus carving it out of someone's chest to give it to me. The rapid shifting beat of my own heart is heard pounding in my ears, but sure, relax.

ERASMUS

22

Just like almost all of the other rooms in this massive home, Lorcan's study is left unlocked. Everything here is open for all of us to use as we wish, except when the house does not want us somewhere. The house is somehow alive and can't be explained. Things will move from where I leave them, and doors I unlocked before will be locked again. When asked about it, Lorcan simply said, "The house is enchanted. If you are meant to be here inside of it, you would be. If not, well, you'll die a painful death."

It makes absolutely no sense to me. Often, I would assume it's Lorcan moving my things where he doesn't not want them to be. He's meticulous like that. What does not add up is how this happens even when he isn't home.

I sit at the large mahogany desk and thumb through Lorcan's

Rolodex. Unlike Clouden and Audelia who use the latest technology, Lorcan is pretty old-fashioned when it comes to certain things, thankfully. It is filled to the brim with names and numbers of those that the vampire has come to call his friends and acquaintances over the years. I'm looking for one name in particular.

When Lorcan came to free me, I heard him on the phone with a woman named Wisteria. I recall him saying she's a brilliant witch, all powerful and intelligent beyond measure. I do not believe Lorcan hands out such compliments without truth as the foundation. As much as I distrust witches I need one at this very moment. The other lady that accompanied him, Justice, I do not want to bother. I get the sense she's even more powerful and I'm not looking to be tossed back into another tomb.

"Erasmus," the witch on the other side of the line says. "It was only a matter of time." Of course, she would have some knowledge of my plans. Most witches have a keen sense of foretelling.

"I have been told you are the most powerful witch of this century." A little flattery typically works wonders.

"Well… if they said *that,* they're lying." There is a pause of silence before she adds, "I'm the most powerful witch *of all time.*"

I am certain she can sense the corners of my lips rising in a smile. I can bet any money that she's probably scrying in a bowl watching me this very moment to see this exact reaction.

"Perfect." Before this little phone call, the witch could have done her research to see exactly what she is getting into. They love to be ready. "I require your assistance, if you will be so kind." Being trusted by Lorcan holds her to the highest standard in my eyes. He tends to flaunt how he has many 'friends' except there are only a handful of those he truly trusts.

"Oh, this is interesting. What's in it for me?"

Always a price. Nothing in this world is free. I knew this before calling her. I half hoped she would want to simply help because she can. "What could I give to a powerful witch that she cannot take for herself?"

Her laughter is borderline seductive. "Why should I take it when I could get others to do it for me?"

She has a point, and she is well aware of that. She is also well aware that I'm in no predicament to turn her down.

"Name your price," I say.

"Well, I need nothing at the moment... however, I can accept an *IOU*." She has me cornered. Being in debt to a witch is not something I would recommend. Desperate times call for desperate measures. I will have to deal with the consequences of this action later.

"Alright. I have two requests. First, I need a potion for everlasting life" *Or a curse*. I think to myself. Something to make Seven immortal like me. If he chooses to and willingly accepts it, then perfect. I'm not sure what I will do if I have to force him to take the potion. We shall see how that little conversation will go soon.

"Second, I need to revisit the past," I continue.

The witch whistles low. "Time travel is tricky, Erasmus. So many mistakes can happen to alter the lives of many."

"I only need five seconds. You can accompany me if you wish. I will touch nothing."

As selfish as it is on my part, I won't change a thing. Altering Seven's path can ultimately lead him elsewhere in his future, thus possibly not ever coming here to Lorcan's house. *That* I can not have.

"I will help you, Immortal Erasmus," Wisteria answers with an air of eloquence as if she has already seen how the play of my events will unfold. I dare not ask her what happens or the reason why she sounds so eager for it. This can go very well for me... or very badly. I'm more than willing to take the chance.

"When can I meet with you?"

LORCAN

23

"Please, have a seat." Seven moves toward the two massive chairs separated by a coffee table between them. He chooses the one to the left, so I settle in to the one on the right. The sunroom in the back of the house is a perfect place for us to just relax together. The knife I keep on me at all times slips back up my sleeve for the time being so we can enjoy this little tea party that I conjured up for the two of us.

"I thought the two of us could enjoy a nice, hot cup of tea together." It's my house after all, what kind of host am I to not indulge my guests with a little southern hospitality? But the human does not seem at ease with being here, and constantly fidgets about while I pour the tea. The sun is setting slowly through the windows that surround my sunroom and it casts a nice warm glow around us. It mimics soft candlelight.

After handing him a cup, I ask, "Enjoying your stay?"

Shaky fingers wrap around his mug of tea as he nods. It's quiet apart from the sound of his heart pounding against his ribcage with obvious fright. I believe even anyone without superb senses can hear it.

"Why won't the house let me leave?" he asks.

I take a sip of my tea and smile. "If I knew, I would surely tell you, dear boy. The house does what it wants to do. It needs you here for whatever reason and I am certain this reason will be laid out for you one of these days." By the rolling of his eyes I can tell my answer doesn't appease him. He accepts it nonetheless.

When the sun finally sets, the room is illuminated from the light of the sconces on the wall. They're set to turn on at a specific time each day. Seven's brows fuse together in thought as his lips part. It would seem he's fighting whether or not to speak freely, and soon gives in. "Is it truly human meat in the dinners?"

I smile on the rim of my tea cup while sipping slowly. "Of course it is."

Squirming in his seat, he appears to be fighting with himself internally again. Eyes fixate on the liquid in his cup, I can imagine the thoughts running through his mind about it. If he had human meat for dinner then just what is in this tea?

"You know," I say softly, "Luring them in is half the fun." Saying this does nothing to ease his nerves. I deduced it wouldn't. Truth be told, it's done the opposite. In addition to his heartbeat hammering away, his breathing hitches as well.

"Oh, don't worry, Seven. You're safe here." Stopping midway from another sip, I smile. "I think."

"As long as Erasmus doesn't push me out of another window,"

he says under his breath. Does he really, truly think Erasmus is the threat here when he sits across from a ruthless killer such as myself?

"You'll never let that go will you?" I ask playfully.

"Would you?" he counters, and the smile that graces my lips is the answer. I'm far too theatrical to just let something so illustrious slide by without taking advantage of it.

"Speaking of which," I begin, "are you aware he's in the kitchen right this second, hovering, to keep his eye on you?"

Seven is finally about to take a sip and instead freezes. He glances at me and then behind us, in search of his stalker. He clears his throat and turns back to face the window, where he seemingly stares out at the yard. I can bet he is listening for any signs of what Erasmus is up to next.

When Seven shifts in the chair to get comfortable, a bit of the stuffing comes loose. It is an old chair after all.

"Oops." I lean forward to push the stuffing back in and Seven catches sight of it. Immediately the blood in his face begins to drain as he puts two and two together. This is not an ordinary chair stuffed with feathers or cotton.

"Lorcan," he says softly, "What is in this chair?"

"This one is stuffed with the finest hair in the world. She was a model I think." Then I ponder on that thought while Seven drops his tea cup. It shatters on the floor by his feet and spills everywhere, creating a nice little puddle of tea and glass at his feet.

"Damn, that was my good China." With supernatural speed I have the broom in my hand and clear up the mess before he can blink again. "I'll keep in mind, next time, to give you plastic."

The Adam's apple in his throat bobs heavily as he swallows back his fear, and whatever questions he has he does not ask. Instead, without looking back, he just heads in the direction to his room. I shrug his quick departure off.

In my solitude, I pull out my phone and send a quick text to Hunter LeBeaux. Just a friendly little smiley face with exclamation marks behind it, to remind him of this adoring friendship we have.

"Oh, that's right. No, she was the Greek actress!" I pick up my mug and down the rest of what's left in it. "The model is in the sofa."

SEVEN

24

ut of nowhere, the walls of my room begin to shake. I jump up from the bed and head for the bedroom door, to seek solace in the hallway, when it slams shut in my face. The window is rattling on its own accord as the space under the window goes from being empty to occupied by a large reading nook. A nice cushion forms, following it is a lamp sticking out of the wall. The carpet beneath my feet rumples to push me toward the window space that just created itself out of thin air. I stand there in shock while slowly running my fingers over the cushion in awe.

"How did you just create something out of nothing?" This defies all laws of science and everything I've ever understood about life.

"You're not haunted, are you?" I ask. The room stills. "You're alive." In some strange way that feels right. This house is an entity of its own. It's keeping me here, as Lorcan said, for a reason. I want to ask that question out loud of 'why' but I refrain. It just gave me a gift and I don't want to sound ungrateful. I already made that mistake before with Erasmus and the heart in the box. This is different. This is *the house.*

Immediately, the book shelf on the far side of the room fills from the top to the bottom with new books for me to read, and to spend time at my new window nook.

"You're trying to get me to stay too, aren't you?" The room is silent again. "Thank you," I whisper and touch the wall before heading out to find Lorcan. I have to call my parents. It's been on my mind for a bit and I can't put it off any longer.

He's in the living room reading a newspaper. "I need a phone," I say.

"Calling the police, are we?" Lorcan's smile is malicious, daring, even as he peeks up from the newspaper.

"My parents. I'm serious… they're probably worried sick."

I can't imagine they wouldn't be. Both Clouden and myself are gone again. Neither of us has popped up for even a second to show we're still alive. Lorcan immediately hands his cell phone over to me, without a care.

But, when I call, they aren't worried at all…

"You're not in your room? We thought you just locked yourself in."

I've done it before. Locked myself in for almost a week before I snapped at the claustrophobia of being locked in. This time they didn't even bother to check on me. I'm thirty-two and I don't need anyone to check on me. Still…

"I'm glad you're out of the house, Seven," my mother says.

I don't even remember how I responded to her. The call ended soon after. Staring into space, I realize Clouden has been right all along. No one gives a rat's ass what we've been up to. They are at peace without me, and truthfully they deserve the peace. I'm nothing more than a burden on them.

"Thanks." I hand the phone back to Lorcan and go in search of the bedroom he is letting me stay in. It's a beautiful bedroom and I should be thankful to even be allowed to stay in it. The colors of the walls are warm and calming and the bed is the most luxurious thing I ever can imagine, with a ton of blankets. There isn't too much furniture and the lighting is so perfect when it's on. This room feels like one big giant hug.

I suppose after Clouden's transition I'll have to figure out some new living arrangements for myself. After realizing how content they probably are, going back to my parents is not an option. Clouden says to stay here. How can I possibly unfold this mess of myself onto these people?

With this thought, I don't even change my clothes, I just flop on the bed and try to force myself to sleep.

It happens just as it has many times before. I wake up drenched in sweat, and it makes me feel like a flood has begun around me. The panic always starts when the flood reaches my arms. Truth be told, there's no literal flood, or so I've been told. It's so realistic to me at the time.

Even all the lights on in my room can not stop the panic that's starting to rise up. I throw the blankets off of me and, almost stumbling out of bed through gasps of air with a door knob fight. I manage to rip the door wide open with more force than I care to. The doorknob ricochets off the wall and bounces it back.

There's a flood rising up and it exists only in my head. Someone can stand right in front of me, point to my dry floor, and turn blue in the face trying to convince me there's no flood in my room. Internally, I'm drowning in a swell of emotions. *That's* the literal flood I feel. Every emotion happening at the same time is drowning me, suffocating me with its vast presence. When I get like this, nothing makes sense.

Clouden is in the hallway, trying to reel me back into reality. It doesn't work. Somehow I force myself free of his presence and I race down the stairs, barely taking them two at a time, until the front door comes into view. I don't even register how it actually opens for me this time. The grass is thick and damp with morning dew under my bare feet. The sun isn't up, and there's darkness all around, triggering yet another wave of emotions in me.

Arms wrap around me and I fight them.

"No! No! Don't fucking touch me! Get off of me!" He covers my mouth and bile rises in my throat. I'm about to hurl everywhere if he doesn't let me fucking go.

"Seven!" Clouden has been screaming my name throughout this entire ordeal, but I ignore it "Seven please, let's get back in the house!"

"*In the house*? With the fucking *maniac* who fucked me with God only knows what and fed me fucking shit?"

"Seven, I need you to breathe for me. Alright? Can you do that?" It's Erasmus talking this time.

"I'm already breathing, that's the fucking problem!" I say a lot of dumb shit when I panic.

"It's not a problem at all. Would you like a piece of chocolate?"

Chocolate?" As if that would calm me in any sense! It only makes me angry for a split second until the coloring of the wrapper catches my eye. My stomach immediately growls and. The next thing I know, I'm walking again, following the bar of fucking chocolate. Their voices are coaxing me. Erasmus' sticks out more than Clouden's. It's something calm and soothing like being wrapped in a bubble bath or like warm chocolate. I can melt into his voice so easily.

"Erasmus, he's having a panic attack. I don't think it's best for him to eat any—"

"You tackle him"—Erasmus whips around to face my brother—"in the middle of the street, and try to cover his mouth, *knowing* his fear of physical contact? Do not *tell* me what *you* think is best." His Danish accent is the most profound I've ever heard.

My brother does not respond. Neither do I. I'm too drained to speak again. Every fiber in my body is slowly realizing how truly exhausted I am. I'm not going to make it with chocolate and... I don't.

I almost pass out right there in the front yard, until Erasmus says, "A little further." So, I push myself to at least get past the threshold.

"Control your human, Erasmus," Lorcan's voice sings out from the upstairs banister. "The neighbors might talk."

ERASMUS

25

During this early morning charade, Seven manages to come out with only a few minor scrapes and some bruising. The worst of it all is his knuckles. They're red and raw with the skin pulled back around tiny open wounds like he may have tried to fight the pavement. I wouldn't doubt it if he did. He was completely unhinged. The fire inside of him momentarily became uncontrollable.

Seven is seated at the table failing miserably at bandaging himself up. His mind has slipped back into place but he's still scrambling for thought. I slide to the seat next to him, purposely taking up his space.

"May I?" I hold my hand out to him.

It takes a moment before Seven puts his hand in mine and I can see he's fighting back the revolting churn in his stomach once more. I carefully clean up the drying blood from his hand and wrap the wounds with gauze. Even though I refrain as much as I can from skin contact, it's still an intimate moment for me. The way he allows me to take care of him at this moment gives me much pleasure.

It's quiet between us, yet there is no tension. His mind is fumbling through thoughts that I want him to be vocal about. If only I can peek inside his head... well I can peek inside of him physically, all I need to do is to peel back the skin, but that's not going to give me access to his thoughts.

"Stay with me," I finally say. "I heard the conversation with your parents. Why not stay here? You *are* welcome."

Seven doesn't speak. The features of his face are loud enough to talk for him so he doesn't have to. His eye contact is far too direct and unwavering in a frozen gaze; a confidence he typically lacks. He's been contemplating this. Clouden has asked him to stay before. He planted the tiny seed and since then, it must've been growing. Realizing his parents are happy without him is the fertilizer which the little sapling needs to blossom.

"Stay with me *and* become immortal," I whisper.

"Why the fuck would I want to live forever?" His voice sounds defeated and the lines on his forehead worry his flesh in more thinking.

"Stay or go. I'm going to give you a choice, Seven." Perhaps this isn't the best time to tell him. Truthfully, it needs to be said sooner rather than later. "At some point, I will press this blade into your skin. You can live or die. It's up to you."

His eyes darken as his gaze shoots up at me. I love the range of blue his eyes become with his change in emotions.

"Again. Why would I want to live forever?"

"Why wouldn't you?"

He laughs shortly. "If I ever get kidnapped again I'm going to have to live forever through the suffering? I don't fucking think so."

My jaw is set before I answer, "Nothing of the sort will ever happen to you again."

"How are you so confident? What's so different this time?" he asks, confusion written all over him.

"You have me."

Staring at the table, Seven's brows fuse in deep thought, as if this has never even once crossed his mind. His hand is palm up in mine still, he has been so far away in his mind that it possibly does not occur to him I'm still touching his skin. Or perhaps he does not mind. That would make all the difference in the world.

"You can't keep me safe always, Erasmus. Forever is a long time."

"You underestimate me." *And this obsession I have with you.* "I know the beat of your heart like I know my favorite song. Every word, every tempo, and swing. I would find you in literally a heartbeat," I coo at him.

Seven says nothing for a moment and then I add, "You also underestimate yourself and what you can be. Nothing like your past will happen ever again because you won't allow it to."

He shifts in his seat and finally retracts his hand. I find it odd how he is more uncomfortable with me complimenting him than the knowledge that I listen so closely to his heartbeat. Right now it is pulsing erratically.

Seven sighs, sounding incredibly disappointed. "You're going to do whatever you want anyway. Whether I say yes or no, so why does it even matter?"

This is true. What matters is how he would choose this life with me. It's a wonderful idea, to think he will.

"Erasmus, what you witnessed last night is who I am—you've seen all of this madness inside of me. "*Why* would you want it to live forever? *You* killing *me* would be a blessing."

"Those panic attacks are not who you are. They're a part of you, that, in time, will leave you. I can help you with it." It's not only a promise, it's a vow. If he picks me, I will dedicate my immortal life to taking care of his every need. Being in that tomb, I witnessed myself go through many emotions; panic being one of them at the beginning. I had to find something to ground myself and we will find Seven's.

It's silent again between us. I can feel his eyes on my face surveying me, and for a long time, I do not think he will speak again, until he actually does.

"Why me?" His voice is low, as if he's hoping I won't hear him. The question isn't a 'woe is me', it is indeed the tone of a serious interrogation.

"Why not you?"

He rolls his eyes. It's not the answer he wants, so I give him the rest of it. "Your mind intrigues me. The way you see the world intrigues me. *You* intrigue me."

He huffs out a breath. "There are plenty of other mentally unstable beings. Are you just going to collect them all?"

I smile. "I think one is enough."

His lips curl before he frowns once more and quickly adds, "And once you're done *fixing me*, then what?"

I'm not *fixing* him, there's nothing wrong with him. I'm freeing him.

"Then we enjoy life."

"Together?" he asks, as if it sounds like the silliest thing he's ever heard.

"Together."

Those deep blue eyes are a canvas of contradictions, swirling again like a kaleidoscope of emotions. He's mulling this over more.

"Think about it," I add. "You have some time."

The knife will drive into him. Whether he lives or dies is up to him, either way, I will have my taste of Seven Wilbrate. The wait will be worth it and the outcome will surpass even my wildest dreams.

LORCAN

26

Audelia probably won't ever comprehend precisely how I found her. Once my mind is set, I will stop at nothing until I get my way. This was proven earlier this spring, when I could do nothing but think of the tomb Erasmus was imprisoned in. Determination is one thing. When your entire world cannot continue until the task is complete, it can be a burden. Finding her is key and, thanks to my heightened senses, I'm able to track her down. I do have the help of the many voices inside my head. They help lead me to her in the same fashion they lead me to my victims. I'm navigating the streets drawn by the subtle traces of her scent and the vibrations her body leaves in the air. She's been avoiding me for some time now, and I've allowed her the freedom to have some fun. I need her home now.

She didn't bother with a coat. She's a fucking vampire and everyone knows we don't need it. I do wish she would do better to blend in before she gets herself caught up in too much danger.. The outfit she chose for her night out completely fit her mood; a fiery, short, little red dress and red heels to match. It's heinous and absurd. Perhaps I'm thinking too much like a father figure, or it could be that I know terrible fashion when I see it. How could she do this to me? Of all the dresses in her closet she takes the one that could be mistaken for a fishing net.

The bar is subtle with slight traces of life tonight. Not odd for a Thursday evening in New Orleans. Every night is the weekend here, so there's bound to be people out and about. Audelia saunters in and, naturally, all eyes are on her as she slips onto a barstool. It's surprising to watch her flirt so casually with the bartender. She's looking around, probably trying to scope the place out to find her next victim. I'm out of sight and I thought to be out of mind until Audelia whispers to herself, "I'm draining one of these fuckers tonight and not even Lorcan himself would be able to stop me."

I could pop out of these shadows and prove her wrong. Instead, I let curiosity get the best of me to see what she's truly up to when I'm not around.

A young man who appears to be no older than Audelia occupies the barstool next to her. He takes one look at her and then says, "You look like you need a drink."

Audelia doesn't even glance his way and replies, "Isn't that why we're all in a fucking bar?"

The young man laughs, and I cringe internally at how forceful it sounds. He's trying entirely too hard already. When she blatantly ignores him, it does nothing to deter his confidence. I'm annoyed with him, and I can only imagine that she is as well. From the looks of it, her patience has grown substantially. She has yet to tear his lips from his face. I imagine she's thinking of something like that.

"Is he bothering you?"

There's another man who appears to inject himself into the conversation. This one is taller, bald and slim. His attire could use some enhancements. Overall, he's not terrible looking. Audelia seems taken with him instantly.

"Well?" he adds to the question.

"If I say yes," Audelia begins, "What are you going to do?"

"If you say yes, I'll bust his head open and eat his fucking brain."

Audelia shifts her focus from the bald man standing to the one in the barstool next to her who began laughing as if he thought this was a joke. She nods, and the new male does not hesitate to do just exactly what he said he would. Without a care that any mortal would see him, he slams a hammer he's been holding into the back of the annoying man's head. Before the body can hit the floor, he peels apart the bone and pulls out a piece of the spongy brain. And he eats it. From my supernatural senses, I can tell he's not a vampire. He's certainly something, though.

"Are you trying to impress me?" Audelia asks.

The man, who I'll call 'her savior'; just for kicks, licks his finger clean of the mess. "Well no... I was quite hungry but... did it?"

Her shoulders lift in a shrug before falling. "If I say yes... Can I watch you do it again?"

The blood pooling in the corners of his lips begins to drizzle down his neck. Audelia is practically salivating at this point, and her savior knows it.

"Next one," he says, "we share." He wipes his mouth with the back of his sleeve and smiles as he leans against the bar counter. No one even regards them. Not one soul bothers with what just happened. "What's your name?"

"Audelia," she replies without hesitation. "You?"

"Cato." His eyes flick around the room,. "They call me 'The End'"

"Oh?" Audelia looks around, too. "Who does?"

Cato smiles wider through a snort. "Anybody worth knowing."

Glancing at the body on the floor, she asks, "Are we leaving him there?"

A simple snap of his fingers ushers in a barmaid. "Be a doll, yes?" He doesn't even have to tell her what to do. She hauls the body away just as quickly as she came over.

"You run this joint?"

"In so many words." His brow pops up. "Are you even more impressed?"

"Maybe."

He holds out his arm for her. "I did promise a share." After just the slightest pause to let him wonder if she was going or not, Audelia slips her arm through his.

"Impress me some more, then."

As they exit the bar, I slip out of the shadows. I do hate to disturb her night but she's got the damn sheriff keeping his eye on me again. If I don't get her ass back in line it will only mean more chaos I'll have to fix.

The next stop is not another bar, as I assumed it would be. They disappear behind a hotel door, and I fight the urge to go bust it down. Audelia is on thin ice with the whole sheriff charade. She's doing it on purpose, and I wonder if she's about to cut up Cato as her next victim. What I find is the opposite. Here she is, completely naked, apart from the thin sheet twisted between her ankles.

"Having fun, are we?"

She covers herself quickly. "Shit, Lorcan!"

"Come now, Delia, you act as though I've never seen a damn tit before." Oh, I have. Many of them. Typically while being sliced into thin layers for my recipes.

Her little friend emerges from the bathroom with a gun pointed at me.

"No use, dear boy. *That* won't kill *me*." I nod at the gun. "Besides, if you pull the trigger while it's aimed at me, you'd do best to fucking run, while you still have legs."

Audelia rolls her eyes. "What do you want, Lorcan."

"A father cannot miss his daughter?" A pout creases my blood stained lips.

She knows better than this. My tone is playful, mocking, even as my head tilts to stare her way. I pay no mind to Cato any longer, and why should I? The only threat in this room is me.

"You're being reckless. The mortals are in an uproar," I say, and before she can retort, I hold up a hand and continue. "Yes, we can take them all on, but at some point they will have enough technology to take on *us*. I would prefer it if you kept yourself under the radar as I've taught you."

My focus remains on her face. As her form does absolutely nothing for me in any other sense besides cooking. I do have manners. "Instantly. Cover your tits and ass and get home. Clouden's transition is coming soon, and we must prepare."

"Mhm. The real reason why you came for me. You didn't miss me. You want me back for Clouden's shit. It's always him."

There it is. Lately, she has been giving quite the little attitude when it comes to Clouden. It's easy to see she is jealous of him. It's all for no reason. I adore them both just the same. Audelia does not seem like the type of girl to entertain such foolish thoughts but I suppose we all have our moments.

"I came for you, darling Delia. You need more training. I've seen the pictures of your recent little victims, and there is progress. You still have much work to do." My lips purse once more in thought and then add, "How the sheriff thought those knife strokes were mine is a mystery indeed."

"Got your attention, though, didn't it?" she snaps.

A perfect brow arches at her question as the edges of my lips slowly incline.

"Is this what it is? A cry for attention? Well. Yes. You certainly got it." Then I look at Cato, who is still watching this little conversation unfold. "Now that you have my attention," I say, while landing my gaze on her once more. "You'd best entertain me."

I have always said there is one danger in this world above all, and the true danger is right here, standing in this room. Should I become bored, it would be dangerous indeed. I leave the hotel room and close the door behind. Repicking the lock, it clicks back in place. I can hear her scoff, probably because this room is so easy to break into. I could've busted the door down, but I decided to opt for a tidier way in. Maybe she'll get the room deposit back.

SEVEN

27

It probably should be a worry, how obsessed Erasmus is with me. In all reality, it's having the opposite effect. There's safety and security because he's always watching me. He's always right there, close enough to me. Erasmus might think he's in control of whatever we are. He's completely wrong. I've learned easily here all I have to do is widen my eyes, pout my lips just a bit, and he's lapping out of the palm of my hand. Considering he gives me a choice to live or die is just another move to try to show he's in control. I can keep batting my lashes at him to keep him at bay.

How long will it last? I don't really know. Maybe it'll buy me more time until I figure this out more. I mean, this is a major choice. He's already made it clear he will try to kill me. I can't comprehend this completely. He's saved me multiple times, mostly from myself, so why would he do all of that just to drive a knife into me? It all boils down to control. The scary part is I should be panicking about this whole thing and I'm not.

It's been almost a week since Eras brought up the 'live or die' situation. I think the little innocent faces I'm throwing his way, sometimes accidental, are dominating his thoughts. *Eras*. Since when did I become so comfortable forming this little nickname? Probably since the moment my skin began to tingle whenever he's near.

"What's this?" I sigh. "If there's more organs in any of these, I'm going to scream." Boxes are covering the bedroom floor.

"Lorcan." That's all Erasmus says as I tear open the first package.

"With Erasmus' help!" Lorcan yells from down in the kitchen. Super hearing, of course, he's listening in.

Every parcel has an assortment of clothing. One box contains socks, another has underwear, and at least three have shirts.

"He assumed you needed something more to wear, apart from Clouden's pajamas. They barely fit you."

It's true. Clouden is taller than I am, so everything is long. I'm a little thicker in the thighs and nothing truly fits. I just make it work because it's all I have here. I haven't asked for someone to go home to grab my things. It's not because I feared they wouldn't. I did not want them to see my parents. They won't ask questions and I think that would only break my heart more. I want to go myself to see their faces, see how they will react to me popping back up, but the front door is locked again anyway. I check it daily. Sometimes hourly.

"Thank you," I whisper to Eras.

Instead of his voice responding, I hear Lorcan yell, "You're welcome!"

Clothing piece after clothing piece, I remove them from the boxes and hang each one up or place them in a drawer.

"He must like company, hm?" I ask Erasmus, regarding Lorcan.

The first night I stayed, there was nothing in the bathroom for toiletries. Come morning, the shelves were packed with everything from toothbrushes to bath bombs. He wasted no time in making sure I have everything a person would need. I have to say it is very heartwarming, despite the complete insanity of the situation.

"I think he cares a great deal for his family... I also believe the house itself plays a part in this."

Family. I don't even bother with the rest of Erasmus' sentence. Erasmus makes it seem like I'm already accepted into this home. He's trying to manipulate me into saying yes to staying here with them, by slipping in words he feels will resonate the most with me. Erasmus is far from stupid. He knows my own family has been broken over the years and he knows I want to belong to something. It's all about controlling a situation.

As I look down at the clothes on the bed, I can't help to think Lorcan likes the idea of control as well. The toothbrush he picked out and the soap on the counter were all there because he chose it, just like the clothes in the box. Whatever he bought, we have no choice but to use it. Don't get me wrong, I'm more than grateful. I'm just trying to point out that it's all about control here, and I'll play this little game.

"Would you maybe grab me something to drink?" I ask. "Please?" I place the shirt down on the bed and widen my eyes at him to try the innocent look on for size once more. Erasmus shifts from one foot to the other. Even though I get uncomfortable looking people in the eyes, I hold Erasmus's stare. For some reason, it's easy to do so with him. The otherwise calm and controlling man falters just from this move of mine. He nods before disappearing into the hallway.

For a moment, there's a triumphant smile on my face. Then I notice the vial on the nightstand. This wasn't there earlier today. A note attached has the words, *'Drink for immortality.'* My innocent doe-like eyes can only get me so far. Maybe I'm *not* in as much control as I think. This game is for the Kings, and I'm just a pawn.

ERASMUS

28

utside the college building a much younger Seven Wilbrate emerges quickly into view and begins the walk from the library to his dorm. This version of Seven is strange to look at in the way he carries himself. There isn't a lot of arrogance in his stride yet it's more than the Seven in the present time at the house.

"I'll give you a few minutes, Erasmus," Wisteria says. "If you touch so much as a leaf that shouldn't be touched, trust me when I say I'll torture you for the rest of your immortal life."

As promised, the witch lived up to her end of the deal. The potion was delivered to my door, and she has taken me back in time to witness this heinous act. No questions asked. This does leave me in a huge debt to her. Technically she can ask for anything. If worse comes to worst, I'll bargain with another witch to take her out. How far will I go for Seven Wilbrate? Who knows, I might make it a game to find out.

"Well," I start to answer in return to the witch. "That sounds a little like foreplay to me."

She swats her hand at my chest. Earlier conversation explained her favor is for women. As far as mine… well, it would seem it is for the one I'm doing all of this for. Prior to this little adventure, Wisteria spoke of herself, highly, of course. She did mention how she needs to get back to the woman she left in her bed to come aid me. The day when Seven came barging in the house shifted a change in me. Prior to his arrival, I was busy preoccupying my time with murder. Now I yearn for this man in ways I can not even comprehend.

So far tonight, there was not another soul out and about in sight apart from Wisteria and I. The abductor knew what he was doing. No cameras on this side of the college, from what I can see. He planned this all too perfectly. Had he not harmed Seven, I would be impressed by his efforts. Terrible for him his is no ordinary human he fucked with. This one belongs to me.

The scene finally begins to unfold and the instinct to protect Seven grasps me for a second. From the information I gathered from Seven, listening to each gruesome detail, multiple times, Wisteria knew precisely where to land us. Seven was not pleased to talk about the encounter more than once, but I needed to see the sequence in complete understanding so I coaxed him for as many details as I could.

I watch as the man cracks the brick on the back of the skull of a much younger Seven. Then as he blacks out, the abductor carries my boy to his car. *My boy.* When did I begin to think of him as this? The first time I laid eyes on him. It only did not resonate at first.

This man, the abductor, has no idea what he holds in his arms. Otherwise, he would not have trifled with him. The car door slams, and the man hurries to the driver's seat before speeding away.

This part is what I need to see.

"Let's get back," I say to Wisteria. She again asks no questions before uncorking the bottle of potion that wraps us in a fog to carry us home to the present time. There is much work to be done still.

"See?" I say with a grin. "Nothing out of place."

"He must mean a great deal to you," Wisteria answers. "Could've botched time, offering him immortality, being in debt to a witch… What are you up to, Erasmus Rasmussen?"

The witch has probably already seen the future. I do not need to answer, and I won't. To speak words into the universe means the universe can use them against you. I will not jeopardize any of my plans.

Whether Seven drinks the vial or not, the man who tortured him will get what's coming to him. There will be no waiting for karma. I am the karma. How can I be this way, knowing I gave Seven a choice between everlasting life and immediate death? This may seem like hypocrisy and it possibly is. My reasons might make up for it later.

Wisteria and I land in my room, where she quickly wraps her hand around the doorknob to leave.

"'Your boy is on the other side of this door, waiting like a puppy for you," she says.

I like the way it sounds out loud. *My boy*.

Those crimson red lips of hers curl, and I have a feeling she's not going to make this easy. With two fingers, she smears her lipstick and opens the door. Passing Seven in the hall, she meets his gaze and holds it, and the devious little thing smiles seductively at him. I can see him trying to put two and two together. There's a taste of the fire again burning in those deep blue eyes. Jealousy scourges through him, and I can not help my little grin that forms because of it.

"Seven," I say, inviting him in. I already anticipate he will decline. As suspected, he does not answer me, instead storms off to wonder what I have been up to with the witch in my room and, of course, jump to incorrect conclusions. If only he knew the truth. I'll let him stew on it for now.

Giving Seven his space does not come easy for me. Since I arrived back from my time with Wisteria he ignores me as much as he possibly can. He's angry with me, though he has no true reason to be.

"Are you finished yet?" I ask.

From his seat at the front window, he blinks slowly and deliberately in my direction. "What are you talking about?

"You know exactly what I mean." Of course I won't make this easy on him, though it really should be. At this point, I'm just trying to get him to argue with me. He's wonderful when he's expressing his rage.

He shakes his head and stares back out the window. "If I knew I wouldn't ask."

"You're angry with me," I say flatly. "A random woman leaves my room and you conveniently have nothing to say to me for the duration of the day."

"It's not my business what you do." His tone is anything but subtle and it only makes me yearn for him all the more. This obsession I have for him has such a tight hold on me. How could he possibly assume I would want another?

"Nej, it isn't. You're still angry and I can't fathom why." Ja, I can. I want him to say it. I want him to admit the feelings he has for me. We are both aware of them and yet he refuses to admit anything. I yearn for him to unveil those true emotions. He's been dancing around it, so hesitant to acknowledge the depth of his affection.

"I'm not mad, Erasmus." Oh, he very much is. Just in the tone of his voice, the way he's tensing up at this conversation, and the sudden increase of his heart rate. Before I can reply to his statement, he triumphantly adds, "Maybe I should invite a friend over. If the house lets you have them, perhaps it'll allow me one too."

He's playing tit for tat. He's not serious. Clouden told me Seven has no friends. He's only saying this to get me riled up and, unfortunately, despite knowing it's a lie, it still pisses me off. "If you want them dead, ja. Invite as many of them as you want."

His nostrils flare ever so slightly in response, a subtle but telling reaction to the tension between us.

"Don't think I won't kill them, Seven. It's what I do for a living."

In addition to his nostrils flaring, his eyes narrow menacingly, in a physical manifestation of the anger brewing beneath the surface. "It's disgusting what you do."

The truth of the matter is, he's right. It is disgusting and disturbing to murder people in cold blood, right in their homes. The majority of them are people Lorcan tells me to end. Some are just for fun. Most of them are criminals and rapists. It's never children, Lorcan has a soft spot for them. I just don't bother. They're boring.

They deserve to grow up and at least have a chance at living. When I go alone, and without a ledger from Lorcan, I just pick one to bring home to have for dinner. Much like shopping at the grocery store.

Seven may claim to dislike my lifestyle. He still eats the dinners we provide and understands what's in them. Even now, as he stares at me with such loathing, there's something more in that gaze: lust. Whether he acknowledges the emotion is there or not, it's still apparent to me.

"Disgusting but, interesting enough, that's not the source of your anger. The woman who left my room is."

Once more, Seven turns his gaze to the window. His lips are thin lines, from him keeping them shut so tight, and he doesn't respond again. The conversation has been a delicate dance, carefully choreographed to reveal the truth. With a victorious smile, I leave to grant him the space to process it all and to unravel the threads of his own emotions.

LORCAN

29

After I make sure Audelia is settled back in the house, I take to the streets for a night out on the town with Clouden. We bumped up his transition to tomorrow as per his request. He fears Seven will leave, if the house allows him to exit. Now that his brother is here, Clouden wants him present for the ceremony. Understandable. Tonight is all about savoring the last little speck of his humanity. It's what we've been training for anyway; when it is time to let his past go, he will fully let it go. There are exceptions to this, of course, his family being the main one. Since Seven arrived, it has become increasingly clear he would be Clouden's downfall, if he isn't careful about it. Recently I tried a few exercises on him to see if anyone else is a weakness. Just as I suspected, there are none. Not even idle threats about his mother or father lift the mask that he wears;

it is only his brother Seven. So, I am thankful for his older brother being in my home.

"Where to first?" Clouden asks with as much enthusiasm as a child who is set free in the candy store. My excitement mirrors his completely. To think of wandering these streets together as vampires, makes my cold, dead heart skip. I don't mind holding back when he's around but once humanity is drained from him, and the supernatural takes over, there won't be any need for restraint.

To answer his question, I hand him a list. All of the eligible suitors for tonight's debauchery are on this piece of paper. He's reading it with a smile.

"There's too many." He smiles at me. "I don't know where to start."

"Give me your knife," I say. When he does, I stab the paper to the nearest tree trunk I can find. Then I pull out my own and hold it by the blade motioning for him to take it.

"Wherever the knife takes aim." He understands and, after a few seconds scrutinizing, he flicks the knife in the direction of the tree. Clouden never misses. The tip of the blade strikes right through the third name on the list.

"There you go then." My lips tug upward. "This is where we start."

As the hours carry on, we manage to scourge the Earth of almost all of them. Between each hunt, we take the body home and toss it in the basement, for later dismembering. We'll save the few left on the list for after his transition. It's no rush at all, but the sooner they are gone the better. I'll just have to initiate the cover up and all shall be well.

Nearing three in the morning on a weeknight, the streets are deserted. We're able to prance around merrily, without care that anyone will take notice of either of us covered from head to toe in blood. Not that many would bat an eye, anyway. This is what makes this city so special. People trust in the lore and magical history of the city, and they just assume we're all a part of it. There's so many people who get into character here, it helps the real monsters to easily blend in, without a second glance. The tourists love to tell us how they enjoy our dedication to the stories.

We pass Decatur and I backtrack a little skip. One of my closest friends lives here and I think I shall pay a quick, little visit.

"Lorcan," Clouden laughs out my name. "Surely you're joking."

I sneak up through the bushes and, with the tip of my knife, I tap on the window belonging to his bedroom. When he doesn't come right away, I keep at it until the curtains yank back, revealing a disheveled Hunter LeBeaux. Wide eyed and giddy with glee, I shake my knife at him as a good morning salute.

"The sun isn't even up yet, Lorcan," Clouden whispers from the sidewalk.

Hunter takes one long look at me covered in crimson. With a heavy sigh, he closes the curtain again.

"Such a lovely man, isn't he?" I ask Clouden as I rejoin him.

"Oh, sure," Clouden feigns agreement. "I half expect him to punch your lights out one day." He laughs and slings an arm around my shoulder.

"Never!" I laugh. "He'd be so terribly bored without me."

We're almost home when I feel it. A tingling sensation begins at the base of my neck, warning me of some kind of danger lurking in these streets, besides myself, of course. Without alerting Clouden, I hold my knife up to the sky as if I'm inspecting it. Truthfully, I'm taking in my surroundings. The air is still enough that even without supernatural hearing I would be able to make out the presence of another. There is *something,* no doubt. Instead of being hasty, I think I'll let it come to me when it is good and ready.

SEVEN

30

Erasmus no doubt means it when he says he will kill me. I must be completely insane to understand this yet still wander about the house unattended. Trusting he's telling the truth about that vial is even more insane on my behalf. What if it's just pure water? Nothing but a trick to have me *think* it's a spell or potion of everlasting life just so he can laugh as I die in his arms. I honestly do not feel Erasmus would laugh. I believe he would be deeply disappointed.

Why do I feel the safest and most secure when surrounded by these monsters? The way Lorcan cradles my brother's face, then holds Clouden's hands and cleanses them for this ritual, helps me briefly understand why he's accepted these people so quickly. Apart from Erasmus wanting to kill me, they have been respectful. Even how Erasmus has laid down this threat is also done in respect. He does not have to give me a choice, yet he does.

I have asked Clouden many times during my stay here why he chose this life. At first, I did not understand it. After spending time with them, I can see it clearly. However, I still can't confirm if this is *my* place. It isn't easy. In staying, I'll just be putting them through the same shit my parents went through. It's Cloud's place, though, and he belongs here just as much as the others do. It's easy to see.

"Should he even be here?" Audelia asks Lorcan as she nods to me. "He's human. Clouden is going to flip."

"Is he?" Lorcan asks.

I can't tell if he's asking if I am still human or if she thinks Clouden will indeed flip. Lorcan is very cautious in many respects. I don't doubt I'll be safe. Even if not, if it's at my brother's hand I die, then so be it. My body stiffens at the thought. Erasmus will kill him. It would be easy to let Clouden do it. I can't picture Erasmus taking the easy way out.

The atmosphere today reminds me of a baptism. Lorcan and Clouden both wear white suits. Both are barefoot, and I know it probably signifies something. I just don't know what. This whole process is foreign to me.

"Are we ready to witness a rebirth?"

I assume Lorcan asks that to the rest of us, but his eyes stay on Clouden. How can someone like Lorcan have such a paternal instinct? Though I adore them all here in this house, there's still much I'll never fully figure out.

"The last few minutes of your humanity."

Laying flat on his back in the center of the room, Clouden's head turns to face me. He holds my gaze only momentarily, until I nod, then his attention is back to Lorcan.

Audelia, Erasmus, and I all kneel in a row not far from them. The lights are off. Candles are lit, casting an eerie, yet warm glow through the room. Fitting for vampires for sure. Maybe a little cliche if you ask me.

Lorcan slowly brings Clouden's wrist to his mouth as if to savor the moment. When he bites down on Cloud's skin, I flinch instead of my brother. It's quiet for a bit, until my brother begins to moan. It's not for pleasure. He is visibly woozy. Erasmus must hear my heartbeat kick up into high gear and he shifts a tad closer, purposely not touching me. I suppose for support.

The next step is when Lorcan slices his own wrist and drizzles his blood into Clouden's mouth. I might be making this up in my head, it looks like Clouden is not reacting to it. The blood leaks out of the corners of his lips, down his cheeks, and into his ears.

"Clouden?" I ask before saying it louder and more erratic, "Clouden!"

His eyes are too focused on the ceiling. The rise and fall of his chest has slowed and then ceases entirely.

"Shit!"

Hastily, I scoot closer to my brother's side. When I feel someone take hold of my wrist, I do not even have a chance to fully process that it's physical touch. My little brother's life is far more critical than my own issues.

All I can see is his life flash before my eyes; our life. I was almost eight when he was born. I was ecstatic to learn our new baby was a boy I could hang out with. The age gap played on us a bit as we got older. I wanted to be with my friends more than I wanted to hang out with Clouden. After my abduction, Clouden took care of me. He was still a child, yet he took over, bringing me everything and anything I needed. He grew up faster than he should have, and I never thanked him for that.

I fight against whatever keeps me grounded. I kick and try to wrench myself free, to no avail. The grip is steady. The flood starts from the inside again. So many emotions well up and I know I cannot contain them all. And I don't.

A hot stream of tears spills down my face, burning my skin in its wake. I'm suffocating in the idea that I could lose Clouden. This can't happen. I fight even harder, scratching, clawing—fuck I'll even *bite* my way to Clouden if I have to— I'm just not strong enough. I have to be strong enough to save him, like he saved me countless times in the past.

My mouth opens and I scream so loud it leaves my throat raw, so loud I can't even hear my own bellowing. My heart is crumbling, falling to pieces, and my little brother still has not moved.

"Clouden…"

ERASMUS

31

Clouden has been gargling Lorcan's blood, trying to breathe around it, and without warning his breath ceases. I knew this was going to drive Seven into anxiety. I'm ready for it. His heartbeat was already erratic, and it immediately kicked into high gear. The possible loss of his brother will damage him in more ways than one. If he isn't careful, he will go into a panic right here. Well, he *isn't* careful. He isn't caring about anything other than Clouden, and it's completely acceptable. Previous distractions I used for his panic attacks will not suffice this time. I can imagine this fear is more dire than ever.

Seven is not fond of physical touch in any way, but this moment for Clouden can not be about Seven. I have no choice but to wrap my fingers around his wrist to stop him. He does not understand how the death of the human means the creation of the vampire. He only sees this as the end, not knowing this is just all a part of the whole process.

Since the moment Seven arrived on our doorstep, there has been a fire barely being kept alive inside of him. Only once have I seen it falter and it was during the panic attack in the middle of the street. Just now, the way he looks at me, I see it ready to erupt. Two rebirths are happening. Clouden is soon to be a vampire and Seven is soon to be what he's born to be. The Phoenix will burn to emerge.

Oh, I beg any god or fate that listens to make Seven drink the damn potion! Live and spread this wildfire. Let it burn everything in its path. I will sit back and happily watch him take everything and anything his heart desires. At this moment, the man I know he can be is rising. There is a violent monster inside of Seven and I would love nothing more than to help him let loose. If only he chooses to let me.

Seven thrashes in my arms, fighting against me. I hold tight. To see him in this rage, taking it out on someone else, would be a beautiful massacre indeed. He's capable of far more than he's aware of.

"He's fine," I whisper. Seven is not listening. My arms are around him, keeping him steady and away from Clouden, while Lordan finishes the transition. He's on the verge of another panic. I lower us both to the floor, slowly, and repeat the words, "He's fine."

Clouden is not dead. Instead, he's suckling happily on Lorcan's wrist. Just as Seven tunes it all out, apart from what his focus is, so has Clouden. Blood is the focus, beautifully thick, warm blood.

My boy reaches for something to grab onto, to help free himself from my grasp, instead he catches Audelia's ankle.

"Get off!" she yells with a slight jerk of her foot. As Seven pulls away, he slices the palm of his hand on her broken boot buckle.

Clouden immediately reacts to the scent of fresh blood. Lorcan is thrown backwards, crashing through the wall with the same ease as a paper airplane floating with the breeze. Clouden is off of the floor and flying toward us. Audelia tries to stop him, and I highly doubt it's to protect Seven. She has a heavy disdain for Clouden, simply because he exists. Jealousy was more or less the fuel for all of their previous fights.

Lorcan shouts at them both. They ignore it completely. Clouden shoves Audelia backwards on her ass so she's sliding against the wall. Her stumble is brief and he's already on her trail again. Before she stands, she snatches the chimney poker and cracks it across his head. She is triumphant for only a moment. Clouden is new and fresh in this game. Once he's on his feet, rushing towards Seven, she catches Clouden around the waist and slams him to the floor again.

This charade is spiraling out of control. Seven is panicking, Audelia is laughing, and Lorcan is finally coming to aid in keeping Clouden away from his brother. Just as he is reaching for the maniac newborn, Audelia tackles Clouden to the floor. Rolling on top of him, she thrusts her head forward to bust his nose. A nice, audible crack gave way to his broken bone. It won't be broken for long. Vampires heal quickly.

Clouden still yanks free from her and races in Seven's direction. The blood is all he can see. Seven's blood. Not on my damn fucking watch. I step between the two, just in time as Clouden is about to take a chunk out of my boy. I reach for Clouden's neck and squeeze. The instinct to protect Seven at all costs is severe. If anything or anyone is killing him, it will be myself. Only I will take his life, and it is only if he chooses me to do so. A few days should be long enough for Seven to reach a conclusion, but, until then, not a damn scratch on his body will be allowed.

My fingers tighten around Clouden's neck, holding him in place. No matter how hard he thrashes, he isn't getting out of this grip. Immortality, along with a bit of strength enhancement, sets me apart from the natural human world.

If Lorcan doesn't act fast, I will break Clouden in half and eat his remains for dinner, just because I can. Over my shoulder, Seven scrambles to his knees. Lips parted in awe. He watches his brother, who has loved him unconditionally and would never have harmed him, want to drain his body of all its blood. I can only imagine what's going through his mind. There's no time to dawdle in thought.

"Lorcan!" I yell, and as he told me to control my human once, I repay that little comment. "Control your newborn!"

Is Clouden going to remember any of this? Audelia doesn't remember any of her human life. It's like she truly was just born when Lorcan found her chewing on that poor woman's shoulder in the middle of the street. Lorcan said it sometimes happens when traumatic events unfold during the transition to becoming a vampire. Maybe Clouden won't remember because of this madness.

Turning to look at Seven, I say, "You owe me."

LORCAN

32

This is a disaster. A complete and utter disaster. Technically, it could've gone a lot worse. I had faith everything would be much better than how it just played out.

Did I believe that Clouden could withstand the pulsating need to satiate hunger? Absolutely not. There was also the hope that, if anything happened, he would fight it. By the looks of it, he can't.

When my adopted daughter, Blair, transitioned from human to vampire, she was easier to work with due to her fear and hatred of hurting others. Yet it made her more difficult in a sense. She refused to feed for a long time, and it made her quite the pissy little thing, at times. Blaze was born a vampire. I always assumed his lineage, some sort of fire mage, also played into his resorting to chaos.

I was above the sway of blood lust, possibly because I consumed the life source as a human, previous to my transition. It was already in my body and I craved it in ways mortals typically did not. I was not typical, at all, to begin with.

The training with Clouden has not been adequate. This is on me, not him, and I will make certain he understands this. Vampires, when newly changed, can be emotional. Blair certainly was for a while. It could have also stemmed from her not wanting to be a vampire. The pact between her birth father and I was not one I could've or would've gone against. Not even for her wishes.

Enough on this thought process for the moment. I have a newborn vampire to tend to. I fear, if I do not retrieve him from Erasmus soon, we'll have an even bigger mess.

Dusting my suit off, it takes me only a few strides to step over the shattered coffee table and take Clouden from Erasmus as he lowers the boy's feet to the floor.

"Well," I say with Clouden's head tucked under my arm, keeping him there until Erasmus can get Seven out of the room. "This was quite entertaining!" Audelia is splayed out on the floor, not caring one bit about the mess surrounding her. Though he is fighting him again, Erasmus leads Seven away. He's a sweet boy who worries for his brother, even after his brother tried to end him.

"Never fear, darling Seven. Clouden will be good as new," I say, to comfort him as best as I can. That is a job for Eras to handle.

Once Seven is clear from view, and the lingering scent has dissipated, I let Clouden free from my grasp. After blinking a few times, the boy's gaze lands on me and, much like a child, when the realization he did something horrible clicks in, he begins to sob uncontrollably.

"Oh, Clouden, dear boy!" I pull him into my arms. "Hush. You did marvelously."

With emotions all over the place, he does not respond with anything more than another sob. I take his face in my hands and smile.

"Come. Let's get you fed properly. Hm? A nice plump, unsuspecting human, and then you rest. Recharge."

Clouden nods. My praise does wonders more for that ego boost he so desperately needed. I picked Clouden, specifically, not because he would be a good killer. No it's because he has an understanding of the mindset. He's perfect, and even more so with the mistakes he makes. His willingness to learn and be taught overrides any little mishaps.

Once I tell him what went wrong, he will work on rectifying it immediately because it's who Clouden is. He is a perfectionist and he trusts me. With an arm slinging around his shoulder, I pull him away to worry about the mess later.

I am quite unsympathetic to many, but my family will always have my heart, even if it is cold and dead.

SEVEN

33

I owe Erasmus for protecting me against Clouden, and he wastes no time cashing in on the debt. I assumed he would force me to down the potion of immortality. He doesn't. Instead, he asks for something much less—a simple glass of my blood.

We both know I am not fond of physical touch, and to retrieve his 'payment,' he will have to touch me. I offered to slice my arm and let it drip into a cup. He said that would be an unnecessary pain.

"May I?"

At least Erasmus has manners and respects my boundaries. This is part of the whole situation I have complete control over. With Eras' hand extended to me, he's frozen in time until I give the okay for him to do so. The King bends to the pawn.

I stick my arm out for him, and Erasmus resumes movement again. His touch is gentle but deliberate as he positions my arm, before wrapping a rubber band around it. Strange as it is, I don't feel like I'm going to vomit. My stomach remains neutral. It's probably because his touch doesn't come as a shock and isn't unwelcome. My mind has been able to wrap around it because I have control over it. If I tell Erasmus to stop, he will. This knowledge makes it much easier to deal with. Trust.

The needle then slips into my vein and, for a brief moment, I feel hope rise in me that it's *the* drug. Whatever the abductor put in me wore off many years ago, the bite didn't. I have been stronger since then, so I'm not yearning for it as badly as I once did. I get the itch for it occasionally, but I'll never scratch it.

My blood pours eagerly into a plastic donation bag. I don't ask where he got any of this equipment from, or why. I have a creative mind and immediately begin to make up stories. Ripping myself from those stories, I decide to talk.

"What would have happened? If you hadn't caught Clouden?" I ask him.

"Nothing. I'd never let anyone get to you." He says it with such a firm conviction that I don't question it.

He's absolutely telling the truth. As long as Erasmus is here, I won't ever be harmed... except by Erasmus, who has threatened to kill me, if I don't become immortal like him. I sometimes wonder if he's even telling the truth. Will he kill me? Why does he protect me just to end up killing me? I don't know why I'm even thinking about this again. Erasmus is an enigma. I *know* he means it when he says he will kill me, so pondering about it is pointless. It's hard not to, though.

"Hypothetically, then," I say, still curious as to what my brother is now capable of.

"He would've drained you. He's a newborn. Lorcan assumed he was strong enough, and he also knew the risk."

"He also knows you wouldn't let him get close to me," I say confidently. I guess I'm conceited when it comes to Erasmus protecting me. Nothing will ever get past him. Nothing. Not even myself.

Erasmus smiles and arrogance floods his features. I fist my hand, and blood pools into the tube quicker. The bag is just about overflowing at this point. Erasmus mutters something low in another language.

"I'm going to donate some blood to Clouden," I tell him.

As Erasmus eases the needle from my arm, he scowls at my words. In that same language, I assume, he speaks again, sounding angry, before translating for me. "You'll do no such thing."

"He's my brother."

"He'll survive. There are plenty more blood bags walking around."

"So, I'm just yours. then?" This is a stupid question. The answer was obvious before I even asked it.

His response is silence.

Anger should well up inside of me. It doesn't. I realize I like this. I like the idea of belonging to him. It feels infinitely safe. It's absolutely ridiculous.

"What if Clouden saves me? I'll have to donate blood to him." Only if Clouden would even ask for blood as payment. I'm playing this hypothetical game well.

Erasmus sets a bandaid on my inner elbow. "I'll pay him some other way."

I want him to elaborate on this, on everything, but he's a little busy eye fucking my blood bag. He doesn't need my blood to live, or any blood at all. He only wants it because it's mine. Erasmus is one of the most intimidating people I've ever encountered. How he's looking at the bag, and cradling it like something absolutely special, makes pride bloom inside of me. I haven't felt joy, about anything regarding myself, in so long that it feels utterly foreign to associate these emotions with anything that came from me. This is insanity.

Erasmus pulls his gaze from the plastic bag to me. The grin on his face does not falter; instead, it blossoms. He gestures for me to follow him to the tea room, and I follow.

ERASMUS

34

The achingly sweet taste of Seven Wilbrate comes as a shock to me. The man is so bitter and cold that I guessed his entire entity was flavored as much. I take another sip of his blood from my glass. He so graciously donated it as 'payment.' I assumed this little taste would dull my ache, unfortunately for Seven, it has done the opposite. I want more.

Seven watches me almost intimately, if I'm not mistaken. His cheeks warm, making the already illustrious scent of his even stronger, as if he's baking from the inside for me. The tension melts from his shoulders, and his gaze does not falter from my lips at the glass. I wonder what he could be thinking. I refrain from asking right away.

I am curious, but I do love when he feeds me these little scraps at a time. Does he enjoy this view? Is he thinking of me taking it straight from the source with my lips pressing to a blood flow on his skin? Seven's sexuality is not something I'm entirely concerned with. It would be easier for me if he's attracted to men. Little by little, just as a story unfolds, so does Seven Wilbrate. He's been through enough traumatic experiences that I highly doubt sexual acts even cross his mind, apart from his nightmares. However, the urge to smile curls within me at the idea of him enjoying me drinking his blood.

To the outside world, Seven is as rare as a penny which can be found on every corner road. If you take the time to look closer, you'll see he is quite exquisite. Maybe it is just my view of him. I am thoroughly intrigued by this man, and now, as a bonus, I am delighted with the way he tastes.

He has said nothing the entire time we've sat together, so far. Curious enough, his focus does not waver from me. This is always considered a victory. He can hardly hold anyone's stare for long—one side effect of his traumatic aftermath—he has no problem keeping mine. I stare just as hard in return. I can see in his stance he's getting quite erratic and fidgety. He wants to cave. He wants to know what I think. And I am eager to hear his thoughts.

"Ask me, Seven. It's killing you not to." As if this is the permission he needs to speak. He can ask me anything and I'll answer him. It just may not be the answer he wants to hear.

He's silent while he thinks for a moment about if he should ask me or not, then finally asks, "What do I taste like?"

I hold up the glass and swirl the crimson liquid around. "Can words truly describe this?"

"Try," he urges as he sits forward to the edge of his seat.

"Seven Wilbrate..." I pause to gather thought. Typically it doesn't take me long to describe this. It is a challenge today to string together the right words. Finally, I say to him, "Your blood is like swallowing a living, breathing fire. There is a gleam to it that's almost undetectable. I pay enough attention I catch it right on my tongue as it slides down my throat. Your blood craves for more."

I also sit forward, and to my astonishment, he does not move away. "I taste a wildness inside of you that's desperately wanting to escape. As much as you'd like to believe it, Seven, nothing is mild about you—especially not your blood."

"All I want is to forget," he says.

"It's not in your path to forget. You must learn from your history. Take the past and mold yourself with it. Create your monster."

A moment settles between us before he speaks again. His voice is barely above a whisper and it does not waver or show a sign of cracking. "How do I let it out, without it taking over me?" he asks.

My lips twist into a clip of a little smile. "You don't."

He is worried about becoming something he is not. What if this is exactly what he is supposed to be?

"There is no toeing the line. You and your monster are one in the same. Once you begin this path, you can never go back."

I hope my words don't deter his thought process. He needed to hear them either way. I will not let him push forward without knowing the full entailment of what's going on. I am a breath away from asking him for the second time to stay with me, when Seven interrupts me.

"And it's stay with you as immortal or die. Why?"

How do I put this without sounding like a maniac? Though it's certain I am. My gaze locks on those bewitchingly blue eyes of his, and I talk honestly. "If I can't have you, no one will."

Outward, this does not seem to bother him, though I wonder if, internally, he understands the depth of truth in those words.

"No one in their right mind would want me," he says sadly.

Before taking another sip of his blood from my glass, I say "Well, no one ever said I was in the right frame of mind, to begin with."

LORCAN
35

This house has been bustling with excitement lately from everything going on. The literal walls are humming with delight at the aspect of being filled with the creatures it has chosen. I figure there won't be anything more to add to our current endeavors, with so much already on our plate. I am incorrect.

The sound of the doorbell ringing is foreign. The last time this happened was when Seven arrived on our doorstep, looking for Clouden. Surely there is no one else looking for my monsters, is there? When I open the door, I am shocked to see such a normal human being wearing jeans and a warm smile. Not a drop of anything supernatural about him. Before Seven's arrival, it had been some time since the house allowed visitors who aren't of the supernatural state to be present at the doorstep.

"Good afternoon," the visitor says with a much too chipper tone. "Might I speak to the man of the house?"

"Oh, you certainly can," I reply. "That would be me."

Before he speaks again, he seemingly freezes up. The natural reaction to humans when they really pay attention to me. Terribly, he fakes an air of shock. "You? Well you're much too young to be the head of the house!"

I have to fight back from rolling my eyes. Flattery will get you everywhere, forcing it is just annoying. "No, my good man," I smile widely. "I assure you it is myself."

Of course when I was changed from human to vampire it was in my early forties and while I possibly do look young for my age he's certainly over exaggerating it a tad bit. Before he can toss another lame compliment my way, I ask, "How can I help you?"

"I'm just going door-to-door to offer our new cable packages, that's all. Hope you'd be interested."

This is indeed interesting. I will not even ask why the house allowed this to happen. Sometimes, it does things just to see how I will react. Well, I will give it the show it rightly deserves if that's what it wants.

"Oh! Yes! Come in, won't you? It's extremely too hot to do business out here on the porch." An easy invitation. After a little internal consideration, he accepts. Most humans tend to think they're overreacting when they get the sense of danger in my presence. If only they listened to their instincts a little better.

As soon he steps in, he glances around the foyer, taking in the exquisite art and sculptures adorning the area. He's already begun talking about the options we have and the packages to benefit me. I hardly watch television, apart from the news to see my work being critiqued by the police, or neighbors and loved ones of my victims. It's quite senseless to even entertain this notion, but I do. And being the good host I am, I offer him a beverage. "Would you care for some tea?"

"No thank you, sir. I have to say this is by far the loveliest house I've been in." At his words, I can feel the walls around us retract just a tad bit, showing me the house likes the compliment.

"He also tried to say I was young," I whisper back to it, in retaliation. Typically it would answer with a shake of its walls or a ruffle of the carpet. This time, the house doesn't respond.

Overhearing that, the solicitor asks a soft, "Hm?"

I just smile at him. The unease he felt is beginning to grow more and more apparent on his face courtesy of the soft furrowing of his brow and the too cheerful smile plastered there. Soon he'll make excuses to leave. It will probably be too late.

"The television screen often flickers. Someone's looked at it already. They say it's not the TV. It's the network's fault. Come see the set up they have for me, it's quite ridiculous."

The salesman shifts uneasily from one foot to the other. "That's... not really my expertise. I can have a technician come and look at that for you. I do have some brochures here of the packages—"

I wave his words off. "It'll only take a second." Opening the door to the basement, I nod for him to follow. "How can you be sure my equipment can even sustain your technology without seeing it first? I can't sign up, unless you help me make sure everything will work together."

His head bobs, slowly, in agreement, and follows me downstairs. The house seemingly lets out a sigh of relief when I close the door behind us, its wooden beams relaxing like a released breath. The air inside clarified like it cleared its throat. Of course it would want more entertainment. As if it hasn't already acquired enough to last four life spans.

SEVEN

36

It's been a few days since I've been allowed to see Clouden. Lorcan says it's because my scent might throw him for a loop, again. He wants me to keep my space. There's been enough space.

"Can I see him today?" I ask Lorcan, hopefully.

After a pause, an almost *no* is sitting on his lips, Lorcan nods and takes me to Clouden's room.

"I'll stay with you. If something happens to you, Erasmus will not be easy to take down." Lorcan laughs and holds the doorknob before adding, "Not a scratch," perfectly mimicking Erasmus' thick 'angry' accent.

The smile tugging at my lips can not be contained. For whatever reason, Erasmus slips into more Danish than English when he's mad. He finally indulged me in a little bit of his history. He's from Denmark. He was forty years old when he became immortal. He didn't tell me why he came here to the United States or how. He only told me he will elaborate at another time. Maybe something traumatic happened to him, as well, and he's just not ready to share it with me yet.

Clouden is on the bed, with a book in hand, lying on his back, with his feet propped against the wall. There is a flicker of his gaze across the pages. It happened too quickly for me to entirely comprehend. He is positively content here. The room is a contrast to mine, with dark walls and dim lighting. For a second, I can't imagine how he can read in here with such little light. Then I remember quickly that his eyesight has recently been enhanced.

"Seven." He says my name almost painfully, and it sounds almost strained sliding from his lips.

My entire body relaxes. I've worried myself sick, thinking he's been in pain after the transition. "Hey. You good?"

There's a smile on his lips, and it's awfully fake as he asks, "Are you?"

He moves quickly to sit up. It's nothing more than a blur to me, which makes my eyes sting. Nothing should be able to move like this. I realize the others move in such a similar fashion. It's probably done a tad slower just for me. Or maybe in general, so other people don't question it.

"Yes." I'm trying to not let him see how nervous I am. I can imagine the rapid increase of my heart will give it away.

"I am sorry, Seven." His voice even sounds different. There's more clarity to it. The pitch is almost soothing to listen to, like a lullaby wrapping itself around you before bed, so you can drift into slumber easily. It's one of the many vampires' luring devices. It's working.

Clouden is saying something else, adding to the conversation, and I find it difficult to pull my attention from the symphony of his new voice. I wonder if this is because he doesn't know how to turn it off yet or perhaps he's trying it on for size, using me as the test subject, since I'm the only human here currently.

Lorcan is off in the far end of the room, pretending to sift through a magazine, to give us the illusion of privacy. He's listening for any sign that Clouden will lose control and attack me.

"Nah, don't be sorry." I try to laugh it off so he won't feel bad. "I mean, everyone else here wants to eat me," I say, honestly, with a shrug. "What's one more?" Out of the corner of my eye, I see Lorcan's lips curve up in a smile.

Clouden smiles too wide and his sharp fangs, in the place of blunt canines, gleam in the light. A trickle of fear spikes inside of me. It's easy to assume this is the reaction humans have when they witness something like this. This interaction is also showing me just how the other vampires here are in absolute control of everything.

"Are you going to, Seven?" he asks, interrupting my thoughts.

Clouden started speaking before this question; I was too enamored, seeing the fangs, to listen. "Hm?" I ask, because I have no idea what he's talking about.

"Join us?"

"Oh," I say. I hoped we wouldn't breach the subject of anything regarding me today. I'm sure Lorcan's ears perk up, listening to my answer. "I—well, I'm not…" I stammer. How can I answer this in a way not to anger or upset him? "Let's focus on you, huh? It's your day."

The way his facial features twist shows me he doesn't want to hear that. He goes with it anyway and allows the subject to slip away.

"When Lorcan says you're good to go out again, I'm taking you to the bar if the house lets me." Vampires can drink other things. It's a matter of wanting to. I mean, I myself don't really want to go to the bar. I'll do it just to please him if it's what it takes. We never truly were able to do these kinds of things before. Not with me being, well, me. For him, though, I'll try. It's long past overdue. I missed out being the big brother he deserved to have all those years.

"And you'll pick who I drain?"

Goosebumps pebble my flesh at the thought. My meaning of the bar is to celebrate with a drink... of alcohol, but Clouden is no longer human. Life will be entirely different for us now.

"Sure. If... if that's what you want."

He nods. "It is, very much."

"Then, it's settled," I reply. "At least you won't need a sweater anymore." I try to lighten the mood. I think it's a failure.

Lorcan appears next to me, just then. "We should let him rest."

I'm not going to argue with him. I don't want Cloud to know that I'm ready to leave the room. It might hurt his feelings. I am uncomfortable being in here with him. For the sake of my brother, I slap on a pout and pretend it upsets me to do so. Lorcan motions for me to head to the door and I move quickly.

Once we are away from the room, he speaks. "I feared your heartbeat would be too much for him. It began to increase the instant he asked you the question."

Erasmus appears in the doorway to where Lorcan led me, and he's doing a quick survey from the top of my head down to the shoes on my feet.

"See?" Lorcan says to him. "Perfect in every way. Not a hair out of place."

Lorcan leaves and closes the door behind me, as soon as I move fully into the room. For one long, drawn out second, Erasmus leans in and inhales through his nostrils, filling his lungs with my scent.

"That sweet scent of your blood pumping, combined with the melody of your heartbeat, is far too intoxicating," he says. "Perhaps your brother is stronger than I initially thought. I wouldn't be."

I believe him. Had he been a vampire, he would have little restraint when it came to my blood. I wonder why he holds back so much now.

"Maybe it's just you who hungers for me like that."

At those words, his eyes darken. He closes the space between us once again. His nose is hovering over my skin, not touching my cheek but I can feel it in my space. If there has ever been a moment that I think Erasmus will splay me open, this is it.

He inhales even slower, this time, before saying, "As it should be."

Erasmus is too close to me. Even though there's no panic coming on, yet, I need to get out of here before it does. It's been a good little stretch without an attack, and I would like to keep it that way. Without a word, I left him standing there.

If there's one room I am in love with in this entire mansion, it's the bathroom. The shower is magnificent. It's so freaking big. You could host a party there, if you wanted to! Seriously, it's unnaturally big. Multiple shower heads line the walls with a variety of settings to choose from. I like the waterfall setting the best. I probably take the longest just getting the shower ready and admiring it than I do actually showering.

However, there is one strange thing about the bathroom. It's always been a luxurious dream of mine to have a house with a bathroom that connects to my bedroom. The bathroom designated to me, back at my parent's house, is in the hallway. I have to leave my room to get to it. Which is fine, it's whatever. Having this bathroom as an extension to my room is just a wonderful little treat. The thing about this bathroom is it's supposed to be shared with the bedroom next to mine. It's an empty one. No one resides in it, so I never worry about someone just randomly walking in while I'm showering.

What's strange is today someone *is* barging in, and that someone is Erasmus.

"Shit!" I yell and cover myself with my hands. As if it helps any. The door to the shower is glass, and reveals everything inside of it. My voice squeaks out the words,"Don't you know how to knock?"

Erasmus' eyes scan over me slowly, and he whistles low.

If my whole body isn't several shades of red, I'll be shocked. "Get out of here!"

"Nej, you get out! This is my washroom."

I almost slip on the soap bubbles. "Yours? Um, no? This one is connected to my room! Yours is across the hall!"

He blinks at me. "Where do you think I am?" Then his thumb flicks over his shoulder to the door he entered from. "My room is right there."

"You're full of shit," I say as I turn off the water and yank the glass door to my shower open. "Hand me a towel."

Erasmus' arms cross over his chest in defiance.

An annoyed sigh escapes through my nostrils. "Move." I'm still very red and embarrassed, but I try to fake through it that this doesn't bother me. Pushing past him, I snatch a towel from the shelf and wrap it quickly around my waist. I can feel his eyes on the back of me, which makes my cheeks heat up even more.

Once the towel is secure I make my way to the door that should open to the empty bedroom next to mine. I fling it open and point inside. "See!"

He's nodding, "Ja, Seven. As I said. It's my room."

"Huh?" I am dumbfounded. The room this door just opened to is indeed his. "How in the hell?"

"I told you," he says. "This is my bathroom."

I'm seriously confused. I didn't leave my room at all, so how could I possibly be in a bathroom that's attached to his across the hall, when no wall connects us? I cross the bathroom in a few strides to open the other door leading to mine and oddly it does. My brain cannot fathom how this is possible. It's not physically possible, at all!

Erasmus stares at me, and I'm out of breath from the intensity of it. "Explain to me how the hell this is real."

In response, he shrugs. "You live in a house made of magic. The possibilities are endless here."

I hate to admit he's right. Nothing about this house is explainable. It won't let me leave, and it's decided to torture me by making me share my marvelously lavish bathroom. I'm being a tad dramatic. I just liked it better when it was only mine.

"Well, I need to finish my shower. Are you going to just stand there and watch me?"

He smiles, and I want to kick myself for even asking the stupid question. "Never mind. You can have it."

I go to let him have his turn in the bathroom, when he moves to stand in front of me. "Finish your shower, Seven."

Ready to retaliate about not wanting him in here, he beats me to the punch and backs out of the room. "Enjoy your spa." I wait until he's completely out, and I make sure to lock the door. Not that it truly matters, seeing as the house can unlock itself, if it decides to allow Erasmus back in.

"Please, let me have some peace," I say to the house while hopping back in the shower, to hopefully relax a bit with the help of the steam and lavender soap.

As I reach for my shampoo, I find two glass cylinders in their place, one labeled 'Salt' and the other 'Pepper.' I groan loudly. If anyone wants to know what it's like as a human living with cannibalistic creatures, this is it.

"For the last time!" I yell, though with their super hearing, they'll hear me even if I whisper. "I am not food!" Over the sound of the shower, an eruption of loud laughter rings from somewhere in the house.

I emerge from the bathroom in pajamas and with a towel draped on my head. Lorcan and Audelia are both gathered at the kitchen island. My bare feet make soft contact with the floor as I move to the counter and place the salt and pepper shakers down.

"Not food," Audelia laughs upon seeing me. "Not according to Erasmus! You're a whole ass snack!"

"He definitely wants a piece of that ass," Lorcan says as he slips a piece of whoever he's dining on this time into his mouth. "Literally. A nice slice of that thick, plump little ass." They both roar with laughter again.

I stop drying my hair with the towel and shoot a glance over my shoulder at my butt. "It's not thick!"

Lorcan points his fork at me. "Those thighs of yours look delicious. *Thick*."

Audelia smirks, "I can't tell if you're being sexual about this or just hungry."

"I am always hungry, darling!" Lorcan licks his fork clean. "Besides, we all know Erasmus would have our heads on a silver platter, if we even acted as if we would come for *his boy*."

Ignoring them, I make my way over to the fridge. Out of the corner of my eye, I see them both watching me, waiting for my response to their conversation. They're desperate for this little gossip. I should shut this shit down, however I'm tempted to play this little game of theirs.

"He would," I say, taking what I assume is orange juice from the fridge. It's an orange liquid in a clear, glass jug. I shouldn't assume anything about the contents of this house. At this point, I don't want to know if it's not orange juice. "Erasmus may not be a good person…" I take a swig of the liquid and set the bottle back on the shelf. "But I suck dick, not morals."

It's a lie. I've never sucked dick in my life. I have never been into men. I dated one girl in high school, before I went to college, and that was as far as my romantic experience journey went. The looks on their faces at my comment is absolutely priceless.

With my 'thick ass,' I close the fridge door. At first, there's shock written across their faces. It quickly softens to smiles. Before leaving, I retrieve the salt and pepper shakers to take back with me. "Just in case he wants a midnight snack."

Echoes of their laughter behind me makes me smile as I go back to my room. I drop myself on the bed and laugh for at least another twenty minutes, because I have absolutely no idea where this side of me came from.

ERASMUS

37

reaming is not for the weak. Those who dream are not afraid to enter the subconscious without restraint, to become vulnerable to the mind that creates the fantasy. In dreams I always find exactly what I'm looking for. Hope blossoms and expels nothing but happiness and everything in my dreams makes perfect sense. Morning comes and everything your imagination creates disappears. This is where the weakness cannot come into play. If I hold onto the dream, I miss reality while it passes by. If I live too fearlessly, the dream is easily forgotten. When I slumber, my fantasies are all consumed by none other than Seven Wilbratte. No surprise there. I still fight between wanting to chew the skin off of him and wanting to ravish him with my body. In the dreams I do both, and constantly.

Last night, I closed my eyes to the vision of the naked Seven in the shower that I interrupted only this time he didn't tell me to leave. Water trickled down, coating the soft hairs of his legs and he let me lap at the side of his thigh with my tongue. His fingers caressed my hair. When I bit down on his leg he locked his fingers and tugged at my scalp. I can't even imagine, in my wildest dreams, how delicious this man tastes. One day I will. I currently sit in the living room trying to etch the scene to my memory forever.

The days after Clouden tried to attack Seven went by slowly. Clouden isn't allowed to leave the house yet and is supervised when he goes near Seven, but it looks like the near attack on his brother was strictly from the way that happened so fast. He obviously was overwhelmed. His feeding was interrupted by another source of sustenance, and like any other animal, he pounced to act on it. It just happened to be his brother Seven.

It's quiet in the house, too quiet. It lasts all of five seconds after the thought disappears from my head, when a throbbing pain replaces it. I'm knocked out of my chair and onto the floor and I'm dazed until I realize that I was hit with something. Clouden is shaking the fist he just struck me with. Faster than he was before the transition, his movements are almost a blur. This time I'm able to roll out of the path of his fist when it comes back around to knock me out. He doesn't stop. He's back to trying to connect with my face and succeeds again. The soft bone in my nose crunches with the force of the inhuman creature's blow.

"*Hvad er der galt med dig?*" My brain lapses, forgetting which language is which and I yell out the question in my native tongue while trying to cradle my face. Of course, it's already healing. It doesn't stop the pain searing through it.

Clouden's answer is another punch to the air, I dodge and am able to spear him to the floor with my body. We tussle around for dominance. I hate to admit he is a bit stronger than myself. I'm just quicker with thinking and slam a chair over his head.

"What is happening?" Seven appears in the doorway as Clouden shakes off the discomfort, and he is back at attacking me. We each grab one another's throat at the same time.

"This is payback for shoving my brother out of the window." The words seeth at me through Clouden's teeth.

"Cloud! *No!*" Seven is almost at his side, and the possessive force that has a choke hold on me about the man kicks into gear. I throw Clouden across the room, but it is futile. He's up and knocks me into the fireplace. Thankfully, it isn't lit. We're ready to clash this time. Both of us have a head start and almost collide into one another if Seven did not step directly in the path as he does. We both have to detour ourselves. Clouden comes in contact with the couch and flips over the back of it. I am thrust at the staircase and slam into the railing. It gives way to my weight and breaks instantly.

Seven comes running in my direction to aid me instead of checking his younger brother for injury first. I'm absolutely shocked by this action. Both of us will live. It is difficult to kill a newborn vampire and I am cursed as an immortal. Even with this knowledge, he still rushes in my direction first.

"Are you okay?" he asks, breathlessly, while holding my face to inspect. I suppose he forgets I heal quickly. I nod and he shoves me down to the floor, mumbling "What an asshole" before going to check on Clouden, to whom he says, "Fucking ridiculous" to. "Are you both finished?" Seven yells.

"I'm getting revenge!" Clouden shouts.

I stand up, fearing his anger will flip into blood rage again. He won't touch Seven, not on my watch.

"I'm fine, Clouden!"

"You could've died!" his brother screams back at him.

"Might I remind you," I say, "You also tried to kill him! If it wasn't for Audelia and myself, you would've drained him."

"I could've died years ago, too, and I didn't!" Seven shouts.

Seven is shaking, his breathing is increasing way too fast, and Clouden notices this as well.

"Seven…"

"I am fine!" Seven yells louder, "I'm *fucking* fine!" The color is quickly draining from his face. The panic is striking him again, and I move into action.

"Clouden, go get him a cold, wet towel. Seven, come by the window."

It's already starting. He wants to run. This time, I will make sure he doesn't go outside and harm himself again. While Cloud is gone, I maneuver Seven to the window. It's not easy to try to distract him from the anxiety while it's happening. I'm not sure if the house will open its doors for him to exit. If the door doesn't open this time for him to leave it might make this even worse.

"No, no," Seven says quickly. "I need to go outside. I need to— I don't know what I need."

"You need to stay with me, Seven," I say. "In this moment. Stay with me." I wonder what he sees while his gaze fixates on me. What's going through his mind? Slowly he's coming back down. His lips stay apart and no sounds emerge. "*Like her*. Just like that."

Clouden has already returned and remains on the other side of the room. When I peek over at him, he nods and leaves with the towel. Seven's mouth closes and his breathing is almost back to normal, but he does not look away from me.

Good. Stay. Just like that.

LORCAN

38

Even though it's been a nice stretch of time, it's not unordinary for Wisteria to pop up for a little visit. She does insist on stopping in for tea at random. I can tell this meeting will be different.

"To what do I owe the pleasure?" I ask. She's in the kitchen where Audelia planted her until I came up from the basement. Naturally, I won't allow my guest to wait too long, so I paused carving the rest of my latest work to come up and see her.

While I wait for her to sort through her thoughts, I begin making a pot of tea. It is doubtful she will even drink it today. I'm doing it for the sake of keeping my hands busy. They're itching terribly to get back to my work.

"Lorcan, I have a request." Wisteria's slender form leans casually against the massive island in the kitchen. Her typical long, dark hair is pulled up into a messy bun at the top of her head. She's completely worn out. "I have a witch who needs a home."

My brows pop up. "The woman who is currently in my living room?" I sensed the other person in there as soon as I walked up the stairs. I knew she was here for good reason, so I waited as patiently as I could for the truth to unfold.

Wisteria nods. "She… I don't want to say she's a problem because she's not. That's not it. I think she's suited to be with someone… more her style."

I, of course, am even more intrigued by her choice of wording. "And what would that *style* be?" With the tea ready, I pour a cup to offer to her. Just as I suspect, she declines so I keep it for myself.

"She's… unorthodox."

Wisteria has seen her fair share of creatures that are far from the normal classification. What is it about this one that sets her apart from the rest she's witnessed?

"Meaning she likes torturing people and eating their spleens?" I inquire.

"Maybe not eating the spleen thing. Yes to the other. She doesn't understand her magic, and I think the environment of my school as her housing area is… complicating things."

The house walls begin to hum. The magic of this place is ancient and it has been protective of me since I inherited it centuries ago. My ears perk, listening to the emotions it gives off. At Wisteria's request, it portrays no denial. I trust that I will know if the answer is a resolute 'no' from the house.

"So, she stays here with me but has classes with you?" I ask.

"If it's alright with you. I think you're just what she needs." Wisteria adds.

"And she is aware and understands what I am? What we are in this household?"

"Of course, I told her well before we arrived. I wouldn't send her somewhere I feel she would be uncomfortable."

I steal a glance at the woman in the living room. She has earbuds for listening to music, but I can guarantee she hears everything we say.

"Alright. She can stay," I reply, and the witch smiles.

Creating a home for monsters has seemingly become my main job. Apart from property investments around the globe, torturing people, and eating them for dinner. I dare say, I have my hands full.

"Virenda Blue," Wisteria calls for the young lady to come in, and she does. Long braids cascade down her back, framing her heart shaped face. Multiple jewels dangle from her earlobes and wrists. She's wearing a sundress that fits every curve of her right along with a conceited smile to match. She is absolutely beautiful.

"This is Lorcan Mortem. You'll be lodging here at his lovely home."

The smile on my face spreads like a crack in stained glass. I extend my hand for a greeting, taking her soft, dainty palm between my fingers.

"It is a pleasure, Miss Blue." Before she can have a chance to speak, I turn my attention to Wisteria. "I've got it from here, darling."

"I'll send your things right away," Wisteria states to the girl. With a smile and a squeeze of Virenda's arm, Wisteria is off on her journey back to the front door.

"Shall we?" Motioning to the hallway, she follows me down the long corridor, up the stairs, and into the second to last room on this side of the mansion. I chose this room for her vibe. Whereas Erasmus enjoys books and art, I feel the house telling me Virenda will appreciate the view from the balcony and the assortment of music.

"Welcome home."

She immediately takes the earbuds out and, with a sense of awe, she slowly enters the room.

"If it's not to your liking, there are others."

She turns to face me. "No, this is amazing. This one room is legit bigger than my last apartment!" The girl turns in a circle, quickly taking in the room as much as she can. Multiple long, dark gold braids swish around her back while she does.

"The bathroom is yours alone, too," I tell her. After opening the door to it, I show off the large tub and separate shower. "Privacy is a high priority here. Though we are almost all some type of supernatural creatures, we certainly hear things. We do our best to respect some boundaries at least."

I'm under the impression she understands, so I continue. "Dinner is typically served at six unless I have commitments elsewhere. Then you'll have to fend for yourself in the kitchen with the rest of the residents. As for the home, you have free rein of it. Just be cautious of others' privacy. I'll give you a grand tour after you relax a bit, yes?" Virendra surveys me with an 'almost too good to be true' air about her before nodding in agreement.

"Treat my space with respect, and all will be well." I smile, trying to be welcoming yet firm. She is still not convinced.

"That's it? No rules?" she asks.

"I find rules are often too tempting to break. Use your better judgment when here. Trust me, the house itself will alert me if anything is amiss." I go to leave, my hand on the doorknob to close it behind me. Before I shut it completely, I say to her, "I am happy you are here, Virendra. I have a good feeling about you." With a wink, I leave her to indulge in some alone time.

As soon as I make my way down the hall I'm cornered by a concerned looking Clouden. His posture is tense and his jaw is tightly locked. "We have a new resident," he says. If I thought he was observant prior to his change it's nothing compared to now. He sees and hears everything.

"We do. Are you going to attack her like you did Erasmus?"

"That was personal," Clouden replies. Yes, it happened because of his brother. His weakness.

"She's very lovely," I say.

"I can see that."

"Just pointing it out."

Cloud raises a brow at me. "Are you trying to play matchmaker or something?"

A hearty laugh erupts from my chest. "Absolutely not!" It's a lie. I might be trying to plant a little seed for him, but Clouden won't bite. I mean, he might if she lets him.

"Something is different about her," he seemingly ignores my comment and moves on to something else. "The air vibrates around her. Can you see it?"

"I can."

As if he's looking through the wood of her bedroom door, his gaze intensifies.

"She's a witch," I say. "It's her magic you can see around her. She hasn't learned to conceal it from other supernatural beings yet." Something we need to work on. I'm not sure how she can achieve this, Wisteria will have to help her. Sooner rather than later, for her own security.

"Interesting," Cloud murmurs.

"Yes, I suppose it is. I can imagine she will bring this house a little more adventure and delight."

I leave him staring at her door. As I make my way down the stairs, I hear him knock. When she opens it, he introduces himself, and there's a smile in his tone I assume he plastered on for theatrical effect. I don't stick around to eavesdrop. There's too much other work to do for me to bother with young adult drama today.

SEVEN

39

Why didn't I just let Clouden attack Erasmus?

He deserves to get his ass beat. Honestly, all the shit he's been pulling I should have just let Clouden finish attacking him. I wonder what would've happened if it carried on too long. Erasmus would've won, and Clouden would cease to exist. If I hadn't intervened, Clouden might be dead. It's Erasmus who is completely immortal. My little brother, though he's stronger and faster, can not overcome death completely.

What absolutely stunned me into silence was how I felt during the panic attack. I wasn't worried about Clouden at all when I should have been. My mind was on Erasmus. I'd forgotten momentarily, through it all, he would live despite any kind of brutal attack. I feared for his life, when it made absolutely no sense to. The panic attack probably should've lasted a lot longer but there's something so soothing about Erasmus' voice. It was hard to ignore the command to stay calm and grounded in that moment.

"Are you alright?" It's Clouden who appears in the doorway to my room asking this.

I've been in here for a while, even missed dinner. I was too hammered with this overbearing onset of emotions. I just didn't have an appetite. My head simply moves up and down as a reply.

"You understand I was just trying to protect you, right?" he asks.

"You don't need to protect me," I reply. "I may just be a human here, but it's fine. Honestly."

Clouden is sitting on my bed with me before I finish a blink. "If you were to stay here... You do need me."

A heavy sigh leaves my chest, and I look at the bottle on my nightstand; the potion of immortality. "I don't think I'm staying here."

The bed shifts, and Cloud is at the windows solemnly peering out. "I really wish you would." For a moment longer, it's silent between us, until he speaks again. "Seven, you're the only weakness I have. You're the only thing in this entire world that I love."

Those words were probably said to make me feel better. They do the opposite. I feel terrible. He worries about me so much. I had the audacity to concern myself with a psychopath before my own brother's well-being.

"Where was this love when you disappeared from me for nine months?" I hate to ask, but we need this conversation to happen.

"It was selfish, Seven," Clouden says. "And if I could change that, I would. I'd have told you or even brought you with me."

"Why? So I can make everyone here feel like Mom and Dad? They'll all end up hating me too."

Clouden's new icy stare makes me shiver. "They adore you. As much as I hate to admit it, Erasmus does too. He just needed to be reminded you're fucking human and could die if some thing happened."

"Oddly enough, I don't think he would let anything happen to me," I say. "Not even you." We share a look that is both serious and comical at once. "You do realize he's going to attack you at some point, right?"

My brother's head tilts and I swear it mimics the same movement Lorcan does. It makes sense they would be similar. Like a father and son type.

"You went after him for pushing me out of the window. He will probably go after you for trying to drain my blood."

"I never touched you, though," Clouden says, almost too quickly.

I smile. "You tried." He wants me to stay here. At any given time, I could die by the hands of one of them and it would be the easiest thing they ever killed. "If the house lets me out, Clouden, I have to go."

Mostly because they'd end up killing me, even by accident. Also because of these feelings stirring up inside of me over Erasmus. I don't like it. Not one bit.

The expression on Cloud's face is difficult to read. I'm not sure why he thinks I'll stay anyway.

I carefully choose my next words and whisper them. "Do you think we can imprison him again?"

My brother's face is almost stone. He's scanning the room trying to focus on anything but me. For some reason mentioning this makes him uneasy. I get the sense that Lorcan would not allow us to lock Erasmus back up. Audelia told me how he released Erasmus and how they slowly became friends over time. Lorcan would not stand for it. I don't want Erasmus gone but how can I survive with him making me feel things I never have.

"Clouden." Changing the tone of my voice, I urge him to look at me and he finally does. "Please. Help me."

ERASMUS

40

That tiny taste of Seven's blood I was granted did nothing to satiate the hunger I have for him. If anything, it worsened it. What started as just a little fun for me is presently internal torture. At first, I would occupy my time scheming and plotting ways to kill Lorcan just for the pleasure of it, and then Seven appeared. There is a constant battle between murdering him and keeping him all to myself. Then I drank his blood, and it completely changed the dynamic. If I kill him, I would get to feast on him only once and then he will cease to ever exist. If he takes the potion, he will be immortal. I'll get to feast on him whenever I want.

Lorcan once said, "As I've stated upon your release, Erasmus. Monsters recognize monsters. There was a distinct feeling that you belong here with me." For a while I lashed out at him over anything. Out of anger, I even told him dinner was disgusting and I never wanted to eat human again. Lorcan simply smiled and replied, "you're not upset that your dinner consists of human organs."

He was right. The typical calm demeanor that I mastered, was momentarily tossed out of the window. At the time, Lorcan was still brand new to me, everything was. I felt emotions I hadn't in many years. Once I sat back down and ate dinner with him, I regained composure. It was delicious, and so was every meal he prepared after that.

Prior to my imprisonment, I was already an unconventional person. Being here with Lorcan gives me comfort that I'm surrounded by the strange and sinister. Lorcan's house of uncommon decor did not bother me at all. The jar of tongues on the shelf in the living room is my favorite. There's a handful of containers scattered around that I'm not entirely sure of the contents.

I accompanied him on a hunt a few days later. He's fastidious about choosing his victims and makes sure the type of person he hunts matches the recipe he has in mind for it. There will never be an unworthy part of a human in our dinners.

"It's all about the flavor," he explained when we were back at the house that night. "I research the selection in the area and only the prime meat makes it to my kitchen."

While he worked on draining the corpse, he happily gave me more details. "Adrenaline," Lorcan began, "is a major factor. The air passages dilate to provide the muscles with more oxygen, resulting in the fresh aroma you smell."

He would carve each organ meticulously and with care before they'd be placed in a container for him to marinate in the seasoning of his choosing.

"When the adrenaline is kicked up, the liver releases blood sugar. It provides the body with energy; a natural sweetener, no refined sugar needed." Lorcan winked before continuing. "The next time we hunt, I'll pick someone not as athletic and you tell me which is tastier for you. The lazier ones leave more of an oily residue on your tongue."

Seven Wilbrate is full of anxiety. His mind creates the hormonal response to stress, and I assume it's what has me salivating just at the thought. The blood that flows through his veins picks up all of that flavor. When I drank the honeyed essence, I immediately became addicted. My obsession for this man already started a long time ago, and now there is absolutely no escaping it.

"If you do kill him," Lorcan says, interrupting my thoughts, "will you let me prepare his body for dinner?"

A growl releases from my lips. He should know better than to even ask that of me. The boy is mine and mine alone. I previously confided in Lorcan with my plans regarding Seven's immortality. After the rocky start between Lorcan and I, it's delightful to have a friend, especially after being isolated for so long. I refuse to share any part of Seven with him or anyone. Ever.

LORCAN

41

"Why is everything so loud?"

The question is from dear Seven who has been complaining of a headache since dawn. Everyone is frazzled by our newest member of the house playing music all night long. Well, she isn't playing the music... The music is her. Her magic is tied to the tune and the symphony she concocts. We don't understand it and neither does Virenda. However, it does not stop her from using it with all her might, at all hours of the day or night. It's blaring to the point of bursting eardrums. She feeds off the vibration and, in return, it would seem they energize her.

Virenda is lying on the floor in her room, watching the music float over her. When she combines her magic with it, it becomes almost physical. She can literally touch the music. It also looks like she can pluck a note out of thin air. Wisteria thinks being here with me will ease her mind and help her to control this power. Of all the places for this to happen! It's always chaotic. Even though there isn't another witch residing here, I believe there's always a method to Wisteria's madness. Virenda certainly does not object to dinner, even knowing what is in it. I doubt she has ever consumed human meat before. She was certainly excited to try it.

Watching from the open, common room area, I peek up from my newspaper to see Erasmus tossing her door open and barging in. He still needs to learn civility.

"Rude!" Virenda responds to his sudden appearance.

Erasmus studies the music notes she brought to life. It is seriously a sight to see. Virenda told me the music notes started to come up when she was around five years of age. Her parents thought it was adorable at first. After a few weeks of constant blaring, they were over it just as fast as Eras is now.

"Det er højt," he yells, and when all Virenda does is blink at him, Erasmus translates slowly. "It. Is. Fucking. Loud. *Unnaturally* loud."

Virenda snorts. "There's nothing natural about this house anyway."

"You're making Seven's ears bleed!"

"Oh, boo-hoo, the human is in ailment," she retorts.

I have to bite my inner cheek to keep the smile from forming.

It only takes Erasmus two strides to be right next to her. He swats at the golden music notes in the air, making the song interrupt and scratch. Wisteria sent her here because she didn't get along with the other girls in the coven. I can imagine she is not going to get along with these housemates either. If he touches her damn magic one more time she just might snap.

"Do not toy with me, woman," Eras huffs. "Not when it comes to him."

If it wasn't for the absolute mania in his eyes, I believe she might have called his bluff. If she knew him better, she would know he is not bluffing at all. Minor inconveniences set him off when it comes down to Seven.

Virenda plucks a musical note from the air and flicks it his way. It lands on his forehead, sizzles, and disappears, leaving a sort of burn on his skin. It too fades and disappears.

"It's no fun to torture you," she says. "You heal too quickly."

He squats down, until he's at eye level with her on the floor. His aura is nothing short of danger falling off of him in waves. She probably should play along and make some alliances with her house-mates. I do love the dramatics, and wish she won't.

"Turn it the fuck down, or I'll break your goddamn fingers off one by one and put them in the next stew." His Danish accent grew increasingly thick at the threat.

He's serious. However, I feel Virenda doesn't take threats lightly. Her lips part and she appears as though she's about to say something else when another figure appears in the doorframe.

"Hey!" Seven says breathlessly, keeping his ears covered. "Would you mind, please, turn it down a bit? Just for a little while."

I hadn't introduced her properly to Seven yet. He keeps being conveniently indisposed when I seek him out. She did know of him, though. I gave her a little rundown of the people who reside here and explained how each one has a vice. The way Erasmus watches Seven probably tells her immediately who the man in her doorway is. At least the human has some manners and is kind about his request. Sure, Virenda is the initial one at fault here by blaring unwanted music in our home. She is a guest here. Doesn't the guest always get the royal treatment?

From my chair, I watch her roll her eyes and with a wave of her hand, she lowers the notes to hover mid-way off the floor, which makes the volume go down. Probably since he asked so pleasantly.

"Thank you so much, Virenda. I need a break. You can turn it up again later." Seven smiles genuinely, and we can all see why the big guy is head over boots for him. Seven is very easy on the eyes, and he's charming, without even trying to be.

Virenda laces each word with sugary sarcasm. "Anything for you, sweet human."

Seven smiles even wider before walking off. Erasmus stands. His gaze does not move from the door until Seven is long gone down the hallway. Oh, the man is absolutely enthralled.

Erasmus glares at Virenda again before heading off in his boy's direction.

"Sheesh," Virenda says to herself while falling back to the floor to indulge in her music, more quietly this time.

SEVEN

42

Time is passing at an alarmingly fast pace. It was summer when I arrived here. Now it's rolling into autumn. Just about everywhere else in the United States they're gearing up for cooler weather. At least, the northern part is. Down here in the south, the heat will stick around for another two more months or longer. I remember waking up on Christmas morning, once or twice, and wore shorts to church, because it just wasn't cold enough to put on pants.

Briefly, I wonder what Halloween will be like in this house. The way things are going, I'll probably still be stuck in here for it. Who knows, maybe Christmas, too. That's one holiday I cannot imagine being celebrated here. Picturing this dark, gothic-style house decked out in the merry decorations is seriously a challenge.

Maybe I can't see it because I'm being distracted. There is more noise in this house nowadays. I'm pretty sure everyone can say that prior to my arrival. Since Virenda got here, it's been *really* loud. Her magic wraps around sounds and music. It's so cool, when you think about it, and it's also so annoying. I'm trying to just deal with it. She and Audelia are like cats fighting over their territory, making even more noise.

"Mind your business!" Outside the room, they're pretty much at it again. Audelia is the one I can hear clearest. She's already jealous of Clouden, and we have Virenda, who can potentially take Lorcan's attention from her as well. I remember thinking, when I was younger and my parents brought home Clouden from the hospital, they'd forget me and just focus on the new baby. It didn't happen, of course.

"Listen, sweetie. This may be your temporary home, but I was here first. I have authority over you."

I wait to hear Virenda's response. Thankfully, it comes almost instantly. "Authority? Are we playing dom and sub?" Even though I'm alone in my room, her response makes me blush. I can't even pinpoint why. It just feels like a natural reaction.

"You're disgusting," Audelia retaliates, and Virenda laughs. "I'll say this only once more. Clouden is off limits for you."

My eyebrows lift up dramatically. Are they fighting over Clouden?

"And so is Cato. That's my boyfriend," Audelia adds.

Okay, they aren't fighting over Clouden?

Virenda laughs again, this time with sarcasm lacing the sound. "I don't want your boyfriends."

"Boyfriend. Singular. Clouden is like a brother to me. You fuck with him, means you fuck with me."

Holy shit, since when? When I first got here Audelia hated Clouden. I pretty much assumed she still did.

I scramble off my bed and peek out the door only to see both women stalking off in opposite directions. Across the hall, Erasmus stands there watching the whole scenario unfold. Until his eyes land on me.

"Wow," I say, meaning the madness we just listened to. He just stares at me. Being stubborn, I stand up straight and hold his gaze too. I'm getting a lot better at it.

Lorcan walks by and stops right in front of us. I can see him in my peripheral vision bouncing his head in from my direction to Erasmus, trying to make sense of what's going on here.

"All of the people in this house are insane," he mumbles as he retreats. At this point, I just want to see who is going to crack first: me or Erasmus.

It's me.

While he's watching me I get this overwhelming sensation swirling in the pit of my stomach. I gulp back as much of it as I can. I realize it isn't bile rising up as much as normal. This feeling is different. It's almost like butterflies fluttering around in there. The emotions become entirely too much for me, and I bolt down the stairs to the front door. One more time I try the doorknob. Naturally, it won't budge.

"Come on," I whisper to the walls. "Why won't you let me out?" Of course, I don't get an answer. "Is this one of those things I need to figure out on my own? Some kind of life lesson?" I'm not sure why I expect a reply. "You let me outside the night of that panic attack."

The house probably knew I needed the air. It's not a malicious thing, though it isn't playing fair either. My fingertips graze the wall-paper, just slightly, and it feels like the wall almost shivered beneath my touch.

"I don't know why you're doing this," I whisper. "I'm going to go insane if I can't ever leave." There is nothing but silence. "Don't make me break a window." Something makes me feel like that would hurt the house, so I don't try it.

"Fine," I say, slowly. "I wish you could tell me how long I'll be stuck here. Am I truly going to live out my days here, like this?" This question should disturb me. It does the opposite and I feel almost at peace. Being somewhere I'm wanted, even if it's with these lunatics, feels wonderfully nice.

ERASMUS

43

The remains of broken dreams are scattered across the floor. The liquid that was once harbored inside the shattered bottle, no doubt has been absorbed into the floorboards. Hope quickly dispels itself from me, in any form. Seven Wilbrate has chosen his path, which does not include a life with me. Or with anyone. He knew the options, and I gave him ample enough time to weigh this. Is it rational, what I'm asking? No. But when have I been a rational man?

To be fair, if it's even an option here, I've waited a long fucking time for Seven to come back into my life. He is why I was thrown in the damn tomb to begin with, yet he couldn't know that. I do not resent him, for it was my own choices that landed me the consequence.

Perhaps, I should finally elaborate. It is my obsession for Seven that sealed my fate many times over. Our fate. I lost him, too many times, with each new life we were reborn into on this planet. Souls reincarnated from one life to the next. I lost him, in every single one of them.

For whatever reason, I remember him in each new life, yet he does not seem to know me. Still, he always ends up falling in love with me in every life we are born into. The last time I lost him, was the last time I would have to be reborn and search for him.

Many, many years ago I seduced a witch. It was a difficult task to take. At the time, I felt like it was my only option. I couldn't seem to find Seven on my own, so I formed a dangerous plan that ended up in madness. The witch was not one to drop her walls for just anyone. She did it for me. I can't say she loved me. I do not care if she did. She was infatuated, to the point of obsession, much like myself with Seven.

"Help me find my friend, my dearest?" I coaxed her, using the obsession of hers for my selfish gain to try to locate Seven in this life. Each past life took me forever to find him on my own. Doing it on my own meant the same fate would happen, and I didn't want to waste precious time, again.

Well, I slipped up too easily. The witch discovered my heart did not belong to her, like I was pretending. She cursed me with an immortal life, hoping I would bend to her will with time.

"You will love me," she commanded. She even tried a love potion, but it didn't last. She figured, over the years, she could urge me to want her, in the same overpowering way I wanted Seven. It was never possible. Using her power she shoved me to my knees, the witch made certain she would show me who was in charge. The vial thrust into my mouth, as she forced the contents down my throat.

Immortality.

"I created you. You are mine, Erasmus." In her eyes, I would have loved her, if she manufactured me. Still, I refused.

It was this life I would always remain to live. Immortality might not be a bad thing. I couldn't die—which meant I could do as I pleased. While I waited for my boy to appear again, in this new life, the witch became more suspicious. It was growing increasingly apparent to her my heart would never belong to her, even if she carved it from my chest. She also held onto the suspicion that if she left me wandering at some point, I would try to dispose of her. This knowledge angered her to the point she gathered her sisters to imprison me in the tomb, where I waited for a long time, before Lorcan found me.

And when Seven... in this life, showed up at Lorcan's house, it was too much to be a coincidence. The compass was proof. It's him. Seven is the man I am destined to be with, in every life, and he distinctively chooses to ignore that. He has to feel this fucking pull to me. He always does. Since he would rather die than be with me, I'll have to wait many more years before he crosses my path again. Can I tell Seven all of this? Will he even understand? If he picked the path with me, I would have indulged him in the story. He has decided otherwise. Why would I waste such breath on the story? It would change nothing.

I gave Seven the possibility I never had—to choose immortality or die by my hand—but he denies himself of a wonderful life. He denies *me* of him. Am I any better than the witch who imprisoned me? No. I'm far worse. I am even more selfish. When I say I will stop at nothing until he is solely mine, I mean it.

"Well, at least when I kill him, he gets reborn again." I eye the knife in my hand, trying to remind myself of what's to come. "Only about thirty-two fucking years to go, until I can find him again."

LORCAN
44

Since Virenda arrived, there has been nothing but tension between her and Audelia. I realize accepting Virenda to stay here with us has raised some emotions. I hoped eventually they would cease on their own. It does not seem likely, anymore. So it might be time I intervene.

"Both of you, come join me in the basement, please," I say to them. "I need your assistance on a little craft."

Virenda glances at Audelia, then back at myself before following me in. I point to the containers on the stainless steel table in the center of the room. They are filled with all different sizes of bones.

"I have too many of these. I don't wish to dispose of them, so what can we do with them instead?"

Virenda just scans each box warily. Audelia is the one who speaks first. "We can make some utensils or something."

"If it is what you wish. You'll need a knife to carve it with," I say.

"What if we did, like, what the kids do in school?" Virenda asks. "Macaroni art!"

Audelia is confused by this. Either she never had to create such a thing or her lost memories don't recall what that is.

"Like gluing them to paper or something…" Virenda adds.

Clouden appears in the doorway. "That's stupid," he says. "It's not useful."

"So, then, we go with my idea: utensils," Audelia states.

"We have plenty of those," Clouden says as he picks up a bone. He holds it up to Audelia's head. "What about hair accessories?"

"Crowns!" I yell. "It's perfect." Digging in the cabinet behind me, I find the fishing twine and rope. "Here."

Truth be told, I don't care what the hell they create as long as they are doing it together, as a family should. I begin to craft with them, and make my own crown of bones, just for the hell of it.

"Well?" I ask them all. "What's the new gossip?" Naturally, I don't care what's going on in the media as for celebrities. So when they start rambling about that part, I just pretend to listen. Celebrities are people who are deemed important for the silliest things: modeling clothes or acting a role in a movie. They do nothing to truly aid in the progress of this world. I do suppose the happiness they bring is enough. However, I think they're terribly overpaid.

At first, it's only Virenda doing all of the talking. She goes on and on about music. Audelia didn't say anything until they both found a cord that tied them together. Some music bands I never heard of. I have, indeed, missed having a daughter. Blair was off living her life, doing whatever it is she does. One day, these two will probably fly the nest, as well. Hopefully, not soon. I'd love to find more about Audelia's past, as soon as we get more information on where to actually start, again. Everything I found recently has resulted in a dead end.

"Lorcan," Virenda says. "Clouden said you pick your victims based on merit, is that right?

As I glance at Cloud, he looks away. I am sure, if he could blush, he would have right then and there.

"Somewhat," I say. "Not all of them. The majority are people I believe the world would be better without. And why waste them, when we can consume them?"

"I thought vampires don't eat food?" Virenda asks.

"We don't *need* to eat. Just like you don't need ice cream, you still eat it for the flavor. I find that I still enjoy the taste of food, after my transition, so I just continue to eat."

"Did you eat them before your change?" she asks. "Humans, I mean."

I smile at the memories that bombard my brain. "Oh, yes." I leave it at that.

Clouden initiates his own conversation and has the girls both laughing. The air in here is much lighter, now that we all came together as one to talk nonsense.

"What do you think will happen with Erasmus and Seven?" Audelia asks. She and Virenda glance at Clouden for his input.

"It's hard to say," he says. "Old Seven would have ignored any romantic advances. He was never much of a flirt or anything, and he really only had a girlfriend in college. I don't even think the girl cared for him, anyway. She was all over the place, flirting with anything that walked." He takes a moment and adds, "After he was kidnapped, when they returned him, he wasn't the same. He's grown so much in the short time he's been here."

The girls both shift in their seats and continue to build their crowns. "And you?" Audelia asks him.

Clouden smiles, baring his fangs in the light as he does. "Oh, I've been with plenty of girls. Can't say they were proper girlfriends, though, just play and run. I'm not committing to anything anytime soon."

Audelia smiles. "I've been seeing someone." She raises her chin.

"We know," both Cloud and Virenda say in unison.

"What about you?" Virenda asks, directing this conversation my way.

My head shakes. "I do not see romance in my cards at all, darling. I like my life just the way it is—with all of you." I place my crown on my head and pose for them with my hands on my hips. "What do you think?"

With lips parted they're all in the process of answering, when a commotion from upstairs shakes the house. The only other two in the house today are Seven and Erasmus. We all glance at the ceiling as I ask, "What are they up to?"

We waste no time in going to see. I steal a front row seat on the couch. The other three disappear to the balcony upstairs to safely witness the madness.

SEVEN

45

Something is... *off*

I haven't seen or heard from Erasmus since the other night. That might not seem like a big deal to most people. This is not a 'most people's' situation. Since I set foot here in this house, I've been like a magnet pulling him right behind me at every turn. He's everywhere, including the air I've been breathing. I can't even remember what the world smelled like before he invaded my space. It's been all him for months and quickly, it's not. I almost feel empty without his presence, lost even. How strange it is. I wanted nothing more than to be free of this man, and now that I might be, I think I might pass out. Something is up. Something is... off.

This is it. Isn't it?

Today.

It's happening today. He's going to kill me. I'd say he's going to *try* to kill me, but let's be realistic here… I'm going against an immortal who is much bigger and much stronger than I am. I need to find Clouden. I thought I was ready for this. I don't think I am.

Will Erasmus ask for any last words? I don't have a speech written up. Erasmus is kind of poetic, in a weird way. Maybe he has a quote or something for me, instead. Maybe, as he slices my arm off, he'll whisper sweet nothings in my ear. Before I can prepare for that, his form appears on the other side of the kitchen island. As if we're finally on the same page, same line, and the same word, Erasmus stares back at me.

No.

That's not right. He mirrors me.

The turn of my chin. The turn of his chin. My lips part. His lips part. We are so in sync with each other that, subconsciously, I can't distinguish myself from him. I inhale, and so does he. My whole life has boiled down to this moment.

Life is futile, when you think about it. There's birth and something in between and then there's death. It's hard to picture life ending, when it's your own. As much as I've endured in this life, I am thankful for it. Everything that's happened was for some cosmic reason. I suppose that reason is for this moment in time. I fill my lungs once more, and I'm smothered with Erasmus' scent. The aroma of his masculinity that's been absent from my air comforts me. I think I'll miss the way he smells the most. I inhale once more, just for the hell of it, and so does Erasmus.

And we're off.

I run. He knew I'd run. He's prepared. I'm at least going to make sure this isn't easy for him. On instinct for survival, my feet carry the rest of me from the kitchen to the hall. Erasmus is on the heel of my boot.

Earlier today, I saw the others go down to the basement. I suppose the madness between Erasmus and myself has pulled everyone back upstairs with us. Virenda's obnoxious music starts blaring through the house again, and the choice of song is ridiculous, but it fits. Lyrics of love sing through the air of these walls. This is Erasmus Rasmussen confessing his love for me. In his own strange way, this is how he shows affection.

He's chasing me around the house like it's a game, and it very well is to him. I'm dodging his advances barely, with just a millisecond each time to get away. We're leaving behind a mess of furniture pieces everywhere. Pictures are knocked from the wall, lamps are tossed to the floor. Lorcan will make him pay for it later. Erasmus is more muscular than me. I have speed and can easily fit in places he has to fight through.

I'm just out of his reach. His fingers stretch behind me, just grazing the soft hairs of my neck, that are standing tall at the possible intrusion. I slow down when I hit the corner of the wall with my shoulder, and Erasmus crashes into me. My elbow connects with his nose, and it instantly bleeds everywhere, but he'll be fine. Funny, isn't it? He's trying to kill me, and I'm worried about his well being. Once I'm gone, who's going to worry about him like I do? I can't run forever. That's why he doesn't mind this last little brawl. In the end, he will win.

If the house isn't in shambles, by the time this is over, I would be surprised. When Erasmus said he would kill me, I wondered if the house would intervene when it happened. So far, no walls move, no shingles toss themselves at us. It's just letting this happen. This part breaks my heart the most. I have a soft spot for this house, even though it's kept me barricaded in. Is this why it sealed me up? Just to be another victim on Erasmus' list of kills. It's not fair. I learned a long time ago, life is rarely ever fair.

My lungs burn. Tears sting the corners of my eyes, not only does the house not interfere. Neither do my housemates. Everyone, including myself, allows this to happen. Something then clicks between us, an understanding that this is crucial to us. There can't be any more running from it, or from him. Nothing but acceptance pours out of me, as I come to a halt in the kitchen and in the way he looks at me, looks *through* me, Erasmus feels it too. This is the moment it all led up to. All of my sufferings will be cleansed from this world.

We stand, bloody and full of this mess we created together. Facing each other, he sees me, and I see him. This time without asking, he touches my chin, so tenderly I think I'll collapse from the softness of his fingers. That will be the end of me in itself. In his eyes, I see my death already haunting him. I won't be the last person he kills, but I'll be the one that matters—the one he gave a part of himself away to.

There is no apology. There's no poem or sensual quote. Not one word is granted to me. In the end, it's just the raw confession of his love piercing my stomach. In the end, there is me, and there is him, and a knife connecting us.

ERASMUS

46

He put up a good fight. Seven became aware when it was over. He stopped running and accepted his fate. I don't ask for permission to caress his lovely face. That beautifully sculpted face is from years and years of genes passed down to mold this perfect specimen. There's so much to say and, yet, nothing to say, at all. Every lingering question was answered. Peering into those big, blue eyes, spiraling with so much emotion, I couldn't determine which was which.

My knife shoves deeply into his stomach. Seven gasps through the pain and instinctively reaches out for me. I would never deny my boy anything he asks for and I hold him up. He doesn't scream. Sharp intakes of air through his nostrils are the only true indication of his pain. He falls into me, and my arms wrap around him as I lower him to the floor. He's shaking, shocked from the excessive suffering his body is enduring. I do not cringe at the sight of his torment and almost look away. Seven will not let me look away. His eyes are fixated on mine, forcing me to keep the focus on him. He makes certain I witness this, until the very antagonizing end. My boy is dying. This is most disappointing. The outcome was obvious when I took notice of the potion bottle broken and leaking on the floor.

Seven's eyes finally close. His heart still beats, barely. His death is not one I truly wanted. It needed to happen. With him gone from this life, I'll have to wait another thirty-two years, possibly longer, to find him, again. If he doesn't want me in this life, there is always another one to try in.

Disappointment tugs at my shoulders while I step over him. I need to find a towel or something to begin the cleaning process. It surprises me that Clouden hasn't shown up to attack me. Maybe the house is on my side and locked up in his room to keep him from this fight. I wish anger would take over me, instead it's just disappointment that's filling me.

Virenda told me earlier this week I've gone about this all wrong. She thinks Seven would have preferred me to court him in a different way. Maybe I should've romanced him better. I went about this whole thing wrong and it's my fault he's dead on the kitchen floor. If things had been different he might have taken the potion. There's always the chance he still would have refused. It was fifty-fifty, no matter which way it's looked at. How am I going to wait another three decades before I can find him again? Who's to say I even get lucky and he gets reborn. I can imagine at some point the soul gets tired of coming back.

The entire time in the tomb, I never wished for death to take me as much as I do today. Carrying on does not seem feasible. Perhaps I can convince the witch Wisteria to reverse this curse on me. She must have a remedy on how to end immortality, if she can grant it so easily. There must be a way. I refuse to carry on like this.

"Hey, asshole."

I freeze. The soft heartbeat that permeated the air, vibrates quickly. As I turn, Seven runs at me in attack mode. It isn't easy to decide what to do next. The sight of him is so breathtaking that I question whether my grief has fabricated this as a hallucination. When he's close enough, I flip him over my shoulder to make positively certain he's tangible and not some apparition. We both end up lying on the cold, hard floor while heaving through lack of breath from the impact.

Seven is up, again, this time more vigilant and uncaring about whether this fight requires physical touch or not. He must be fighting the revulsion. Either way, I'm on cloud nine. And he does something I never would've expected. He bites me. The ache in my shoulder is a sharp, yet glorious feeling. I yank him by his hair, slam his head into the wall, and he fucking laughs through a bloody nose.

At this point, Seven has lost his shit completely and tackles me in the living room, where Lorcan is sitting on the couch. He's obviously pretending to read a newspaper, seemingly unaware of the madness. As we roll through, trying to choke each other out, Lorcan lifts his legs. He's completely unperturbed by any of this.

"You both have a mess to clean when you're done..." He turns the page of his paper and glances our way for a second. "...doing whatever it is you're doing." Perhaps he is paying attention after all.

Seven's fist connects with my face. I immediately bash my forehead into his, cracking both of our skulls. It takes only a second and I watch the previous bruise on his cheek slowly disappear. He did it. He fucking did it. He took the potion.

Grabbing his wrist, I stop his next blow just before his fist can connect with my cheek. Seven ceases fighting me finally; instead, he's slowly coming to a stand, and I follow suit. The knife I stabbed him with is still lodged in his stomach.

"May I?" I ask. He's confused by the meaning of my question until his gaze goes to where my eyes flick, and he nods. With an arm around him, I retrieve the knife. He isn't silent anymore. He's cursing me to every god there is.

"You didn't say it would still hurt!"

I chuckle, "You didn't ask."

The blood pouring from his stomach begins to slow, until it completely stops. It didn't help that his body healed around the knife before I could dislodge it. Seven looks at me with complete earnestness and sincerity. His hand ball into a fist as he grasps the front of my shirt, so tightly his knuckles turn white.

"You can't leave me, Erasmus," he says. "I hope you know that. Not ever."

Of course, I know. Just as I wanted him to, Seven quickly became dependent on me. I'll have to make sure to prance this win in front of Virenda to show her that doing things my way typically ends up how it should. The realization is beginning to wrap itself around me tightly. He chose this. He chose *me*.

"If you think you're obsessive, you haven't seen anything yet. I'm not just yours, Erasmus." The beauty of that fire burning steadily inside Seven lights up the blue of his eyes perfectly. He licks his lips before speaking again. "You're also mine."

There you are, wildfire. There you fucking are.

Seven laughs softly and frees his fist from my shirt before he holds his hand out for me, and I gratefully accept. He does not revolt, and he does not heave at my touch as his fingers tighten around my hand. I could weep for joy at this moment in time. As we step over the mess we made, Lorcan screams from the other room to clean it up, and I will. First, I'm taking my boy upstairs to celebrate.

LORCAN
47

"Oh, Wisteria, it's been so entertaining in the house these days!" While on the call with Wisteria, I'm technically still working. The phone is cradled between my cheek and shoulder as I carve up a few slices of thigh from my previous victim. I could cook it whole and let the skin crisp up nicely, but I need a different recipe tonight. I'll pan sear this one with a nice glass of A positive.

"Erasmus tried to kill Seven, thinking he didn't take the potion. The little rascal did indeed. When he got up and mauled Erasmus, I could've just died from laughter. Granted, I was in the living room when the debacle started. It was still quite humorous. The girls, Clouden, and I were doing crafts when Erasmus and Seven started their little feud. We just had to go witness it for ourselves! Apparently Clouden was in on it, too. I wondered why he didn't rip Erasmus' head off when he stabbed his brother. Anyway, they left the house in shambles for a bit. Worse than children, I swear! Of course, it was myself who cleaned it all up. They were too busy upstairs in Erasmus' room."

"Were they making out, finally?" she asks.

"No. The fools were dancing around the room to a ridiculous song from the '90s. You know, the one that pretty blond sang. Oh, what's the name of it? I can't even remember. The '90s was an era of decent music too. It was the '80s era that was my favorite. Not for fashion, of course, those damn shoulder pads were hideous."

Wisteria laughs in my ear, and I'm still sawing away while I continue the conversation. "Virenda tells me she and the others are getting along much better these days as well."

Thankfully, because I still can't quite understand the fiasco they started. The only part that made sense was perhaps Audelia was playing the Queen Bee, letting Virenda realize her status. Whatever the reason, they seem to be over it for now. When Wisteria brought Virenda here she believed we could make her be more at ease. It took a little while, but she's come along.

Wisteria laughs again. "Your home is positively wonderful, it sounds?"

"I would have to say 'yes'." And it's true. Having all of these creatures in this house together has been a challenge. I think we have adjusted quite well. "Looks like we have just what we need for the time being."

"I'm so happy. Virenda is doing well there with you. She's been completing all of the assignments I send her. I don't know how you do it, Lorcan. Whatever it is, keep it up. "

I can't say if there will be more people calling this place a home any time soon. Then again I did not see any of these coming at all. It happened quickly, too. For the longest time, this house was empty except for myself and presently it's filled with people and their noise. Beautiful noise.

Speaking of them, Erasmus has just arrived inside from the yard and left his muddy shoes by the front door. "Absolutely not." I lower the phone briefly to yell in his direction, "Pick those up!"

It's difficult to sound angry when I'm brimming with so much happiness.

"Yes, well, Lorcan do be careful."

Wisteria wouldn't just tell me to be careful unless she has a reason to. I won't question it. I'm afraid if I do, it could alter whatever is going to happen and make it all the more dreadful.

"Call me later?" she asks.

After we hang up it dawns on me I need to fill in another person with all these little details of my life. I press the speed dial for Hunter's number. It goes straight to voicemail, and I happily leave one with a much more simplified version of the tale.

SEVEN

48

omehow, I actually manipulated Erasmus into thinking I didn't take the potion. This was by far the greatest ploy I have ever pulled off. Thank Clouden for that. He taught me the little ins and outs. Initially, I asked him for help to imprison Erasmus again. Everything about him frightened me. The feelings I have for him changed my mind. I'm desperately afraid of how I feel for him, but the fear wasn't enough to change them.

Pretending that nothing changed was a little bit of a challenge. I had to become an actor. For me to accomplish what I needed to, I needed to be in a certain mental space I typically am not in. I may have overdone it, though, because my anxiety increased majorly once I took the potion. The acting part was so Erasmus would think I was still human. He couldn't know I was panicking because

I drank the potion. He would have to think it was just an ordinary occurrence.

It was taking so long for him to kill me, I almost thought he wouldn't. I wondered how to trigger him to make it happen sooner. Clouden came up with the idea after I took the potion to refill it with water and smash the bottle on the floor. It would make it seem I was angry and just broke it.

It worked. He did try to kill me after that.

I find *how* he tried to murder me romantic, and it should tell you right then and there I'm not right in the head. He held me so close when the knife penetrated my skin. It felt like we were dancing intimately together. In a way, we did.

As strange as it may be, whatever is between us feels infinitely right. I was meant to take the potion. I'm supposed to be here. I'm supposed to be with him. Clouden may have left home on his own accord to make his own choices. I can't shake the feeling fate knew I would follow him. Something in this universe knew Clouden leaving would ultimately push me to this path of finding Lorcan's house... and finding Erasmus. Don't ask me to explain how I can feel so connected to a man who has been promising to murder me, and would have succeeded if I did not drink the vial of potion. It doesn't make sense, but this is how it's meant to be. I am where I am meant to be.

Anxiety slams into me. What if he leaves? What if Erasmus decides sometime down the line I'm not what he wanted? He will realize I'm the biggest mistake of his life. I've become too dependent on him, on knowing he's there. One day, he might not be.

Panic rises like bread dough, this is seriously nothing new in the life of Seven Wilbrate. This might not be healthy. Let's be real here,

I am not the sanest person in the world. Even if I was mentally sane, I have a feeling that no matter what, meeting Erasmus Rasmussen would have still shaken me. Would I have been able to survive a separation from him even then? My gut says no. At this point, I'm falling apart just at the nightmare of Erasmus leaving me. What even are we? I'm already feeling an attack coming on at the uncertainty of it all.

The room is closing in on me. The hypothetical flood builds up inside my skin, and the need to breathe is even more dire than ever. How ridiculous is it? I've brought this upon myself, but it's pretty much how it happens each time it does.

The blankets are tossed to the floor, and my feet are carrying me down the hall to his room before I can muster up a defensive thought. I doubt he'll mind. When I burst open the door to his room, Erasmus looks absolutely enchanted to see me, even in such disarray, from what I can see of him anyway.

"It's fucking dark in here!"

I'm not sure why I chose those words as a greeting. This is one thing my anxiety does to me—it says whatever the hell it wants to. How can he sleep in this darkness? Granted, I am aware that your eyes are closed the entire duration of slumber. What if he needs to grab a drink of water in the middle of the night? Surely he would trip! Not that it matters. He's immortal, so I suppose it makes sense he sleeps in pitch black darkness. It feels like a void, a beautiful void I am about to make my own home inside of. Just standing in the same room as he is, I can feel the panic begin to loosen. The flood waters are slowly starting to recede. It's this feeling of comfort I need and he's the source of it.

ERASMUS

49

ong before the door to my bedroom flew open, I heard him coming. It was the once soft breath quickly turning erratic that stirred me from a deep sleep. Across the hall, Seven's voice was muffled but clear to me. He alone is the only one worth my attention, and it is always solely on him. I can sense instantly when he is distressed. Still, I wait for him to come to me. I'll try not to interfere unless I deem it completely necessary, as I did previously when he ran out in the middle of the road.

"It's too fucking dark! I can't see!"

The soft fragrance of vulnerability coats his skin like sweat. In a half roll, peeking over my shoulder, I see Seven's chest heaving so arduously it was a wonder how he's still standing upright.

"You can see in the dark," I say softly and roll back over. He's panicking, but he's safe.

"No!" he shouts. "No, it's dark as fuck! I can't!"

"Close the door, Seven."

"It feels— It feels like… I can't see, and it's—it's…"

"You can see. You found my room." I still do not turn to look at him. I'll crack if I do. He needs to pull himself back to reality, and if I coax him every time, he won't be able to do it alone. As much as I want him solely dependent on me, I will not be entirely selfish now he is immortal. "You don't need to use your eyes to see, Seven."

"That's what eyes are fucking for!"

Then I recall how he would cease all action when I said three words to him, so I say them out loud for this moment. "Stay with me?" I ask, and there it is. It's as simple as that. Those three magical words together trigger something. Immediately his breath is slowing. His pulse is still beating irrationally fast but he's not shaking as roughly. The familiarity of those three words sink into him. I found the antidote, and I am beyond thrilled it's me.

Seven nods. I pull the covers back on the empty side of the bed that my back is facing, and Seven slowly eases under them. His body still jerks and convulses from the onset of panic, but I can already feel him begin to relax. Once he calms, oxygen hits him like liquor, potent and immediate. The silence in the air is pregnant with an unasked question. Even with my back to him, I can still feel it.

"What is it, Seven?"

Permission is all he needs to speak. He wastes no time asking the question. "What are we?"

"Immortal," I answer back without thought.

"I meant… us." The panic still shifts in his voice. Somehow, he pushes through it to breach this subject.

"Labels are for the mundane, Seven," I reply.

"I like labels. I like knowing what something is."

Of course, he does. In his mind, he's labeled the world with his imagination. This relationship is something we share together, so he wants my input on it.

"You can't always know what everything is," I say.

There is a hard silence before he answers, "I just want to know *this*."

"What would you have me say, Seven? Friends? Lovers? Husbands? Do any of those terms fit us?"

After a pause, he says softly, "No."

It's quiet between us, again. Unanswered questions still linger in the air. Once more, he waits for permission to question it. I wonder if he realizes how good of a submissive he is. He makes a sound as if to say something and stops.

"Yes, Seven?" I ask.

"I can just come in here whenever I want?"

I'm fighting a smile while I answer him. "Yes, now go to sleep."

Remarkably, he curls against my back. Between the goosebumps on my skin and the fire in my blood, I fight the urge to turn and face him, to pull him flush to me and keep him there for always. He presses his forehead to my back and sighs. The air is finally clear enough for him to relax.

"Don't try to murder me in my sleep," he says. I can feel the smile on his lips without seeing it. Even if I did try, I wouldn't succeed anymore. He is immortal.

I smile and say, "Not tonight."

LORCAN
50

"Will somebody get the damn door!"

The incessant sound of knocking throbs abruptly through the large mansion, pulsating to each crack and corner. Everyone is home. I can hear Virenda dancing in her room, music blaring. Audelia is on the phone, yapping away with her boyfriend Cato. The clink of glass chess pieces tells me Clouden is playing a solo game. And Seven and Erasmus are upstairs probably having a damn staring contest again. They tend to do that a lot.

Enhanced hearing helps me detect a thumbtack falling on the carpet from miles away, and it is nothing compared to the pounding of a fist on the front door this instant. I am covered in blood up to my elbows, digging my hands deep inside the corpse that is lying flat on my workstation. Their lips parted and eyes glazed with death, my victim is a universe of its own accord. Easing out one organ after another, I set them in a basket to stock the fridge later.

The pounding continues, which means no one in this whole damn house bothered to answer it. I can sense the person at the other side of the door is not human, and when I finally take the time to focus on catching their scent, I freeze on the spot. That fragrance I am intimately familiar with and recognize it instantly.

An urgency tugs at my core. Neglecting the body on the table, my feet manage to carry me away from my work, suddenly on a quest to beat everyone to the door. I take the stairs two by two and accelerate from the basement.

Clouden is almost there to answer the door, and with a bloody hand, I yank at the back of his shirt to pull him backward.

"Hey! You said to answer it!" he says, stumbling a bit.

"Go away, changed my mind!" I snap.

My fingers, wet with the blood, slip around the doorknob, and for the life of me, I can't get the damn thing to open! I'm half a second away from just yanking the door full off of the frame when I finally manage it. The house is playing its little tricks again.

The man on my porch is waiting patiently, and biding his time by taking in the scenery of Canal Street, until the creak of the door pulls him back to this moment. When he turns to face me, it is then my cold, dead heart might have thumped once behind its rib cage. The familiar grin I remember is almost hidden under the same deep mustache and beard. It's there aiding the soft crinkles of his eyes.

I exhale his name like I'd been in possession of it since the day he left those fifty years ago. "Callinicus.,"

"Hello, Lorcan." The same husky tone of his voice has not changed a bit. Of course, why would it? "You look happy to see me?" It is a question and a statement all at once. What he sees on my face is indeed happiness. What he often fails to understand is why.

"Of course, I am, Cal. Come in."

I hold the door open for him, and as he passes, he locks his eyes with mine until it's impossible to continue inside, without looking away.

"I'm happy that you're happy to see me. However, I do come with some news." He shifts from one foot to the other. He's coming off as a bit worried.

Blood stains the door as I close it. I ignore the mess, something I rarely do.

"Oh? And here I thought you stopped in for a visit because you missed me." I chuckle.

He smiles, and my words, though playful, are held true. Cal did more than miss me.

"I came from the near future, and from what I can see, Lorcan, there is a band of vampire hunters who are after you. They're not too keen on the recent killings over the years and are adamant about your demise."

I throw my hands up. He meant well, but he's taken the element of surprise from me! It's not every day people catch me!

"Why are you telling me this?"

Cal shrugs, "I'm not even sure. Perhaps to see what you do next."

"Oh, you shouldn't have told me. You took all the drama out of it!" I whine playfully. This can't be the reason he stopped by. There's more to this story than he's letting on. I'll have to let it unfold as it does.

"You can still make it theatrical, though," he says. "You always do."

This is the truth of it. Everything, and I do mean everything I do, is always done in the most poetic, dramatic, and theatrical ways possible. Cal knows this all too personally.

"I always do." Like a spell has been broken, I blink and realize my manners have been tossed from my whole being. "For fuck's sake, Cal, you let me drawl on and on without offering you a drink!"

"Oh, Lorcan, please... I know where the fridge is." He makes his way toward the kitchen. I beat him there. Supernatural speed and all.

"You'll not lift a finger in this house. Let me make you a special pot of tea," I say with a devious smirk on my lips. "Like old times."

"Like old times," Cal repeats. He takes a seat at the counter barstool and asks, "Do you know where I can get this fixed?" He holds out his watch. It is the watch that helps him glide through time. Cracks cover the face, and the hands are bent.

"Cal, what did you do?"

He shrugs softly. "On my way in, there was a little accident. Tripped down a flight of stairs."

From the perfectly intact attire, not one shred of fabric out of place. I see no indication of a fall. There's also no fresh blood, not even a scratch of skin that would give evidence to the claim, and I refrain from mentioning it as well.

"I can contact my friend Wisteria. The witch will possibly have a spell to rectify it."

He grins. "Thank you."

"Anything for you, my darling Cal." This comment is not entirely true, considering our shared past.

When it is ready, I pour the tea. "Well, since you're here for this little visit, you must tell me everything about your travels. Leave no details for the imagination."

Cal takes one sip of the tea, and his eyes close. When he opens them again, I have a feeling he was lost in memory, then he looks down to the liquid in his mug. The flavor of this tea is one he probably never tried before and I doubt will ever forget it.

"Where to even begin?"

The corners of my lips rise to reveal razor-sharp fangs as I talk once more. "Seventy three years ago… when you stepped off the front porch. Do not stop talking until your story lands you right back here again."

He begins, and it takes him a few hours to tell me of the lifetimes he traveled.

SEVEN

51

If it was not for the traumatic piece of shit experience of my past, would I have been married by now with kids? I'm at the ripe age of thirty-two, and everyone I once called friends has their own beautiful families. Would it have been a woman I settled down with? I have never been attracted to men, and I didn't think of them in any way romantically. I had one girlfriend right before college. It wasn't anything serious at all. The only person who has ever touched me intimately is Erasmus. Unless you count my abductor, that was not intimate to me. That was abuse. And at first, even Erasmus' touch was always just to my hand or face, after he asked me for permission. He never oversteps my boundaries, though the line is becoming thin for him.

In a way, I am thankful for everything I've gone through. It landed me right where I needed to be. I'm sitting on the counter while Erasmus sets the oven to preheat and grabs ingredients to make cookies, because I mentioned briefly, two seconds earlier, I wanted something sweet.

"How do you do it?"

Erasmus does not look up from gathering the ingredients as he asks in return, "You are obviously not asking how I make the cookies?"

"No."

It's obvious what he and Lorcan do when they leave the house together, even though neither of them have ever really gone into full detail. While he mixes everything in the bowl, I wait a moment before adding to my question.

"Killing someone. Is it as intimate as when you tried to kill me?" I'm sure he hears the emphasis on the word 'try' in that comment since he did not succeed.

"The art of murder is always intimate," Erasmus answers as he molds the cookies on the baking sheet. None of them are uniform and some are smaller than others. "Your murder was entirely different."

When he does not elaborate, I ask, "How?"

"Because it was you," Erasmus says just as easily. "Your finality would have disheartened me. Knowing you were completely gone, in a world I would always have to be in, would have wrecked me."

"I could have just lived."

After some time, Erasmus places the cookie sheet in the oven and turns on the timer, when he finally replies, "You would not have been immortal. I wanted you to be equal to me."

"So I can kick your ass right back?" Of course, I have to be cocky about it.

The corners of his lips turn up, "So you can kick my ass right back."

"How?" I urge, almost whining like a petulant child who hasn't received what they want quickly enough.

Erasmus' hand then splays onto my stomach and presses down, urging my body to lay flat on the counter. He takes the tip of his knife to trace a slow line down my chest. When it reaches my stomach, the muscles there contract.

"First, I would slice you open, starting from the chest to the bottom of your belly."

I should not be enjoying this as much as I do. Honestly, I am.

"And then I would peel the layers of your skin apart." He pretends to pull back my flesh, and I imagine my stomach open and raw, showing off all of my internal organs to him. Why do I want him to be happy with what he'd see?

My voice cracks, and somehow I form the words entirely. "That's not how you tried to kill me."

"As I have stated before, you are not everyone else. Your death would have been treasured. I do not keep souvenirs, but I had plans for your heart to be secured somewhere I could easily reach."

Knowing he would keep my heart made my pulse quicken. His ears perk up, and I know he hears it. "You'd have eaten the rest?"

"Of course. A tasty morsel like yourself? I would not have wasted a single scrap of you."

We both smile because that's certainly true. As odd as it is, I feel comfort knowing I would've been a meal for him to enjoy. I still can be.

"And now?" The words come out a little more rugged than I expect them to. The atmosphere change shifts everything inside me.

"I am going to get my taste," he says.

Blood rushes to my cheeks. "You make it sound so romantic."

"It should be."

"So…" I begin softly. "When you peel my skin off, you'll bring me roses?"

"If that is what you wish."

"Surprise me."

His lips curl again, and I pull him by the front of his shirt so his mouth hovers above mine. I bite his chin hard enough for the flesh to become red with my teeth indent.

"That was very naughty of you." He smiles.

"Are you complaining?"

"Nej, my perfect boy," Erasmus says slowly. "I would never complain about you."

His praise is like a drug to me. Where there was once an itch from the abductor drugs, praise from Erasmus felt like scratching it finally. Perhaps he's right. I'm a perfect boy, a 'foolishly perfect, little submissive thing,' as he says. I'm so eager for more of those words coaxing me. I'm a hair away from kissing him and desperately wanting it. From never wanting anyone to touch me, to wanting to be consumed utterly by Erasmus, frightens yet astounds me all at once.

The kiss is a breath away.

And then the damn oven timer goes off.

I almost tell him to let the cookies burn, and that I'm burning inside for this kiss to happen. Fuck the cookies. I don't say it though. Against his better judgment, and mine, he goes to the oven to take out the dessert I no longer have an appetite for. The kiss has been lost in translation.

"I am glad I did not kill you." Eras grins as he opens the oven.

"But you did," I reply softly. "You killed my pain. The loneliness. You killed the Seven Wilbrate, and who I was before Erasmus Rasmussen came into my life." That man is long gone. Years of therapy couldn't help me. After these months with Erasmus, I am better than ever. I feel something I never have before... I feel deadly.

There is something he wants to say. He refrains from actually doing so. He can tell when there's a question on my mind, and I'm slowly understanding that skill. The vibe in the room shifts. It isn't anything tangible that changed but it's there. Then, a smile tugs the corners of his lips, and the mood in the room shifts once more. He's elated, and to be perfectly honest, so am I. I find myself internally asking 'What's next for us?' constantly. Erasmus once said to me he tasted a fire simmering in my blood. Well, It's about time to let it burn.

ERASMUS

52

As much as I hate leaving Seven's side, more work still needs to be done. He does not ask where I go or what I do. I am confident he has his suspicions, though I doubt he will ever get it correct. I have been swamped lately with my own personal agenda, which wraps itself around Seven. Everything I do is subject to my boy. This will be the most prominent, most important thing I have ever done.

The license plate number I procured many months ago on my adventure with Wisteria, led me to this building. I wonder why? It is not the right place. As I make my way through the hall, no portrait in any picture frame matches the profile I am looking for. Faces of this family line the walls. Not one of them is who I'm here for. This is not the home of the man who stole Seven Wilbrate all those years ago.

After another unsuccessful night, I emerge from the house. The street is dark. Cars and parts fill the front yard of this home, and from what my line of vision shows me, partially the back too. Whoever lives here is a mechanic, no doubt.

The sound of a door creaking open quickly pulls my attention away from the vehicles. The neighbor is outside, bringing his trash can to the street. It's a little late at night for that. Who knows this man's schedule? Perhaps he works strange hours. Or he can simply be nocturnal.

It's right then, when the man turns to go inside, I see his face in the street light's flickering glimmer. The image of a younger Seven Wilbrate being carried off by the abductor slams into me. That face, the one right in front of me, is the same apart from the aging process of humans. My heart flips and turns with excitement.

"There you fucking are," I whisper.

Funny how it works sometimes, isn't it? Sometimes you seem to be in the right place at the perfect time. As if, for once, the universe is on your side. Do I trust it? No. When the universe grants you a favor, it will come with a bill to collect soon enough.

When Wisteria and I traveled into the past, it was to acquire as much information as I could in a minimal amount of time. I memorized every line and feature of that man's face and license plate number, as he drove off with a younger version of my boy. After much research on my part, the license plate led me to this home I stand in the shadows of. Perhaps the process would've been faster if I asked for assistance. Lorcan is relatively fast when locating people. I wanted to do this part alone. This is personal.

The man went back inside and closed the door behind him, completely unaware of his fate being sealed. It dawned on me how he did it. No leads to him in case his tracks weren't covered precisely. Instead, everything could point to the neighbor. The tenant next door obviously works on cars. The abductor possibly borrowed one for his little adventure that day.

I would have been impressed at his efforts to cover his tracks, if only he chose someone else to torture in such a state. Sadly, he did choose Seven Wilbrate as his victim. Seven is mine, and what is mine shall be taken care of.

I'm starting with taking care of the man who caused him so much pain.

When I return home to scheme and plot more, the most awful sounding music is playing. Seven is singing loudly and belting out the lyrics as if from his heart, while Virenda sits on the floor and orchestrates the whole thing—something about a kiss. It is unstoppable and impossible and perpetual, or something like that.

It's adorable. At the same time, my eardrums are on the verge of bursting out of my head for relief.

"What is this racket?"

Immediately they both face me with ridiculous expressions lining their faces and, together in unison, exclaim, "It's Faith Hill!"

As if I'm supposed to know what the fuck that means. I stare at them with my ignorance while they both begin singing along again. It could be worse, I suppose. No sooner than I thought that, Seven dances, yes, dances over to me. Still singing, he circles me and purposely belts out loud enough to try to get under my skin with it. For kicks, I play along and pretend to be insanely annoyed by this. It ultimately makes him do it more, and trust me, I am more than fine with it. His company alone is what I seek. Let him believe he's bothering me. It might only push him to do it again, and again, and again.

"Awful boy," I say, and indeed the brat does as expected—he sings even louder.

"I am so excited you finally asked me for help!" Lorcan claps. He's a little too pleased that I need his assistance with the abductor, and after I barely even explain my plan to him he's already on board, grabbing his gloves.

"Don't make me regret asking, Lorcan."

He laughs and then asks, "How do you want to do this?"

We both stand on the sidewalk across the street from the abductor's house, contemplating the best way for us to tackle this scenario. I would have liked to lead Seven here and then kill the bastard, but the house still won't allow Seven to leave, so I will have to bring the abductor to Seven. It would be easy for me or Lorcan to kill him ourselves. I think it'll be more beneficial for Seven to do it. If he wants to.

"He has cameras all over." I point to the few of them I noticed when I came earlier. " We just need to knock him out. No killing. We save that part for Seven if he wants to do it."

"Do you think he will?" Lorcan asks.

"I'm not sure. We will let him decide the man's fate." The monster that lives within Seven wants to come out and play, I am sure of it. He just needs the nudge.

"You're faster than me," I say to Lorcan, which makes his chest puff up with conceit. "Could you get past the security cameras and shut them off?" If anyone can do it, it's him. He's been in much more difficult circumstances than this without alerting securities.

"Do you want to time me?" Lorcan smiles widely as he asks this. "My record right now is 2.3 seconds. If I can beat it, I get his left arm as a reward."

I huff out a "Nej."

"Fine, fine. I'll do it just for our little human."

He says it on purpose. There is no 'our' when it comes to Seven Wilbrate just 'mine'.

A simple blur in the air is the only indication Lorcan is on the prowl and no longer standing next to me. It isn't even two seconds before his head pops out the front door and he waves for me to come inside.

The inside of the house is dirty, dark and damp, exactly what you'd expect from a disgusting psychopath. The smell of mold permeating the living room is too much for me to breathe in. Lorcan nods to the hallway and I follow him to the only door that has light coming from underneath it. We stand before it, and Lorcan presses a finger to his lips, as if I would make a sound to alert the fool we are here. It is pointless though, Lorcan kicks the door in the very next second.

The man at the computer desk is almost the exact same as the man from the past. The only difference is additional lines on his face and a few gray hairs on his head. He jumps up and fumbles for his phone when Lorcan snatches him by his throat.

"Are you sure you want to wait to kill him, Erasmus? I could snap his pretty little neck and he would be done."

"Nej," I say, simply, and make my way over to them. The abductor is trying to thrash about, but Lorcan holds him firmly to the wall. I study the features on his face, then glance down at his hands. Those fingers were the ones that caused my boy so much pain. I'll have so much fun breaking off each one individually and forcing them down his throat.

"Take your time, Erasmus. I won't get tired." Lorcan smiles and the adbuctor's eyes widen at the sight of his fangs. Whimpers are softly coming from him, thanks to the force Lorcan has. He knows just where to hold so that not much noise can come out. He can still breathe. Barely.

"You might have thought you got away with it. All of those years ago, there was a boy you abducted from the college courtyard. You tortured him and then dumped his weary body on his family's door-step."

The abductor only makes a gurgling sound in response, and Lorcan loosens his grasp a tad bit, so that he can inhale a breath.

"The police couldn't find you. The FBI couldn't get anywhere. Thirteen years later, and you think you made a clean escape." I lean in so my face is inches from his. "I found you and you're going to pay for what you did to him."

Lorcan's manic laugh shrieks out loudly, and the abductor glances his way. "I think when we truly get started, you'll wish you were dead."

LORCAN

53

al popping up at my doorstep was only partially a shock. After all, we never truly leave each other on bad terms. Sure, we have our differences. That never stops him from returning to my home. This time he says it's to warn me of danger. I don't entirely believe that to be true. I'll play along with it and see.

"Well, Wisteria said she can swing by Friday to take a look at your watch," I say.

There's the watch matter too. How convenient it broke right before he got to my home. The watch is his way to travel the world at any time, whether it be past or future. As far as I know, he's been the owner of it for many years. Centuries, at the very least.

"Crash on your couch?" Callinicus asks, and I am utterly taken aback by the absurdity of this question.

"On the co…" I start, exasperated. "With all these rooms I have free? Nonsense, Cal, you'll take a room. Second or third floor?" It was already known I will not take no for an answer.

"I couldn't possibly impose." He says it with the most charming, sickly sweet smile.

"Hush. You're a guest in this house," I reply. "And while here, you'll be treated as such. Come. I'll show you to your room."

If one had told me my future here, I would have positively laughed in their face. I have indeed learned through the years, monsters need to look out for one another… including myself.

"Pick the one furthest from Erasmus and Seven," Audelia says tartly as she walks by. "Oh my gods, do they go at it all hours of the night."

Cal laughs. He doesn't quite understand what she means, I'm sure. "Any room is fine."

"Lorcan, he's never going to get any sleep. Put him on the third floor," she orders. "It might be far away enough that he'll manage!"

"Yes," I say softly. "Those two have been going at it these days." None of us here are safe from the noise as we can hear the faintest pin drop across the house. Cal's senses aren't heightened like the majority of us here. Still, I doubt he'll be safe from the commotion the other two seem to create in the middle of the night.

"It's cute and all," Audelia says, "but some of us need sleep. Maybe I'll spend a few nights at Cato's."

My brows pop up knowingly. "As if you'd get any sleep there…"

She flicks my shoulder playfully as she walks by, leaving me to bring Cal to a guest room. "Come." I wave at him to follow, and he obliges.

We pass my room and I take notice of him glancing towards it. I can bet his mind is filled with memories of the past times we both entered there together. I push those thoughts out of my mind quickly.

"Here we are," I say, opening the door, and I let Cal go in first.

He glances around slowly before turning in my direction. "Thank you," he replies.

"My pleasure, old friend."

The corners of his lips turn up, softening the edges of his face. It is as though he's about to say something, when the sound of Seven's voice comes thundering in.

"You can't expect me to believe that!" Seven yells. Erasmus returns fire in Danish, probably on purpose just to make Seven even more annoyed, and it does. They're both hollering at one another for heaven knows what this time.

Cal's brows raise at me. "I assumed you meant noises of pleasure…"

I smile in return. "Trust me, it is indeed a pleasure to them." They seem to love arguing. Although I pick the room furthest from Seven and Eras, the noise is still loud enough to make it up here, including with Virenda's music and Audelia banging on her door to lower it.

"Well, I'll let you try to get some rest," I say to Cal. "Freshen up in the bath if you need."

Closing the door behind me, I mutter about getting us all noise-canceling headphones. An even better idea is procuring Seven and Erasmus a small house in the back yard so they can bicker all day and night as they wish to.

As I move to descend the stairs, the house itself does something it hasn't done in a while; the house constricts. Though physically, they do not move, the walls feel like they tighten around me. A warning. I steal a glance back to Cal's room. All is well. The house, however, does not agree with him staying here. Just as I sensed his arrival was peculiar, the house indeed senses it too.

SEVEN

54

Lately, my life has been an adventure of the grandest. The people I have surrounding me have all made it possible. Going from a below average human being to a relatively moderate immortal is astounding. Assuming this was the highlight of my life, and there will be no other excitement, is fine with me. Erasmus is not fine with it.

"I have a surprise for you," Erasmus says. He's just returned from outside and smells of soft florals and lush green grass. I miss going outside.

"Is it a dog? It's a dog, isn't it?" I playfully mentioned the other day we should have one for all of us in the house. I had a dog as a child. It ran away or was stolen, and we never picked another after.

Erasmus' answer is a smile. I have a slight feeling it isn't a dog. I won't let the thought go, simply because he has yet to deny me anything.

"Come with me," he says.

Closing my current read, I get up and go along with him. It isn't easy to focus on the floor beneath me when Erasmus is so close. My gaze flickers over to him, and results in me tripping over my feet a time or two. It pulls in a laugh and a 'foolish boy' from Erasmus. I almost wonder if he's convinced the house to let me out but we just head to the basement.

"If you have a dog in a cage in this basement, I'm going to bite your damn ear off, Erasmus."

Erasmus turns the doorknob, opening the door quickly, and we descend the steps in darkness. I've been down here a few times, and the lack of light always makes me nervous. The light switch is at the bottom of the stairs, for whatever reason. Claustrophobia would set in if we didn't emerge as quickly as we did to the large open basement. I stand in the middle of the dark room, waiting for the light to come on, and partially panic. He might keep me in the dark, but he doesn't. The fluorescents light up the room from one end to the other.

It all happens too quickly. Behind Erasmus is a man I do not recognize but Instinct tells me exactly who it is.

"Erasmus, wh—"

I never finish the question. The man who destroyed my life has just hit Erasmus with a lamp. In horror, I watch Eras drop to the floor.

Not dead, I remind myself, Erasmus can't die. He still does not move. This brings on an even larger fear. Frozen on the spot, I can not fully process what happened because I do not understand it all. Why is the abductor in the basement? I flee from the scene as fast as my legs can carry me up the stairs, screaming the whole time in case Lorcan or one of the others can hear me. This room is soundproof and thanks to my shitty ass luck, the door is fucking locked.

Immediately, I'm choking for air, breathing oxygen around a sob. Why did Erasmus bring him here? Why here? Has Erasmus betrayed me? Is he working with this psychopathic lunatic? There is no way. Absolutely not. Both my heart and brain say no. This is something else. Right?

Taking my distraction as a win, the abductor races up the stairs at me. With every ounce of strength my body holds, I fight him and the revulsion of his touch. His hands are at my throat, and immediately my body recoils. Those hands stained me so thoroughly in the past, the ones I thought were just a mere memory, are here in reality once more—a literal, living nightmare.

Heaving up everything I ate, and then some, does nothing to waver him whatsoever. Covered in my vomit, he still fights around it. Grabbing at his shirt and clawing at his skin, we tussle against one another for what feels like an eternity. This could've gone much easier if I just used my brain instead of focusing on the panic. I'm on overload. Even immortality has not honed in on my panic and the ability to think under pressure. I must be more machine than man at times, short-circuiting and spazzing with an overbearing panic attack. My system is shutting down, slowly fading into a faint.

And I'm at this man's mercy for the second time in my life.

When I finally come to, I want nothing more than to die. How could this happen again? Why the fuck did Erasmus bring him here? My brain doesn't give me a chance to recover before it begins bombarding me with questions. Only one of my wrists is bound to the wall. This time, it isn't a simple rope holding me there. He used a metal shackle to ensure I won't get out. Probably one Lorcan has for torturing people too. Speaking of Lorcan, he has to come down here at some point, right? Where the hell is he? I can't help thinking he has betrayed me too. Is this all some elaborate plan to torture me for the rest of my immortal life?

I was doing *so* well, making so much progress with myself. With one moment in time, I'm jerked back to the small, insignificant man I was before. Nothing makes sense.

Across from me is another prisoner. The way my heart muscles contract, one would have thought I'm about to go into cardiac arrest. It sure fucking feels like it. The abductor has Erasmus bound the same way I was all those years ago. Both wrists are secured by rope. Is it the same rope? Did the abductor keep it as a fucking souvenir and brought it with him tonight? Eras' ankles are restricted too. A blindfold is covering his eyes. His body is limp against the restraints, he's still knocked out.

"I don't know how you found me." The voice I was never granted permission to hear before makes my stomach convulse, just knowing it comes from him. "I left no trace of me on you."

This time he wore no mask. Allowing me to see him is supposed to be a gift, I assume, since he thinks to kill me this time. Trust me. I wish I didn't take the potion so that he *could* kill me. He's going to have a fucking field day torturing me over and over again, because I can not fucking die. Immortality has its perks. This is not one.

"Now you're awake, let's have some fun." He taps Erasmus' cheek. He doesn't move. Did he drug him? Wouldn't he heal over the drug, or is this some chemical not even immortality can fight?

My whole body stiffens as the man carries a large rod toward Erasmus. Is he going to do to Erasmus what he did to me all those years ago, and make sure I witness all of it?

"No," I say through gritting teeth. Then I shout much louder, "*No!*"

Tugging at the shackle, tears began to glitter in my eyes. Erasmus won't die. He's still going to feel it. He'll have to live with himself like I had to all these years.

Save him. Save him. Save him. It's all I keep repeating internally. I can not allow this shit to happen, *not* to Erasmus. I *will not* let this happen. *I can't die,* I remind myself. It's the only thought apart from Erasmus resonating in my mind. *Use what you know, Seven. Don't panic. Stay alert.*

I scream then, so loud I'm sure the walls will come crashing down on us from the force of it. My throat is raw with this intense need to vocalize every emotion I have shoved inside of me from all those years ago. I tug and pull so hard at the shackle on my wrist, it starts to cut into my flesh. It tears through my veins, and with one desperate tug, it slices partly through to the bone. The pain is beyond imaginable. It isn't enough to free myself just yet. I have to do it again, this time hard enough to break through it. Fresh blood is pouring from the wound. I won't stop. I can't stop. I use the shackle to tear the rest of my hand completely off.

The whole time I'm mutilating myself, he's watching me. At the moment, the fear I witness in the abductor's eyes is powerful. He's afraid of me. There is no time to savor this. I lunge myself at him. This time the feeling of him does not make me recoil, instead, I yearn for it. I want him to feel me and how deadly I am becoming.

My fist, the one I still have at the moment, connects over and over with his face. Blood coats my hand and splashes up at me. His nose is done, for sure. His cheek is sunken in but I can't stop. Not until a hand is on my shoulder.

Wide-eyed, I gasp and immediately thrash out at it, unsure of who it could be. Erasmus stands next to me, smiling. "We want him alive, Seven. We are far from done with him."

Out of breath, shaking, and riding this adrenaline rush, I blink at him, unable to truly understand. Since my escape, my hand has grown back in place perfectly as if it was never gone. Breathing is still difficult, but I somehow manage through it. This whole thing is like a dream, mixing with a nightmare at the same time.

"Stay with me." Erasmus cups my face in his hands. Just like he's whispering an incantation, I'm under a spell only he can conjure for me. Resolve and comfort washes over me like rain. The calming sensation Eras' voice gives to me does not diminish this fire bursting into flames inside of me. It simply contains it for the moment. This is what Erasmus meant. This is what he's been aiming for.

The monster living inside this skin of mine has come to life today. I see it reflecting in Erasmus' eyes, looking back at me. His monster and my monster are the same. We are the same. And while millions of people harbor their own monsters, mine is connected with his in a way it can never connect with anyone else. There's something in his soul and mine links us. I can't explain it, but it's there.

"I told you. You would never let it happen again." Eras' voice cut through the silence. "My knight in shining armor. Slaying all of the dragons."

Erasmus lifts my blood soaked hand; the abductor's blood. Erasmus inspects it. I'm still in complete and utter shock.

"May I?" he whispers.

Despite knowing exactly what he means to do, I nod my approval. I trust him to do whatever he wants. He pulls my hand to his lips. His tongue peeks out between red lips and licks up the palm of my hand.

The monster inside me stretches to fill each gap and fiber of my body. Something awakens inside me, and it's hungry for blood. For vengeance. And for Erasmus.

ERASMUS

55

I t was probably wrong of me to play the damsel in distress part. It was indeed required. Seven would've undoubtedly saved himself from the abductor. He just needed a little more push to do it. By pretending to be unconscious, I waited to see how he would react when I knew the abductor would try to attack me.

Perhaps manipulating him with the whole scenario is wrong. My moral compass has never truly cooperated. Had it tried to point me in another direction, I would have broken it anyway.

Seven did much more than I expected him to. When he ripped his hand off, I reveled, and pride flooded through me. Not only would I do anything to keep him safe, he would do the same for me. That wasn't why I did this, though. I wanted Seven to realize he could save himself *and* me if anything came down to it. He needed to see

THE HOUSE OF DEATH – ERASMUS

himself in a way that would forever boost his confidence. No longer would he second-guess himself. Tonight will always resonate in his mind as one of the greatest accomplishments of his life.

I tell him how Lorcan and I kidnapped the man. I leave out the part of how I found him in the first place. Today is not the day to explain about the witch bringing me to the past. I explain how we carried the abductor home. It probably looked like we were bringing a drunken comrade home in New Orleans. Being splattered in blood would not even be questioned. Stranger and far worse things have been witnessed on these streets. Lorcan busted the abductor's chin even after I told him we needed the man in one perfect piece. He couldn't help himself.

Alarms of fire trucks blared loudly a few streets away while we walked. Before Lorcan and I left, we set the house on fire, just in case we left any DNA on accident. Not that we couldn't take on the humans, we did not need them on our tracks creating extra drama.

The air is smothered with Seven's emotions, filling it with adrenaline, happiness, and power. Covered in blood, he smiles at me. It is the purest and simplest thing I have ever seen.

When we secure the man in a cage, ensuring he will not escape, Seven reaches for my hand. "Thank you."

"Anything for you, my perfect boy."

"No, Erasmus, I mean it. Thank you. I— I can't explain all of what I'm feeling. It's like… like something inside of me— It's—

"Awakened?"

"Yes." Seven nods quickly. "Yes, exactly."

I can not stop the smile forming on my lips.

Seven has something inside of him desiring to escape. The moment he stormed into the house, I sensed it. It's easier to call it a monster when I cannot pinpoint exactly what it is. Perhaps there is no mortal name for it at all... yet.

"I'll be right here to help you."

"It's so strange. When I ripped my hand off to get out of those shackles, I felt so connected to you. Like... I felt so possessive of you. I do not want anyone else to touch you in any way." Seven laughs softly, but he's struck with sternness.

Seven's brows fused in thought once more. He feels the connection we've shared previously. I knew he would. He can't reach it just yet.

"I just..." he says. The abductor in the cage groans in pain softly. Seven is so far in thought, I don't think he hears. "I just..." His head shakes a bit. "I have to be with you."

One day I am going to fill him in on our past. The ones before this life we are currently sharing. "My foolish boy. You are with me. And you always will be."

The blue of Seven's eyes darkens. There's a thousand unspoken words in them, a depth of feelings he can't express yet. I can smell the arousal rolling off of him, amongst other emotions I have learned to decipher. When you're locked in a tomb with nothing to do, you learn to make the most of it. I won't act on these emotions tonight. This night has been a win in so many ways for us. I want to savor them all perfectly.

"You did this all for me," he says, as he finally glances back at the man in the cage. "At first I thought you brought him here to torture me for the rest of eternity. I regret thinking about it but it did cross my mind, just so you know." Seven's face is flushed and full of shame. "Trust is so difficult in times of adversity. I should've known he was here against his will, when he knocked you out."

"To be honest, I was never knocked out," I admit. Seven glares at me then his face softens. "You needed this," I say. "You need to overcome your past. I thought the best way to do so was to bring him to you, and let you finish him off, your way."

"What if I hadn't wanted to, Erasmus? What if it would've only traumatized me more?"

I shake my head. "Nej. I see it in you. You want him to hurt, just like you did." Again, shame takes over my boy's face. I lift his chin to look at me. "Do you regret this?"

"No," he says. "That's partially why I feel guilty. I don't regret wanting to hurt him." Seven's eyes deepen again, then he smiles at me, and the monster inside of him smiles at me too.

"Now." I take Seven's face and glance at the cage the man was locked in. "Shall we have a little fun?"

After we departed from the basement, I left Seven upstairs in the common area to relax. Nestled in a large chair with a blanket, a book in his hand, and a hot cup of tea is on the table next to him. I doubt he's actually reading. He's been staring at the same page for a while now. I leave him to it and disappear to my room. I'm gone only a few minutes when I hear an unfamiliar deep voice out there with him.

"Reading something good?"

Curiously, I peek through the crack at my door. Callinicus. The man Lorcan invited to stay with us is hovering over my boy. Seven appears nervous looking up at him and fumbles for a reply.

"Oh. I-I don't really... I just started it.."

Callinicus exhales a laugh through his nose and I want nothing more than to break it off. He reaches for the book and closes it briefly to see the cover. Seven moves his hand out of the way so he doesn't touch it.

"Ah, a classic. You'll enjoy it."

I'm gripping the doorframe so hard I wouldn't be surprised if I find splinters in my skin.

"I think... I just lost my place," Seven says. He flips the book open again and frantically starts turning pages.

"That's my fault. I'm so sorry."

"No, no it's okay." Still turning pages, Seven doesn't look up at the man. "I'll figure it out."

"When you're done, you should tell me your thoughts. I am curious to know what others think of the story."

Seven's heartbeat is kicked into frantic mode. Sweat beads form above his brow. "Oh, I, um... I don't know."

"Are you well?" Callinicus asks, and moves closer to Seven's chair. "You look terribly flush all of the sudden." His hand raises in the direction of Seven's arm. My boy is looking from side to side, shaking his head, and breathing heavier. I was going to let him do this on his own, but I can't allow him to panic like this without intervening.

"Do not fucking touch him." It takes every ounce of restraint I have to keep from tossing Callinicus over the balcony. "You're alright?" I ask Seven.

"I didn't mean to offend you," Callinicus insists as he glances my way.

"It is not a matter of offending *me*," I say. "In case you haven't noticed he was trying to relax before your intrusion." I might be a tad over doing it. I can't help how possessive I am of Seven. Maybe it's jealousy pushing me to keep this new man away from my boy. "May I?" I ask the question to Seven and he nods. The palm of my hand cups his chin, ushering him to look up at me. When he does I can hear his breathing begin to normalize once more.

"I'm fine," he says. "Thank you."

"Anything for you, my perfect boy."

Brows raised, Callinicus takes a few steps back. He's mumbling something about the strange folk who reside in this house. Good. Let him believe we are odd. Maybe he will keep away from what's mine. I might be wrong to want to keep Seven all to myself. I don't care. If he only needs me, then he won't ever leave.

LORCAN

56

The news blares on the television in the kitchen. The pot on the stove is almost bubbling over thanks to being distracted by the reporter talking. First they shared the weather, next about the local school raising money to pay off children's lunch debts. Why this country feels the need to make children pay for their food is beyond me. I make a mental note to remind myself to send in an anonymous donation to cover the cost. Then I wait, a little too giddily, to see if the abductor's house will appear on the screen.

After almost all of the other reports, it finally airs the one I'm waiting on. The house is in flames on the video sent in by neighbors, while the reporter's blame it on faulty electrical wiring. No one was home at the time of the fire they say, thankfully. No, no, the owner is alive... for now. The neighbors appear for an interview and answer a few questions. They say they don't know him very well. He's always gone and probably left a cigarette burning or something. They don't seem sad that his home has gone to ashes. One patron says he's glad the house is gone. It was nothing more than an eye sore.

I throw my hands up and laugh. "See, I did them all a favor!"

Quickly the scene changes to a new breaking news report about a man who was accused of trafficking local women has disappeared. They give a brief detail about him and show a picture in hopes that if any citizen of this city knows his whereabouts, they should call in immediately.

I could call in and give them a tip that he's about to be dead. It probably wouldn't be wise of me. Instead we're having him for dinner tonight. The large industrial sized crawfish pot out on the back patio will boil him alive. There won't be anything left, either, not with the appetite I have worked up today. The pot on the stove is just a little side dish we will enjoy later. I turn off to let it simmer.

Our dinner has to soak in the boiling water to absorb the many seasonings I added in, and my mouth is watering just thinking about it. This is a different approach tonight since I didn't skin or debone anything. He was paralyzed after I toyed with the spinal cord, and contorted to fit in the pot before filling it up with water almost to the brim. He can breathe thanks to the makeshift snorkel attached to his mouth. After tasting the water I add a bit more seasoning, then I turn on the propane and wait for the water to heat up, in which he will feel every degree of the temperature rise. He makes some noise, a little scream here and a wailing there. It is, as always, music to my ears. Once he begins boiling, all sounds from him cease.

"According to this recipe I found, it says to boil the crawfish for 2-3 minutes, however, this isn't crawfish…" I stand there by the pot with my hands on my hips. "Best let it go for five."

SEVEN

57

When you think of a torture chamber, I am almost positive a dark, dreary room comes to mind. Perhaps it is so humid the ugly brick walls are dripping with a feverish sweat, leaving a slick sheen of conspicuous moisture everywhere. Maybe you see old, rustic tools coated with dried secretions, hanging from sharp hooks.

This basement cellar isn't as one would have expected it to be at all. The smell of bleach and chemicals invades your unsuspecting nostrils. Flip the switch, and a bright, fluorescent light is born to flood the room. It has a contradiction of cleanliness to what your thoughts perceive this kind of place to have. Everything is pristine down to the marble floor.

A large, stainless steel table is the throne at the center of the room.

With the press of a button, a whirring sound opens a cage to lower long chains of hooks holding up a body by the mere skin of its back.

On those hooks is Mister Abduction. I should have his name by now. I don't. I wanted to know his name for a long time. I've realized I don't need it. Hanging over the table, Mister Abduction can make no sound. His lips are carefully sewn together for the time being. Oh, they won't stay closed for long. I want to hear his words, his pleading. I used to want to hear the 'why,' but I'm not intrigued by it anymore. It was fun for him to have me against my will. The consequence of that fun is about to begin.

Eyes wide, he is suspended from the hooks, unable to move an inch. Just like I wasn't able to move when he bound me. On my back, I slip onto the table to lie directly under him. His eyes are searching, curious as to what I have planned. Nothing major for this moment. I just want him to see me. I want him to see what I've become.

I lay there for a long time. I'm looking up at him, the way he used to just stare at me in his dark room. I was never blessed with seeing his face before this. The difference here is I want to see him.

With the knife in hand, I poke his belly with the tip, just enough to make him inhale sharply. A few drops of blood drizzle down onto my shirt. There is an undeniable urge to feel it on me. One button at a time, I open the front of my shirt, baring my chest for the blood to commence. When it doesn't, I raise the tip of the knife to poke him again. It goes a little deeper this time, and his body jerks at the invasion.

As the tiny droplets of his blood bounce onto my skin, my nostrils flare with a sharp annoyance. It isn't enough. A few more holes will do the trick, and soon my chest is covered with more dots of his life source.

Erasmus is soon at my side, surveying the mess.

"May I?" he asks. Unlike Mister Abduction, Eras never touches me without asking.

Of course I give him the okay, though I genuinely do not know what I am agreeing to. At this moment, I feel too much like a god to care. His finger swipes across my chest and then he pulls into his mouth. He's already had his first taste of him when the man's broken nose bled on my hand.

"I like his flavor," Eras says, and anger bubbles inside of me. He's supposed to only like my blood. That's irrational, of course. You can have multiple favorite dishes.

"Better than mine?" I ask. Eras fights back a grin. He doesn't answer me. I knew the answer before the question was birthed.

He slips the whole palm of his hand across my chest. He holds his thumb to my mouth. I wait so long to move the blood drips from his finger and onto my lips. I lick them slowly. He's right. The flavor is unimaginable. Grabbing his wrist as my head lifts from the table, I meet the palm of his hand and slowly swipe my tongue across it. There's something more than the blood I taste, though, and it does not take long to understand it. It's so delectable because underneath the layer of blood it's flavored with the sheen of Erasmus' flesh.

My lips stay apart, and some force of nature leaves them precisely as is, like I forgot how to close my mouth. Erasmus is between my legs, pushing my naked thighs apart.

Where did my clothes go? Where did his clothes go? Why did I even care?

"May I?" he asks again, and with my mouth still open, like a panting dog eager for a treat, I nod.

I do not recoil from the pain. Instead, I eagerly invite it. Unlike when the abductor forced things inside me, the stinging, burning sensation only lasts a moment.

Blood is everywhere between Eras and me as a steady stream pours from Mister Abductor's body from above. Erasmus used it as a lubricant. I should be appalled by this. I am instead quite the opposite and aroused even more.

Arousal. Such a foreign concept to me for so long. It's been over a decade since I imagined myself in a physical predicament with another. Yet here I am.

Eras' fingers dig feverishly into my outer thighs, and his thrusts quicken. "Come with me," he says as he always has to me. This time in a very different sense. The tone of his voice is much more demanding, much more rugged than it typically is. The look in his eyes is always full of passion, and tonight it's bubbling over. It's as if he controls where my gaze is trying to go. I can't look away. I want to see what my abductor thinks, but I can't look away from Erasmus.

"Come with me," he says again, this time urgently. My whole body tenses as if he has complete power over it. He does, though. He truly does.

We probably sound like a stampede of bodies crashing into one another. And we are. We are more than us. Soon, we're both soaked between layers of blood, sweat, and my release. When my head falls back to the table, I'm breathing so heavily that my chest twitches and stutters. I might never breathe normally again.

Only now do I look back on Mister Abductor, who dazedly looks down at me in return. I'm half smiling.

"See?" I say in a harsh, crackling voice and laugh. "You didn't destroy me." My mouth opens to catch another drop of his blood on my tongue as it falls from his chest. "You created me. You created this."

Just then, my eyes open at the sound of the door creaking open. Dazed, I look around the room, confused at what has happened. Erasmus is walking in. Though the shirt is unbuttoned, my clothes are on as I lay under Mister Abductor's steadily bleeding body. Apart from poking at him a few times with the knife, I dreamt the whole scene up. Erasmus is looking at me as if he and I just shared the fantasy in my mind. Glancing at my blood covered chest, he asks, "May I?"

This time his question is not in a dream. Through parting, panting lips, I nod to grant him permission. He glides his fingers across my chest, pooling blood at the tips, and brings them to his lips for another taste.

ERASMUS

58

It has been a wonderful evening slipping easily into a wonderful night. Seven and I prepared dinner while the rest of the house lazed about enjoying their leisure time. Now that everything is in order, we stay at the table. Since arriving here, we have rearranged the seating chart. Each chair is adorned with gold plates drilled into them, and carved into the gold is each of our names etched in perfect cursive handwriting belonging to Lorcan. Where Seven used to sit across from me, I happily moved my chair to be next to him.

"Will you all join us?" I ask the rest of the household.

With the abductor lying flat on the table, Lorcan takes his seat at the head of the table. We have the abductor hooked up to an IV and oxygen to keep him alive. He's paralyzed at the same time, so he can't entirely move. Lorcan can not contain his glee.

"Are we having sushi?" he asks.

Seven tries not to smile at Lorcan's comment, but it's inevitable. All evening a seriousness has overtaken my boy, and understandable so.

"Well then," Lorcan sneers. "Let's all enjoy this meal Erasmus and Seven have graciously prepared for us."

There is silence amongst us momentarily.

"Seven?" Still standing as he spoke, a knife is held out in Lorcan's hand for Seven to take. "Would you do the honors?"

Seven has not looked away once from the abductor, until Lorcan flips the blade around so the handle is outstretched to him. Slowly, Seven's fingers curl around the base of the knife. If there was a way to open Seven's mind and feel the thoughts running through it, I would do it. I will force him to tell me later what he's thinking, though. Not uttering a single word, Seven brings the blade to the abductor's mouth and he cuts free the thread that bound the man's lips together.

"I want to hear you scream." The chill creeping through my body at hearing this tone come out of Seven's mouth explodes at the base of my spine.

Everyone else at the table listens and observes. They're well aware tonight is more than just having dinner; it is a liberation. We wait patiently for the next installment.

As Lorcan sits, the feast begins. I watch my boy looking at his utensils, carefully choosing the one to use first. None of us will make a move until Seven does so first. This is his night, after all. He decides on the spoon. A breath passes and his arm lifts to move so quickly I almost miss it. The scream retching its way out of the abductor's lungs gives us all the signal that he has been impaled. The blunt tip of the spoon broke through the tender flesh of the man's thigh, the spoon rigid until Seven yanks down, spreading the wound to open it even more.

And cue the begging and the pleading.

"Already?" I say. "One small scoop, and you're asking for us to end you. I don't think you granted my boy any kind of reprieve when the tables were turned, did you?"

He isn't looking at me, though. The abductor's gaze is tearful as he prays to the ceiling. "Is there even a god up there?" He has the nerve to ask such.

"If there is," I say. "I doubt he would come to your aid. We might eat him too if he tried."

"Dig in." While he scoops the flesh out of the wound he made, Seven says this, and I can not stop the chuckle erupting from my chest at his little pun.

"Foolish boy," I say, and he smiles even more, though I can see the unease behind his eyes. The unease is not for what we are doing, it is for something else entirely.

As Lorcan begins slicing and peeling off the skin of the man's leg, the abductor sings a beautiful song of his pain, making Lorcan dance in his seat.

"Hmm," I say to Seven as I lean closer. "Electric knife on each of his fingers? Surely his cock. Might shove it down his throat if I tire of his screams."

Lorcan takes slices of flesh and sets them on Virenda and Audelia's plates. They honestly do not look excited by this. It's the understanding that this is a family event. Everyone will eat what is served for Seven's sake. Audelia takes the abductor's hand before chomping down on a finger—the sound of broken bones and tearing ligaments fills our ears just as much as his wailing did.

Clouden is next. He swipes a knife blade across the abductor's stomach. Blood oozes quickly to the surface and spills from the fresh wound. Clouden's nostrils flare as his glass presses to the man's stomach, so the blood slides messily into the glass while coating his hand and everything else it touches.

The more we carve from him, the more we devour, and the more the abductor's sobs season his flesh with salty tears. With forks clinking on the plates and gulps taken from glasses, we all knew not a piece of this meal will be taken for granted.

Halfway through dinner, the abductor stops making any noise. His chest is not rising and falling. The look in his eyes is distant.

"*No*." Seven demands.

Even though we induced his life with medications, the abductor is still dying. The table shakes with the added force of Seven clambering on top of it. Glasses are knocked over, and plates are broken under his weight. Seven doesn't care about the mess. Nor do any of us, for that matter.

"No. No. No! I'm not done with you yet! Fucking *live*. You asshole, I said fucking live!" Losing all restraint, Seven shakes the man by what is left of his arms—lumps of battered flesh.

This is not something we can control. Seven knew when we set the abductor on the table this would be the man's end, and out of all of the choices, Seven chose for him to go out this way. I wondered if he would make it all night. Seven hoped he would. Now my boy is in a fit of rage and despair. It hasn't been a long enough pain to compete with the months he endured at this man's hand.

"Seven," Lorcan says softly. "We will carve the rest later. Erasmus, take him to go wash up, dear."

Seven isn't moving. His head presses to the remains of the man who had abused him. He's sobbing so loudly and it breaks my heart to hear. I slip my arms around him, slide him off the table, and into my arms to carry my boy up the stairs to our room, leaving Lorcan and the others to clean up the mess. No one complains about this chore, because tonight the cleaning is anything but a job. It is a renewal.

His body is limp with each step up the stairs, almost dead weight in my arms. "Stay with me, Seven."

Through a sob, he whimpers and buries his face into the crook of my shoulder. It is half of a victory today. The abductor is dead. The other half is a defeat. The abductor is *dead*.

LORCAN

59

I feel terribly bad for Seven. It would seem this dinner did not go according to his plan, at all. We did all we could under the circumstances. However, it is a dinner I will remember for many years to come. What a clever boy. I didn't think about having them alive *while* I ate them. Surely the man could've lived a lot longer. Next time we'll figure out how to make it happen. I am quite positive there will be a next time, seeing how absolutely creative this was. Since Seven picked out everything, the plates did not match the mood. I would've opted for the gold, but it's neither here nor there. It was perfect no matter what.

While Erasmus carries Seven away the rest of us begin to clean up the mess. Audelia and Virenda are once again still partially on the outs with one another. Tonight, they don't bicker. Even Clouden is silent. As he reaches for the knife that's in the abductor's kneecap I stop him.

"One moment there, Cloud." With my phone in hand I snap a photo to save for Seven to commemorate later. "Let's make this a little cheerful for Seven. Everyone in the photo."

Audelia quickly runs her fingers through her hair and Virenda is already standing behind the corpse. She lifts one side, and Clouden holds the other, so the dead man is propped up. Audelia pops up behind him, smiling brightly.

"On three, everyone say 'Murder'!" I hold up the phone to video and grab a photo as they all play along counting down to yell it out. Of course, I have to shoot one with myself as a selfie while they remain in the background.

After this, the mood changes. Virenda turns on her magic tunes while we pick up the broken glass and dishes. Clouden and I carry the corpse to the basement where I leave him on one of the large stainless steel tables, until Seven gives word on what to do next. I will not take any of this into my hands without consulting him first.

There is a soft knock at the front door. I answer, knowing already who is on the other side. Callinicus smiles back as Virenda dances by behind me to her music, along with Audelia and Clouden who waltz terribly to the tune.

"Am I interrupting?" Cal asks.

"No, just finishing dinner. Are you ready or would you like to come in?"

Cal peeks behind me to the other three, who swiftly change from waltzing to doing one of the most obnoxious dances—The Macarena. I roll my eyes and internally pray that he is indeed ready for our night out.

"I think we should leave them to it. I have no desire to have a dance party."

I pretend to pout. "Well, aren't you just the party pooper tonight!"

He holds his arm out, and I nudge it with my elbow. It is a lovely gesture on his part. I do not wish to be public with anyone in such a manner. Holding his hand or even his arm would give him the notion I am looking for something more. I'm not and won't ever be willing to do that again, with anyone. As per his request, we're going out for a night on the town since he's here in the city, until his time device is fixed anyway. He might as well enjoy it.

Unfortunately, I probably won't. Callinicus is partially a fan of my work, but he doesn't entirely like the process of it. He and I met many years ago when I was still a fairly newborn vampire. My bloodlust was under control. My temper still was not. He was in an argument with another man in a tavern, and seeing as the other gentleman had a gang of followers to interfere, I figured at least adding myself to the sequence Cal would have a chance. Of course he did, I slaughtered them all, including the barmaid and other patrons who got in the way. He was thankful I saved him, but when I dragged each body to the basement of my home, he worried he would end up there too. Wisteria believes Cal is only my friend because he is too afraid of me to be my enemy. I think she's wrong. Who wouldn't *want* to be my friend?

The streets are bustling with patrons tonight. Most of them are not so well behaved. It's to be expected in New Orleans. People come here to escape and live the legends of the city. We take a streetcar. I have no choice but to be mashed in between Callinicus and an unfortunately scented male, who needs more than deodorant to mask his horrendous odor. This damn city is always filled to the brim with people, though it does make it easier for me to blend in, or try to at least.

Cal didn't tell me where he was taking me tonight, and I have my suspicions just from the route we've been on. It's confirmed when we stop in front of the Saenger Theatre.

"A broadway? Darling you shouldn't have." Oh, I'm glad he did. It's been ages since I've been to a play of any sort. The last one I attended tainted my taste for it. I guess I'll give it another go. Cal holds the door open and I slip inside into the cool air of the building.

"It's a good thing I'm dressed for this," I say to Cal, as he appears beside me.

He laughs. "You're always dressed for this."

This is true. I do love my suits. Ralph Lauren makes a pretty penny off of me multiple times a year when I have them shipped in. So, to say I'm always ready for something extravagant is an understatement.

To make the night even better, the seats are wonderful. Grand suites right in front. The crowd around me disappears as the lights dim. Even Cal is gone. It's just me and the orchestra. Figuratively of course. There's no better way to witness theater than to immerse yourself completely in the play.

When it's over we file out of the building with everyone else. Instead of waiting for the taxi, we go on foot.

"That was marvelous, Cal! Thank you for such a treat."

"It was, indeed." He smiles in return, however, it does not reach his eyes as it used to.

Since he arrived back on my doorstep, the air between us has changed drastically. I can't say if it is his travels that make him appear weary perhaps. It's different this time..

As we round a corner to take a side street, I backtrack a few paces to where a homeless man sits with a sign representing his bad luck. I pull out a wad of cash and drop it in his cup before returning to Cal. Continuing our walk, I hear the distinct sound of laughter along with bellows of delight as the homeless man counts his earnings from me.

"You know he's probably just going to go buy alcohol with it, right?" Cal asks.

I shrug. "It's his choice what to do with it. If it makes him happy, then so be it. He won't be hurting anyone, only himself." Seeing as he doesn't have a car to drink and drive he'll just match the rest of this drunken city.

Cal shakes his head. "They won't learn if you constantly give them handouts."

His comment makes me cease walking. "Is that what you genuinely think?" I study him for a moment before moving again. "I think he doesn't *have* to learn anything, if he doesn't want to. It's not my business, Callinicus." Something is indeed off with this conversation between us. He's never had an issue with this sort of thing before. "What has made you change so drastically over these last fifty years?"

He doesn't answer right away. "At least I did change." As we walk on I ponder what he meant by this.

"Come now." I smile wide. "Say what you mean."

We come to a stop in front of the house. With his hands in his pockets, he stares at me for a moment, carefully picking the next words he will speak.

"I mean playing 'Robin Hood'. All of this." His hand waves at the house before going on. "When will you get tired of killing these people, Lorcan? You know some of them don't deserve it."

As soon as he says it, I can tell he wants nothing more than to take it back.

The smile that seemingly forever stains my face falters, just for a second. "We're all still playing at something, aren't we, Callinicus? What is life if not a game, hm? The rich and powerful are in control of everything. They can easily help the ones who need it. Most refuse. Too full of greed. If they can be selfish..." I lean in to make my words drive into him. "Then why can't I?"

When he doesn't reply, I stand upright again. "As for when I'll get tired of this, I don't believe I ever will." With this remark I open the little gate leading up to my porch and leave Cal there on the sidewalk.

I think I'm more confused than ever with his actions tonight. Is Cal here as an old friend visiting another? Or is he here to persuade me to stop my work?

After closing the front door behind me I snap my fingers. "I forgot to send Hunter the email!" The issue with Callinicus is already dismissed from my mind. The text I sent Hunter previously didn't seem to go through and perhaps he hasn't checked his voicemail yet. I'll send my friend a little email to remind him I am indeed always thinking of him.

SEVEN

60

There's not much I can tell you about what happened after my abductor stopped breathing. It happened too fast. Many months of having to endure him, only for him to die after less than an hour. In a way, I feel cheated.

The pain of knowing he is gone completely overwhelms me. I should've jumped and cheered for joy. In its place is this sudden and demanding sadness. Not for him, no, of course not for him. I feel it for me, and for the vengeance I didn't get to savor, the revenge I wasn't truly rewarded.

Through the fog of my defeat, Erasmus carried me to the bathroom, and when he set me on the counter, I vaguely remember hearing him speaking to me.

No. He's singing to me. The words don't make any sense, and at first, I assumed it was because my brain is all over the place. It's because he's speaking another language. His native tongue of Danish. It mesmerizes me, and I don't even know what he's saying. Honestly, the comfort is he's sharing this with me.

The whole time he's singing, Erasmus takes his time peeling the blood-stained clothes from my body. I don't panic much at his touch, anymore. I feel like I should, but I'm too numb to care. I didn't notice how much blood covered me until this moment. If I was in a normal state of mind, I might've argued with him about wasting his time. Forget being careful with my clothes, I would demand he tear them off. He has the hands of a killer, yet his movements are gentle. Before I can even think to object, I'm back in his arms.

The bath water turns red as Erasmus sets me down in it. I always felt small in this enormous tub. Tonight, I feel molecular. I almost fight the soapy sponge touching me. How ridiculous is it that I want his blood to stain my skin forever? I think once this is gone, he will truly be gone, and there is no turning back time to gain more of it.

How evil am I? I wanted him to suffer more than he did. Do I care that he died on the table under our hands? No. Does this make me selfish? Possibly. I deserved to be greedy after what he did to me. Sure, I didn't die. I can't tell you how many times I wanted to.

With each sponge swipe, the past is slowly being cleansed from me. My emotions are everywhere. Everything is too soft, too easy. There's this burning need for Erasmus to scrub my skin off.

Despite the abductor dying too quickly, I should be happy. At least I had a good meal with my family. This thought tightens my chest, and then laughter erupts, frantically and hysterically from my throat. It startles Erasmus, momentarily freezing his movement and ceasing his singing. After he makes sure I'm alright, he resumes cleaning me. He's chuckling along with me, despite not understanding why. I don't even know why. It still feels good.

Erasmus doesn't ask questions, and he doesn't offer words to complicate my mind even more. It's his presence speaking volumes to me. Perhaps it was the stupid puns earlier at dinner about my abuser being dead and gone from this world, or maybe it is just simply because. We're both cracking up with hysteria and it makes the moment even sweeter. This is certainly a night I will remember for the rest of my immortal life.

ERASMUS

61

leave Seven in his room and, after making sure he is tucked in the bed, I go to the backyard for a moment of fresh air. Even out here I can make out Seven's heart beat. Besides Seven, the only thumping hearts here are mine and Virenda. Audelia, Lorcan, and Clouden's are all silent. Seven's is often erratic. It never has a steady rhythm to it, especially now. After he took the potion, it didn't change. I had no idea he indulged in the potion or when he even took it. The foolish boy tricked me, and I still randomly chuckle to myself about it. He took it. That's what matters.

His heart is hammering and skipping beats all over the place, so I go back inside to check on him. Seven is a lump under the covers, and every few seconds his form bounces softly. He breaks my heart when he cries. I wish I could go back in time again and make sure the abductor lives through this whole debacle, just for Seven's sake.

"Are you just going to stand there and watch me cry?" he asks.

Without a word, I sit on the edge of his bed and watch him. He's looking out the dark window into the night.

"I can hear yours too," he whispers, and at first I'm confused by what he means. He didn't have to look up when I was standing in the doorway… to know I was there. He heard my heart.

When he sits up, I think he's going to kiss me. He doesn't and just stares at me.

"We're a pair of creeps, aren't we?" he asks. That's not why he's staring though. He's picking my heartbeat out and deciphering it from my own. It is so much more than that. He's listening with so much attention I am certain nothing can break his focus. I'm in tune as well, listening to the drumming sound of our symphony. After some time the beats of our heart are pounding in sync, thrumming together perfectly. Seven's eyes widen and then he sucks in a deep breath of air, changing the pace of his heartbeat. Shock is written all over his features. "How'd we do that?"

I can not reply to him. What words in the modern English language can describe this? So, I leave it unanswered for the time being.

When I get up to leave, he reaches a hand to grab my wrist, stopping me.

"Thank you," he says softly. "I mean it. For everything. The abductor. The potion. All of it."

Seven Wilbrate never has to thank me for anything in his entire life. I will do anything he asks me to, and anything he doesn't ask me to. Like this, with the abductor. I'd do it all again, over and over if I needed to.

"Do you need anything?" I ask.

Seven shakes his head. "Not really. No… Maybe? I don't know."

"Should you decide you need anything, all you have to do is ask."

His gaze has emotions in them that I only briefly witness before the question leaves his mouth. "You'll give me the moon if I ask for it?"

"You'd better be specific in your requests," I say. "I have heard that a modern term for the moon can also mean pulling down your pants and showing off your ass."

Seven laughs, much like he did in the bath. It is full of some sort of raw hysteria like it's been building up inside of him for a long time.

"Okay," he says with a smile. "I am in need of a dog."

I roll my eyes. He's requested this before and I have yet to fulfill this one demand of his.

"As I answered before, it remains the same. I shall see what I can do, Seven."

"It's not hard. You just go to the pound and adopt one." He counters with a mischievous air about him.

"I believe it is much more complicated than you're making it out to be."

"Is it?" Seven's brow pops up with the question. "Well. If I could leave the house, maybe I'd show you. I mean, there's plenty of strays out there who need a home."

I sigh. "I'm sure Lorcan would just love it, don't you think? Dog hair on his beloved suits."

Once more, Seven snickers out a laugh. "Seriously, I'm good. I think. I mean, I don't think I need anything." He glances around the room. "I have everything here."

He does. He really does.

LORCAN

62

Well, this is entirely unexpected, indeed. I am down in my cellar with the man's remains who caused Seven's trauma. He's dead, as he should be, since we practically devoured him whole. Sadly, he died before we could finish dinner. I didn't have the heart to eat without Seven there, despite the hunger pangs I felt. It was satiated with leftovers from a previous meal, though.

After calming himself, Seven has requested for me to show him the correct ways to cut him up.

"There are many, many ways, dear boy. You simply let the knife guide you."

It is easier said than done. There is a technique to it. You must let your heart guide you, and having a steady hand helps. We learned that Seven is not as steady as he could be. He will be fine with some patience and more practice.

"Try here." I draw a line around the shoulder area in a circular motion. This time Seven takes my direction to heart, and a perfect cut has been made. The childlike smile on his face is adorable.

He wants to do this as the finale of his escapades to seal the deal; to be the last person who touches this man.

"Your face was the last he saw before he died," I tell Seven. "I know he went rather quickly for your taste. If it helps, you were the last thing he saw. It was such a powerful moment, Seven."

"I hadn't thought of that," he says while making a sleek little cut at the man's throat. "I've been so absorbed with the realization he's gone, I didn't think of anything else."

"Understandably so. Your first kill, was it not?" Of course, it was, and he nods the confirmation.

"A perfect opening act." I wink at the boy. He just peers at me, unsure, yet certain of what I mean. This won't be his first and only kill. I can see it in his eyes. Now he has a taste for it, this is only the beginning. Oh, what a perfect way to start. It's great to get the revenge your heart burned for.

"May I come in?" Erasmus stands at the door waiting for approval not to interrupt. I wave him in with my free hand, the one not peeling skin from bone.

"Of course, darling, join us in this adventure." I half wondered why Erasmus did not join him here. Perhaps he assumed Seven might wish to be alone with me in this endeavor.

It is silent while we work. Erasmus is an antidote to Seven's anxiety. The vibe in the room softens when he approaches Seven's side. The boy's hand is steadier and more in tune.

The only sound to be heard is the unmistakable pop of a bone breaking, the squelching of bodily fluids, and the soft breathing of the two immortal men next to me. Here and there is a light 'plop' of a kidney or liver onto a platter.

"I have no idea how you found him." The silence is broken with Seven's statement. "And I don't care how you did it. I'm glad you did."

Erasmus does not answer. Seven is the only one in this room who doesn't know what Erasmus did. I know because I was there helping and I know the rest because Wisteria is quite the gossip with me over tea. Her little adventure to the past with Erasmus was a tale she was bubbling to tell. And how he is in debt to her because of it—and the potion Seven drank.

They both stop harvesting organs to peer at one another. A look is shared, a longing gaze in each other's eyes, and Seven closes the distance between them. Of course, I can't keep the smile on my lips to myself. The two men are ridiculously adorable together, and despite being ruthless killers, they are soft for one another. I highly doubt that I am capable of such intimacy anymore, but they are lovely together. What they share, though, is not anything I ever want for myself.

They pay no mind to me across the table, carving away at the muscle and meat of the corpse—and who could blame them, honestly? They are enamored with one another. God help anyone who tries to stand in their way of each other. Although just for entertainment purposes, I would love to see someone try.

No words have been spoken, and trust me, none are needed to convey what each one feels. Love and adoration smother the air. Had I needed to breathe, I'd have suffocated in it. Covered in blood, Seven's fingers caress Erasmus' cheek lovingly.

It's written all over Seven's face. He wants to take things further, but he's afraid, and with good reason considering his past. They have yet to move, and I doubt either of them will. If I could bet, I'd wager a full bank account they will stay staring in awe at one another, well into the morning. Seeing it is getting quite romantic here, I sneak away silently and leave the two gazing longingly at one another over the dead body. We can package the meal tomorrow. It won't be spoiled. If it's still intact by then.

SEVEN

63

I t's been quiet in the house lately. Of course, the reason is obvious and I hate to admit it's because of me. No one knows how to act around me anymore. They're all walking on eggshells, even Erasmus and, especially, Clouden. Neither of them have even tried to talk to me about anything that's happened.

After Erasmus checked on me he didn't bring it back up. I get the feeling he's not going to talk about it again, unless I bring it up, and I haven't even seen Clouden to try. It kind of annoys me how he doesn't bother to see if I'm alright. I suppose he assumes Erasmus will take care of me. It shouldn't even come to that. I'm so angry with myself. I'm angry no one else has bothered with me. It's no one else's job or responsibility. I'm my own person. I'm grown. I should be able to tell others when I need something or something's wrong.

Instead, I just bottle it all up because I don't want to burden anyone, anymore than I already have.

Since this whole debacle started, I haven't had any panic attacks. I feel anxious. It's just naturally how I am. Why should I feel it at all? I'm immortal. What is there to fear anymore? This thing has undeniably turned me inside out. There's still plenty to be afraid of. I just need to find a new way to contain it. I'm not sure the old ways will be sufficient any longer.

"My psychiatrist would have a field day with this," I say aloud to myself.

I can't just pick up a phone and tell her how I feel about killing my kidnapper. I'd be sentenced to life in prison, and since I can't die, it would be a long time behind bars. Still, I could mention other things I need to talk about. My feelings for a man who pushed me out a window for one. I should not be having butterflies in my belly every time he looks at me. I'm sure he did go to great lengths to find the abductor for me, and he did give me a heart in a box. This isn't normal. This isn't natural, but these feelings inside of me are.

Perhaps it's nothing more than Stockholm syndrome. If that's the case, I'd be in love with the house itself, since it's what's actually holding me hostage. Unless Erasmus has made some kind of deal with it to keep me locked in. I would not put it past him. I have all of these questions yet only one sticks out the most.

Does it really matter?

Erasmus did horrendous things. Does it matter? Does it matter if he would do it again? There is one thing I'm sure of and it's that Erasmus will burn this entire world down if I ever ask him to. He won't even demand me to tell him why, he would not beg me to leave it as is. He would simply do it.

That's it. That's what matters.

Time is such a fickle thing. Not long ago, the first autumn leaf fell to the ground and we're getting close to ending it. The calendar on the wall is showing the date as October 31st. Halloween. I'm still here, just like I thought I'd be. So much has been going on, Lorcan didn't even decorate for the holiday. It could be he never does, I just expected something to be hanging up to prove the season. Maybe a corpse hanging from the chandelier, anything. There's not a pumpkin in sight. I used to love Halloween and autumn the most. That was before, when I cared about anything. Slowly a passion for life is coming back.

Sitting at my window, I watch the sidewalk fill with children in costumes making their way from one house to the next. They all avoid this one like the plague, and I can't blame them. They don't even seem to notice this building at all. I bet it's the house protecting them, keeping them far away from the monsters within. Something tells me Lorcan wouldn't hurt them. Scare them, yes, not harm them in any way.

It's crazy this house, of all houses, doesn't have any kind of decoration outside. I'm actually angry about it. I press my head to the coolness of the window and let out a deep sigh as I close my eyes. The carpet next to me shakes, and I peek one eye open at it. It bunches up in a circle then spits out something orange at me. I catch it just in time, before it can smack me in the face.

"A pumpkin!" Not just any pumpkin, the most perfect pumpkin I've ever seen. I hug it to my chest. Either the house can read minds or I'm just unmistakably sad about the Halloween mess and it can sense it. I'm sad about other things too, but this is the house trying to cheer me up. It's working a bit. For now, anyway.

More pumpkins are popping up from the rug, strings of orange lights prance their way to hang over my bed. The ceiling has transformed to resemble the night sky complete with a full, fat moon and twinkling stars. A large cauldron appears in my lap, filled to the brim with all of my favorite candies. On the wall across from my bed, a projector starts showing a movie.

Erasmus returns from the kitchen with two mugs of hot chocolate in his hands. He stops just after the door closes behind him and takes it all in. The room is suddenly so different from when he went downstairs earlier. I'm still sitting at the window nook where he left me.

"Do I even want to know?" he asks.

"Happy Halloween," I say. "I'm glad the house didn't let us forget it."

Erasmus hands me a warm mug and sits across from me at the other side of the window. "Being in the tomb I lost all sense of time. It could've been Halloween everyday for years and I wouldn't have known."

I'm at a loss for words. It's easy to forget he was stowed away for so long. "I'm sorry you were stuck in there."

"I can argue with the gods about it, one day. Today" —he steals a candy bar from the bucket in my lap—"I'm going to try one of these." I watch him unwrap it and take a huge bite. His nose scrunches and he spits it back into the wrapper.

"Not to your taste?"

"Nej, disgusting," he says and grins. I can see specks of chocolate smeared between his teeth. "I bet you taste better."

Instantly my cheeks burn from his comment. He said it before. He's reminding me he wants his taste of me, and one day he will get it. Just as he promised to kill me if I didn't take the potion, he promises to take a chunk out of me. The little bag of blood was just a sample. He still wants the real deal.

Lifting my chin, I hold out my arm to him. "Then try it."

The smile fades from his lips, and Erasmus looks like a bus just slammed into him.

"You don't mean it," he whispers.

"Don't I?" I took the potion after he didn't think I would. He questions this, as well?

Erasmus just stares at me long and hard, until I shove my wrist up a bit higher. He takes it, wrapping his fingers around my skin and never losing eye contact with me. Blood is pulsing in my ears and I can't decide if it's from his touch or the thought of his teeth digging into my flesh. It's probably both.

He lifts my wrist to his mouth, and my lips part watching him. I can't believe I'm letting him do this. Why wouldn't I? Just when I think Erasmus is going to chomp down, he does the unthinkable. His lips press the tiniest kiss to my wrist instead, leaving me breathless.

"Not tonight, Seven," he says. "Soon, but not yet."

Slowly, I pull my hand back to my lap, and we watch the last stream of the trick or treaters disappear from the sidewalk. My thoughts are on the tingling sensation his lips left on my skin.

ERASMUS

64

The mood did not change the next day.

"You look perturbed." So many thoughts are seemingly going through Seven's mind, and he's lost in them again. I fear the abductor dying could possibly have traumatized him.

"The abductor is dead," Seven replies, completely drained. "And I don't know how I feel about it. In a way, it's freeing... liberating. In a way, I almost feel lost."

"You've never had this before," I say. "Nothing is holding you to the past any longer."

I shouldn't be focusing on his lips, yet I am. My tongue sizzles with the anticipation of kissing him. I can not be the one to make the first move. Not for this. I have to allow Seven to take it from me, when he is ready and not a moment before.

"All of these years. I wasn't sure if he was dead or alive. I didn't care," he says.

"And now?"

"I want to do it again." The fire smoldering inside Seven has definitely been set aflame. "Take me with you on the next hunt. I would've enjoyed this one more, if it wasn't for being overwhelmed by his quick death."

Of course, I'm pleased by this. It's something I've been waiting for. Seven understands now. Our monsters are one and the same.

"I want to liberate people, Erasmus," he continues. "Not to hurt the innocent. I don't want to be like him."

I'm curious what those words truly mean, and I have my suspicion. "I am to have a moral compass?"

"Didn't you? For this?" he asks, and he seems afraid of the answer.

"Nej," I say. "This was done for love. For you. I am no hero."

"I'm not asking you to be, but you're just picking a human to maim... I mean, how fun is that?" Seven asks. "They can't win against you, so let's make it like a game. For us."

He's trying to manipulate me, just as I manipulated him before. I should be angry at this little move of his but pride swells inside of me instead.

"I'll gather a bunch of them," he adds. "As much information, and as many of them as possible." His words become increasingly urgent. "I will never let you starve, and you will always have a choice in this, just as you have let me choose my path. Let's do something with what we have. Let's help other people who were just like me, and who can't get their revenge for themselves."

I do not care a damn bit about anyone else or if they get their revenge. What I did with the abductor is because I love Seven and only him. I don't care if other killers walk the earth. They're not my problem as long as they stay far away from this house. It would seem my boy wants to use his immortality for the greater good. How can I deny him?

"As you wish, my perfect boy."

"Do you know what I wish for right this moment?" He smiles through the question.

My eyebrow pops. "I am certain it would be a dog."

"Well, yeah…" Seven laughs softly. "But it's been established that's a firm 'no'. I *really* would like a bath."

Without further questioning, I ran the bathwater.

The shirt on his back is already gone before I can make a move to help him out of it. Such an impatient thing. As he wiggles to tug off his pants, I stop him. The question of 'May I' is there, ready to fall out of my mouth. The look on Seven's face gives me approval before I can ask it. Just as I wanted him to, he's dropping his walls for me. Though the question isn't truly required any longer, I will still ask if I perceive it essential to do so.

Taking his hands, I press them to the counter behind him before slowly peeling the clothing off him. I take my time undressing him the rest of the way, savoring this between us and remembering every line of his body. The beautiful thing he is.

"Erasmus… You don't have to do this."

"Foolish boy, I know. I want to. Let me care for you."

Seven rolls his eyes. I take off the socks from his feet. Before I let him stand, I press a kiss to his ankle, and it results in Seven's chest rumbling with a soft chuckle

When the tub is full, I turn off the water and hold a hand out to help him get in. Seven smiles, amused by my efforts. He takes my hand and lowers himself into the tub.

"*Foolish man*," he says, mocking me, and a huge smile spreads across my face.

"Only for you."

He's submerged in the water, laying back against the tub while I begin to wash his hair. The sensation of my fingertips gliding through his dark locks pulls a deep moan from his chest.

"You're spoiling me, Erasmus," Seven coos.

"Ja," I reply. "That's exactly what I intend to do."

He reaches wet fingers up and touches my face lightly. I turn my cheek to press into his palm. Those lovely fingers curl, almost urging me down to him and somehow resisting at the same time.

"How did you end up locked in the tomb?" It is a question I figured he would ask someday. "When I asked how you two met, Lorcan told me he found you there." Seven is genuinely curious. Something I love about him.

"It is a long and complicated story. I would love nothing more than to tell you but only at the right moment."

Seven does not say anything in return.

"You trust me, ja?"

He lifts his head up just a tad to face me. "With everything." A fire burns brilliantly in those majestic blue eyes of his.

"Then trust me, this is not the right time, yet."

The story will make much more sense once he is aware of our history. Our true past. The many past lives we fought to be together, and how it led up to the moment of me being imprisoned in the tomb.

Seven sighs, it is more of a happy and content release than anything. Then he says, "This is the happiest I have ever been." His eyes are closing as his head falls back against the tub, and his lips curl deliciously into a smile.

I believe him.

LORCAN

65

There I sit at the mahogany desk of my study. Eyes and thoughts engrossed on the computer screen before me, I scan over the numbers for this month. Apart from being the brutal murderer I am, there are two other jobs I excel at: being a father for my family and investing in properties across the world.

I watch the numbers on the screen drastically drop, first down to the hundred thousands and, within minutes, just thousands.

The identity of the hacker was easy to trace. How ignorant the person must be to not know my accounts all have the best security money can buy. Sure, they can get into my accounts. It doesn't mean they'll come out. Going over the information given, it was too simple to track down my hacker. This person must be an amateur trying to be sneaky or they're just very stupid and careless. The first mistake she made was hacking my account. The second mistake was thinking she would get away with it.

To hack someone, you need to be smarter than your victim. Obviously she is not. After finding out the exact location of my little hacker, I waste no time and go to her. Why not pay her a visit? She wants my attention, right? She's got it. She sits there behind her keyboard, looking quite smug with herself as the numbers in my account decrease and hers increases substantially.

"Well, well, well."

She damn near jumps to the ceiling at my whisper in her ear. When she turns around, her face instantly goes pale. I snatch her hand from the mouse and grasp it firmly. I survey each finger with a smile. She's completely frozen, barely moving, apart from the increase in her breath and blood pulsing through her veins quickly.

"Excited to see me?" My lips turn up into a broad smile. "You should be." I nod to the screen. "I've come to collect back what is mine."

"It wasn't me," she says hurriedly. This angers me to my core.

I slam my free hand on the desk and push her head to the screen before us, so her cheek is flush to it. "I think we both know better." She's picked the wrong one to hack, and then lies about it with significant proof right before our eyes. "This account is mine." I release her face from the screen to turn it to look at me instead.

"The question... what to do with you?" My head tilts from one way to the next as I stare at her. She keeps trying to pull away. It's a certainty here: no one gets away from me if I don't want them to. Flicking open my knife, I pull her hand in front of my eyes. I have it all mapped out on precisely what to do. I do so love the theater and dramatics involved in stretching things out.

My eyes cast to the tip of the blade, and I turn it three times in my hand right before digging it slowly under her middle fingernail. Oh, the lovely scream developing from her is beautiful to hear.

"I think I'll start with the middle finger. The phrase 'fuck you' came to mind." She probably is far from listening at this point and possibly can't hear me through the writhing and sound of her screams. What do I care? The torture is half the fun.

As she falls from the chair to her knees, I yank the knife from her and, this time go with the pinky finger, shoving it deep once again under the lining of the nail.

"Maybe next time you'll think twice before hacking an account that belongs to a serial killer." She cries again in agony, and my face lights up with a smile. Naturally, she tries to fight me, kicking and punching with the other arm. Her attempt is futile. I twist her wrist with a flick of my own, and a distinct *crack* fills the air.

"Have we learned a lesson yet?" She convulses and nods through the sobs. I am hardly finished with her. Quickly, I pull up the chair next to her and slam her hand down on the seat.

"I don't think you have." With a twirl of my knife, I slam the tip of my blade into her hand, slicing straight through her skin to the chair. Pulling it from her flesh, I twirl it again before resuming to slowly carve away at the knuckle of her pointer finger. One hard slice, and I could've broken the finger free of the hand. It would be too easy. I want her to *feel* the pain she's caused. With each sawing, she is screaming so loud I believe for certain her lungs will bust. Oh, how lovely it would be if they did!

Once the finger is fully separated from the hand, I perch it between my lips like a cigar and go for her middle finger again. I shove my knife down at the knuckle, separating it from the hand with one slice quickly. Blood squirts in every direction, coating us both. She's seated on the floor when I crouch down to her level and dangle her middle finger in the air in front of her face.

"Here. A trophy of your 'accomplishment.'" I smile and the blood from the other finger between my lips seeps into my mouth then spills out the corners. "And the middle finger to once again signify 'go fuck yourself.' Now, you can literally do it."

I leave her there, alive. I'm not going to kill her. No, that's not what this was about. There is no song of death to follow through in my head for this one. She didn't deserve to die by an artist's hand. She will live with what she's done. A punishment has been bestowed in her honor. One can rest assured she will think twice before hacking my accounts ever again. If she can even use her hands after tonight.

Perhaps I am upset with other scenarios and I am taking it out on this woman. Well, no, let's be completely honest she deserved this little reprimand. Callinicus left a little before this charade began, and I do suppose it caused me to be deeper in my feelings.

"Your friend Wisteria fixed my watch," he said. "Once again, Lorcan, I thank you for your hospitality. I don't know where I'd be without you."

"Anything for you, dear Cal."

"I hate to leave in such haste, but there's work I need to do."

I nodded. "I understand. Work is never done. You'll stop again, soon? Don't let another seventy-three years pass by before you decide to come visit." I'm not much for hugging and Cal didn't even try to. Instead, he shook my hand.

"Oh, Lorcan. I promise to come visit again, very soon."

He saw no other reason to stay around. I do believe his presence was more than what he made it out to be. He's up to something. I'll find out what. Maybe I have placed too much on my plate. The turmoil I am subjecting myself to is far too much a human emotion. This must be rectified. Immediately.

SEVEN

66

The members of this house are something else. I've been in my room, staying away from them all to just try to make sense of what's happened and how much my life has altered. I can't make heads or tails of why I feel so defeated still about Mr. Abduction being gone. It's a hard one to process. The whole scenario is like a dream. Erasmus found him and we killed him. *I* killed him. It felt liberating but at the same time, I've never killed anything other than a houseplant. This has weighed on my mind heavily and stays there consuming me.

I shouldn't expect too much privacy with these nosy monsters around. Audelia is the first to come in. She hands me an envelope. Sitting on the floor by the unlit fireplace, I open it and give her a smile. Inside are pictures of them cleaning the mess after the abductor died. In a way it opened the wound again, not as much as it should have. Lorcan is holding the camera in one, taking a selfie with the rest of them and the dead body. I suppose he wanted to capture the moment, in case I would like another memory of it. It is disgusting and thoughtful all at once. The bags containing his remains won't last forever, but these photographs will.

Audelia and I are laying on the floor in quiet when the door creaks open again. Clouden and Virenda join us. The silence is gone with their presence.

"So, you took the potion," Clouden says as he sits next to me. "*And* you're staying."

I nod. "I'm staying."

Thankfully he doesn't ask me why. I do not have a straight up answer for it. It is a magnitude of components that made up my mind. Erasmus is the main ingredient but there are others. Clouden, Audelia, Lorcan... Virenda too. Mostly myself.

"I called my psychiatrist and told her to forward my letters here. I'm probably overdue for a session." Is psychiatry even a necessary component anymore? Just so she doesn't bother my parents, I changed the address.

Clouden talks again. "I wanted to come visit you sooner. I know when shit hits the fan you don't like to be smothered." He's right.

"I called mom," I say. "Told her I was with you." There is a tad bit of annoyance in my tone. "She and dad are doing just fine." Clouden was right. They didn't seem worried about me at all. I was a burden to them.

"What are you and Erasmus?" Virenda asks with a cheeky little grin. She and Audelia exchange a glance, telling me they'd been gossiping about us. Of course they would. It is kind of difficult to answer this question. We're a lot of things. I can't put a label on us, because I don't think there is one that truly fits.

So, I settle with saying, "We're just us."

"I told you," Audelia says. She pokes my ribs, and we both laugh. "I told you he was into you when he pushed you out of the window!"

"Yeah, yeah… It was a weird fucking way to show someone you like them!"

"It's like kids," Clouden says, his head resting on my chest. "Remember in third grade I pulled the girl's hair? I kind of did it because I liked her."

"Yeah," I laugh and flick his forehead. "You didn't try to kill her, though!"

"Same thing, just… yours is the adult version."

The girls start talking about something else, and Clouden chimes in here and there with them. I'm lost in my own thoughts and they all seem to drift to Erasmus. Even if I did feel something for him, would I be able to offer him anything intimately? The dream I had in the basement the other night terrified me, in more ways than one. I don't even know where to begin with allowing myself to open up to him in that way, or if I ever could. Erasmus never asks anything about my sexuality, or if I even want to indulge in any of it. He never makes any attempt to pressure me in any way. To be honest, he's relatively pleased to have just my presence. It's the strangest thing but also the most comforting.

"Do you think we'll get anyone else in this house?" Audelia asks.

None of us answer right away. I never thought of the possibility of other people in this house. The rooms are vast, the walls themselves can make more rooms if it wants to. Do I want it to? I sort of hope we don't get additional people. Not yet, anyway. I like this family we've created here. Well, the family Lorcan put together.

"If we do get more people the next one better be hot," Virenda says.

"Are you saying none of us are hot?" Clouden asks curiously.

Virenda rolls her eyes. "I meant like single and hot."

Cloud throws up his hands. "Am I not both of those things??"

"Yeah, but you're like a brother. I can't even look at you. Besides, Audelia here has placed a threat. You're not up for grabs."

"I only said it because you were new and needed to know your place!" Audelia shouts. "And to point out none of us are just toys."

"So he *is* up for grabs then?" Virenda asks.

I snort a laugh and they all turn my way. "Sorry," I say. "I never thought I'd see the day when my little brother would be the focus of women fussing over him."

Virenda gasps. "Have you seen him?"

"You know," Cloud says, "I do kind of look like you, Seven. So, it means you're automatically considered hot too."

I just lay there shaking my head. "I'm too old for this kind of conversation. Hey Virenda? Can you play "This Kiss" by Faith Hill?"

"He's not too old. He's just too 'taken,'" Audelia sings out the words.

My cheeks heat up at her comment, and I wipe at them, pretending to be overheated. It's pretty pointless. They all know. Erasmus knows. I know. It just is what it is.

They start talking again amongst themselves. It's about Erasmus and I, of course. Like their words conjure him, he appears at the door. He doesn't come in. He just looks at me briefly and leaves. One day we'll talk about everything. Today isn't the day for it, yet.

Since I've come to the realization about staying here, perhaps the house will let me out.

"I'll be right back," I say, and scramble my way to the front door. "This is it, right? I've accomplished what was asked of me. I've decided to stay." There is a nice pause for dramatic effect before my hand wraps around the doorknob and I turn it.

Nothing. The knob won't budge.

Feeling very defeated at this moment, my hand drops from it. There's something else still incomplete, and I am confident I know what it is.

ERASMUS

67

eatly placed on the counter is a press of fourteen ziplock bags of various shapes and sizes.

"I took the liberty of packaging him for you," Lorcan says to Seven. "Well, what's left of him after our little feast."

I can see the wheels in my boy's head turning. This is the finality of the man who once abused Seven, but even though it transpired, I can still see a look of turmoil in Seven.

"He's gone."

"Yes," Lorcan says, and we look at each other, not sure how he will react.

Seven nods. "I have so many questions. Why... me?"

"My dear boy, why not you?" Lorcan answers before I can. "You are scrumptious." He pinches Seven's cheek, making him smile. It isn't what Seven is looking for.

"To be honest, Seven, does it matter?" Lorcan asks. "It could have just easily been anyone else. You might have just been in the right place at the right moment."

"What if there's more? What if he did stalk me? What if he knew it was going to be me? Did he do this to other people? Surely, it wasn't just me."

"Maybe you were his type," I say. "I'm sure you're delicious." Masking the hunger for him that tries to appear in my eyes is not easy. Despite the seriousness of the conversation, I want to devour him.

"Perhaps it is not for you to understand, Seven," Lorcan says warily. "The mind of a psychopath or sociopath is not an easy thing to pick apart. Many attributes would have led you to be his one."

Lorcan would know all about it, wouldn't he?

"So," Lorcan carries on, "we can stand here wondering the if's and why's, or we can put it to rest with him." His dark eyes glance down briefly before back up to Seven. "Or… you can go back in time and ask him yourself."

He's looking at me. What game is he playing with those words?

"Erasmus. What's he talking about?" Seven stares at me with a distant look in his eyes. He blinks slowly and I can tell he's confused.

"Now is as good of a time as any." Lorcan has pointedly fixed his focus on mine.

"It's how I found him." Without averting my stare from Lorcan, I answer Seven. "The witch brought me back in time to witness your capture."

The room is quiet, right up until Seven yells out with anger so loudly I am positive the walls will come down around us. "You could've altered this!"

Lorcan just stares directly at me. I am still not certain why he picked to disclose this little information to Seven. I am sure time will tell us. Or simply, he just desires entertainment. I would not put it past him.

"You could've changed the past, and you selfishly chose not to? Why?"

I turn to look at Seven. His eyes are wide, and his cheeks are flushed with the anger boiling in him.

"Perhaps a better person would've done it. You would've done it. You are selfless and beautiful and worthy. I could not and will never see past anything that keeps you to me. Do you regret that I did not change the circumstances?"

He hesitates momentarily, mulling this over in his head, and just as quickly as he became upset, his anger wilts. It softens with the whisper of one word. "No."

Lorcan is placing each bag into a large container. He's labeled both of them with Seven's name.

Seven closes the gap between us, his chest almost pressed to mine. "If I have to walk through hell to get to you, I will. I'm sorry, I yelled. I'm a little shocked, but I shouldn't be. You'd do anything to keep us together, even if it meant *letting* me walk through hell. I made it out alive, and in a way, I suppose I'm stronger than before."

I will not apologize to him. I am not sorry for this, so saying those words would mean nothing and hold emptiness.

"I only would have changed it so we could have met before all of it happened," Seven says. "Maybe none of it would have happened at all like it did. You'd have been way too protective of me to allow it." His voice is much calmer. "Maybe it would have been you to touch me first. Not him."

"Would it have been me, though?" I ask. Not that Seven and I have even done anything remotely close to intimacy, apart from the soft romantic touches to his cheek. Perhaps this is what he speaks of.

"Yes," Seven laughs. "I know damn well no one, not one soul, would have managed to lay a finger on me if you were around back then. I had a girlfriend. She wasn't my priority... my career and school were." At the mention of school, I see a flash of sadness in his eyes. He never let it go. It meant a great deal to him. "You'd have probably killed her or something, just to get her out of the way."

I shrug. My boy is discovering me all too well. "An easy obstacle to overcome."

The corners of Seven's lips curl up slightly as he answers, "It would've been nice. I do think this way is better."

The yearning to touch him takes over, and my hand cups his cheek of its own accord.

"Også mig." *Me too*. Despite we have yet to even kiss, this is the most intimate situation I have ever been in.

A soft tapping gets our attention. Lorcan has packaged everything in the bin and closed it tight.

"All for you, darling," Lorcan says. "No one will touch this box. It'll be safe down here for when you need to nibble something bitter." He winks at Seven before making his way up the stairs. "Oh, Erasmus. Wisteria said she would like to call in one of the debts you owe."

Seven's body goes stiff, and through gritting teeth, he asks, "What. Debts?"

Exhaling heavily, I reply, "Kræft æde mig." I glare at Lorcan, who simply winks my way before completely disappearing upstairs.

"Let's talk in the bedroom, Seven."

Shaking with more anger than before, Seven pulls away from me and storms off up the stairs.

What fresh hell am I in now?

LORCAN

68

The night Clouden and I went out right before his transition, someone was following us. They'd made it far too obvious and whether they wanted it to be or not was the question. Multiple times I'd been out since then and they relatively stayed to themselves, so I suspected they were trying to conceal themselves from me.

At first, I brushed it off as being one of the police officers. Perhaps the sheriff watched me. He hadn't ordered anyone to follow me in years. If I was to guess, when Audelia pulled her little stunt like she did, the sheriff might've been worried I was going off the rails. The police had better training than this amateur stalker. Whatever they were up to, they did not hide themselves very well, and currently I have him tied to a chair in my basement.

"Do you know what the main flaw was?" I ask. He can't answer, though, because of the gag in his mouth.. Scrutinizing every little detail about him, I circle the chair to just take in this pathetic creature. "Do you know what I am?" I ask. "Oh, where are my manners?" Removing the gag, I ask the question again.

He coughs out the answer. "A killer."

"Yes, but *what* am I?" This time my face is directly in front of his, fangs bared so he can properly see them.

He refuses to answer. I know he is aware. How could he not be? "If you know what I am then you'd have been much more careful." I touch the throbbing pulse at his neck and smile. "You must be foolish to come after *me*, human."

I have the distinct thought he isn't working alone.

"Your main flaw was not masking your scent. As a human you can't help your heartbeat. When you go hunting for deer wouldn't you conceal your scent?" This man is no true hunter, he is nothing more than a human caught in a debacle that he can not escape from. "Whoever sent you must have a death wish for you."

"Why do you think someone sent me?" he asks.

I pick up my knife from the table. "Well, maybe no one did but are you stupid enough to send yourself on a suicide mission like *this*?" I wave my knife to show *this* means me and my basement along with what I'm about to do to him.

He just simply stares up at me.

"You haven't followed me long. A few weeks. What knowledge have you acquired in this timeframe, hm?" I ask. Of course he won't answer me. It is time for a little more drastic measures. I planned to play nice. I can see now it won't be going in that direction.

The stalker is bound to the chair by his waist, legs, ankles, and wrists. There's no room given for him to even wiggle in the chair with how tight the ropes are. Of course, I tested them. If he blinks he might miss it coming. His hands are clutching both armrests, and now a knife is piercing the skin and stabbing through to the chair.

Oh, he responds to *this*.

The echoes of his wailing grow tiring after another moment. "Well if you'd answer me, I would not have to resort to such violence. This is only the beginning. Comply and I won't have to keep you in agony."

This time he does reply, and it is a very sound "Fuck you."

A deep sigh escapes my chest. "I did warn you." I hurl the knife down into his other hand. If he tries to move his legs they don't budge at all. I think I'll reward myself later for tying them so perfectly.

"I'm just getting started, darling. Just wait until I splay you open to pull out your intestines. Don't think death will take you quickly. I can make this last a lot longer than you think."

"Alright!" he yells. "It was the man. The one you were with."

My brain wracks through the 'men' this can be, and I already have an idea. The tip of a new knife's blade is pressed under the stalker's chin. "Which man?"

It can't possibly be Erasmus, can it? We did venture out together to the abductor's house to retrieve him for Seven. There's also Clouden as a possibility. If it's Clouden I will set him on fire, watch him burn, and put out the fire just before he dies to start the process all over again. Either of them being the person to aid this fool will break my heart completely. Typically calm under pressure. Tonight I waver, and my fingers twitch with the rising of my temper.

His head lifts to look up at the ceiling hoping to catch a break from the pressure of the knife. "The one, your friend. I don't know his name! He has a device he wears. He just paid me to keep tabs on you. He's a vampire hunter!"

"And he hired an amateur," I say. This is all the evidence I truly need. Though I'm pissed off it's Cal, I am absolutely relieved it's not anyone in my home who has betrayed me. I should trust them more than I do. "Hm, was this so hard? It isn't like *you* were the one betrayed by a friend. Next time, you'd do your best to comply with your kidnapper." I'm not careful when I pull the knives out from his hands.

"Too bad for you there won't be a next time."

This isn't the first time someone I call a friend betrayed me. When you've lived as long as I have, this sort of thing feels common. Over the years, for as long as humanity will endure, I can guarantee one thing will always happen: deception. Kings of our past were deceived by so called loyal patrons. This aspect of life will never die. I should feel something about this happening to me again. I don't. I can't say I'm even numb to the emotion, I've just been well acquainted with it so much it doesn't even bubble to the surface any longer. Loyalty is not something you'll find in all of your friends, unfortunately. It is best to weed those out accordingly.

I am at my desk finishing up writing a letter to Hunter LeBeaux, to at least let my true friend know he means the world to me. The stalker's finger is perched between my lips like a cigarette, and every so often I chomp down on the bone as I seal the letter to be sent to the post office tomorrow. Here I am stewing in my rage, which aids me to create a plot to kill Cal. The scheme is a simple one that will unfold as soon as I leave tonight. It's a pity I have to do it but this cannot go without punishment.

Well, there's been a turn of events... I don't even need to leave my house anymore to fulfill this plan of action. I sense him walking up to the front door, and he pauses before ringing the bell. Probably trying to come up with a good cover for the dirty work he's been playing at. I won't rush to answer it this time. Why would I? The excitement is gone. Downstairs, someone lets him in. There's not much time to think of what to say to him. Words aren't even necessary anymore. I'm just adding the final touch to my notes when the door to my study opens and Cal walks in with an oblivious smile on his face.

"I couldn't leave without properly thanking you, Lorcan. The watch is like new again." He rambles on and on about a new play coming to Broadway. I pretend to ignore all of it and continue writing scribbles on a piece of scrap paper at this point. I can't look at him.

"Tell me, Cal," I say, cutting him off. "How stupid do you think I am?"

Cal looks at me with an air of innocence. I know a mask when I see one. The house does too, that's why it gave me a warning when he first arrived.

"You're not stupid at all," he says.

"Then, darling, why would you ever try to deceive me?"

"I'm not sure I follow you." His tone remains calm. It's his heartbeat giving him away. An innocent man would have no reason for it to be pounding the way it just increased.

The corners of my mouth tug upward ever so slowly. "Your little stalker didn't make it."

He finally gives way and the invisible mask slides off.

"Was this your plan? Come to 'warn me' of others when it was you behind it the whole time?" I let him have a chance to answer and he doesn't. "How odd you would even have knowledge about such a scheme, if you weren't somehow involved with it."

Cal thinks quickly. Naturally, I am a great deal faster. He tries to spin the dial of the time turner on his wrist. With little effort, I reach him and knock it from his fingers, causing it to fly across the room.

"What was the end plan here, Cal? Were you going to kill me?" We are directly in front of one another, face to face, almost nose to nose. "You have to be more creative than this little shenanigan."

"I want *you* to stop killing," he says. "The plan was not to kill you. Just to imprison you."

The laughter barks like a volcano eruption from a deep pit within my chest.

"You are visibly insane," he adds. "You always have been. What you think you're doing isn't helping anyone."

My hand is around his throat slamming him into the wall. "Visibly insane." I repeat his words through gritting teeth. "And yet here you are befriending me and spending time with me. Ah, this was just part of the plan all along wasn't it? What did you do? Go to the future to see how this would all play out? Did you honestly think you'd win?"

"I don't," he says through a strangling breath. "Another might."

"Might?" I ask. "You did all of this and don't even know if what you're fighting for will even happen? I did not think you were stupid, Cal, but here I am drawn to this conclusion. I assume you thought to gain my trust even more with those little date nights, and then what? Move in for the kill at some point? Probably the next Broadway show. I can already imagine it."

He's suffocating from my grasp, which isn't even my full force yet.

"We could've been good friends over the years, Cal. Such a waste. I hate waste." I shake my head and loosen the grip I have on him to let him catch his breath. "Ah well, at least I finally get to say we're having a friend for dinner."

SEVEN

69

"Are you out of your goddamn mind!" The anger inside of me can't be contained. Erasmus just finished telling me of all the little fucking debts he owes the witch—and why.

First, she brought him back in time to witness my capture, so he could find the man in the present, and we could take care of him. We didn't need to do this. I'm so glad we did, but he did not need to put himself in debt over this.

The second, is the vial of immortality she conjured for me to be like him. To live forever. I never asked where he acquired it. It never crossed my mind. Once again, I'm more than happy he got it, however, there could've been another way of getting the potion.

"So, she can ask you to do *anything* not once but twice!" My stomach is turning, making me sick. What will she call him for? "What do you think she's going to ask you to do?" Fear is wrapping itself around me. It isn't just written on my face it's etched in the tone of my voice as well.

He shrugs. He's too fucking calm about this!

"Erasmus, the thought of her asking you to sleep with her or—"

"She's a lesbian, Seven. It won't happen."

I relax just a bit, but it's not as much as I would hope to. Who is this woman? I don't know what she wants with him! Eras is mine, he belongs to me and she will *not* take him from me.

"She is a powerful witch," I say. "What would she want from you?"

"Don't know," he says. "I am certain I will find out soon."

How soon is soon? How long do I have to freak out over this?

"What if it's something— What if she wants something you can't give her?"

He shrugs again.

"Stop fucking shrugging!" I shouldn't raise my voice. How can I help it? He is driving me nuts with his carelessness of it all.

"Seven, everything will work out. You have to trust me on this," Erasmus replies.

"I trust you! I don't trust *her*!" The number of people I trust can fit on a tiny scrap piece of paper.

"*She* has given me this life," he answers loudly. "I will repay her whatever she wants."

He might be ok with this, I am not. "That's not comforting, considering we don't have a clue what it is, to prepare for, Erasmus!"

He moves quickly to hold my face in his hands. I'm sure by now he sees the panic rising, ready to pull me under the waves.

"I will handle this," Eras says softly.

My chest heaves as the millions of scenarios compile in my head at once. I don't know this witch, and I can only imagine she is capable of powerful things. She can move time, and she can grant eternal life.

"No, Erasmus." A strange and unfamiliar calm washes over me. Panic ceases for a while, and in its place, I feel something much more powerful: fury. "I will handle this."

I watch Erasmus' eyes flicker from pride to worry. Oh, so *now* he's worried?

"We have to be careful about this, Seven. I made a deal, understanding that I would one day have to fulfill it. Breaking a contract with a witch is not something I suggest doing."

"Being in debt to a witch isn't something I suggest doing," I snap back at him..

"It was for a good cause. Selfishly, I got what I wanted, and so did you."

I take a breath and exhale long and slow. "If what she asks for is something that I don't deem worthy of you, of us, I'm going to kill her."

The corners of Eras' lips turn up quickly. "You'll try to kill a witch for me?"

"No, Erasmus, I'm *going* to kill a witch for you. Only if she asks you for something stupid. I'm immortal. She can't hurt me."

"She can imprison you," he whispers.

We lock eyes, and for a second there, he is trying to tell me a bit of his story.

"You won't let it happen. Besides, as long as you're with me, she can lock me where ever the fuck she wants to. End of story. I don't need anything in this world except you. Everything else is a luxury. I need you."

I'm right, and he doesn't say anything. He doesn't have to. Those honey-brown eyes are pouring unspoken words into me, and I hear every single one of them.

ERASMUS

70

even's anger lightens as the days pass, but I can tell he still has the debts on his mind. To ease him a bit, I decided today I am going to tell him about the compass.

"You have my compass," I say to him.

Seven is seated at the reading nook by his window with a book in hand. He looks up at me confused before he understands what I mean.

"Oh, yes!" He scrambles from the window over to the dresser where he digs around for it. "I meant to give this back to you, ages ago. I was going to trade it back for my knife. The one you took when I stabbed you and you pushed me out the window."

He holds it out for me. Instead of taking it, I tell him to open it. Seven does as I command, without question.

"Where is it pointing?" I ask him.

"Uh. To me," he answers..

"Turn around."

Seven hesitates briefly and then turns his back to me. "Where's it pointing?"

"Still to me, Erasmus. It should be pointing North. It's not moving." He hands it to me and I accept it. This time as soon as he hands it over the dial shifts a tad bit then stays locked on him.

"I think it's broken," he says.

"Move to your left."

I keep the compass at a height that we can both see it. He does and as he moves those few paces, the arrow moves with him.

"This is weird," Seven says.

"I want you to walk from one side of the room to the other. Watch the compass as you do."

Seven's feet slowly take him as I direct, and the whole time the compass follows his movements.

He's watching it in awe. "Give it back, let me see something."

I hand it over to him again.

"You move from left to right."

As he demands, I move from left to right. The compass needle does not budge one bit. It stays completely still, focusing on him.

"The compass was meant for me to track you," I say.

"I don't get it."

"Do you not?" I ask. "From the moment you stepped foot into this house, Seven, I was like a magnet drawn to you. I can't explain it all. I do know this; I belong to you. In every life you have ever had, including this one."

The witch's flaw was she left the compass with me. She wouldn't dare try to open the tomb again to take it back. I'm sure she was afraid I would escape. Or maybe she knew it would torment me if the compass arrow started moving and I couldn't reach Seven. I have come to realize I didn't even need the damn thing to begin with. I would have found him all on my own. Fate would have led him to me again.

Seven remains still while processing my words. I'm not sure if he connects it at all, but it is a start that I could give him. I wait for the million questions to form from his lips. In the place of words he chooses actions. Seven closes the space between us, inclines his head, and kisses me. His arms fling around my neck and I'm wrapping mine around him in return. Words are absolutely unnecessary, our bodies communicate on a primal level, speaking directly to each others' souls.

Virenda's music blares through the house with the damn song about kissing again. It's pivotal and subliminal. How ironic this is playing right now—as if her music is somehow tied to us, as well. She always plays the silliest little music pieces, especially this one Seven is so obsessed with. I am far from listening anymore. The only sound I care to hear is Seven's breathing, the beating of his heart, and the soft murmur he's exhaling into my mouth.

I do not lead him in this, instead, I let him completely control it. His mouth becomes hungrier, more demanding for me to give him everything. And I do not deny him. There is an urgency to this kiss, a desperate yearning to crawl inside my mouth and let me swallow him whole. I would devour him.

The divide between us is only physical. Anywhere else, and you would never know where I begin and Seven ends. When he breaks the kiss, his eyes are still closed. His lips, plump and raw, curl lazily into a smile.

Breathless, Seven speaks as he lowers himself back down to the floor. It did not occur to me he needed to be on his tiptoes just a bit to reach. "I couldn't wait any longer," he says. I do not have to ask him to reiterate what he is saying. "I thought you'd take it. I thought you'd kiss me first."

The corners of my lips roll over into a smile. "When have I forced you to do anything?"

With a shrug, he answers, "Maybe take a potion or die!" He laughs and then adds, "You're demanding. Dominance just radiates off of you. I thought you'd just... I don't know, dominate."

"I am very patient, Seven," I say. "It is much more than you think. We are equals, and in time you will see and understand this."

This might not be true. The hold this man has on me is nothing short of powerful. Seven nods, and I can see the workings of his mind slipping into place.

"You must trust me completely," I say. "Feel safe and understand I will never harm you. I will never just take from you, only what you give. You give yourself to me, and I shall take whenever I want."

"I did," he replies. "I took the potion."

"Verbal consent. I want to hear the words, Seven. Tell me I may do as I please with you." My nose trails softly under his jaw. "Whatever pleases me."

"Why didn't you ask this sooner? You've had me all along!" Seven laughs out the words.

"You needed to be ready. I knew you'd take it upon yourself to take what I am always willing to give you."

There is a pause, not because he's thinking about this. I like to think he imagines us in ways he never thought he would be again. In the world of his mind, he is creating. I love watching him. His lips part just slightly, when he's lost in a dreamlike state.

"I am yours to do as you please," he says. There is a slight bit of fear shaking his voice. It's only audible enough if you know what his tone is typically. I know him inside and out. This means the past still holds him, and with good reason. However, I will not do anything to him in any way that will bring his trauma back to the surface. Unless you count pushing him out of the window. I will make sure when I take him, he will enjoy every second of it. Not a thought of the past to haunt him ever again.

"My perfect boy. And I, yours."

Seven leans in one more time. "I'm still mad at you," he says onto my lips with a tender kiss sealing those words. Before I can retaliate, he's pulling me by the wrist out of the room. "Wait. I need to try something."

We stand in the foyer at the front door and Seven is just staring at it. The house hasn't let him leave since he arrived, apart from the first panic attack. It has been a puzzle that's been driving him crazy.

"Take my hand," he says to me.

Without hesitation, my fingers lace with his. He turns the door-knob, and when he does there is a soft click as the knob loosens finally. The door opens the rest of the way on its own, and Seven smiles wide.

"I knew it!" he says through a laugh. "I fucking knew it!"

"What?" I ask.

"It's been waiting for me to accept it." Seven looks at me again, my head cocks to the side in curiosity and then he says. "That I am absolutely in love with you."

There are no words to convey my emotions at this moment. None are needed. His next action makes me all the more speechless. He doesn't leave the house, instead Seven closes the door.

LORCAN

71

"Lorcan, it's getting late. We can finish making dinner if you'd like us to do it today." Virenda opens the door to the basement and follows the sound until she is standing in my view. Just as she rounds the corner I spoon out an eyeball to place in a jar.

"Damn," she says.

"Is it that late already?" I ask, looking up from my workstation. "I completely lost track of it all!" The meat grinder is still messy and full of bits, the tables are all covered in blood and other bodily fluids. I would like to clean this before I go to dinner, but as I begin the walls start to shake. The floor is pushing my feet until I'm at the door. "I won't leave the mess!" The house is trying to make me leave the basement. I put up a fight. It's not an easy thing either, fighting with a supernatural building. In the end, I just let it win.

The table is already set and each member of this family is dressed up beautifully for dinner tonight. The windows to the house are open allowing the crisp autumn breeze to accompany us. Thanksgiving hasn't been celebrated here for many years and I'm awfully excited to dig into the lovely cornucopia of flavors and colors that are presented at the table. The star of this banquet is a recent senator who was convicted of an array of heinous crimes. He's been glazed and garnished with fresh herbs and sliced into nice bite sized portions for us all to share. Glistening, flaky pie crusts call from the other end of the table which consist of an assortment of the classics, like pumpkin and apple with my own little twists in them. A vibrant holiday picture if there has ever been one.

After many lonely years, this not so little house of mine is finally brimming with life once more. Ironic to say since so much death has happened within these walls, and by my hand, of course. Residing under this roof is more than just people. They are family. Each has grown increasingly into their true forms in just a short time staying here. They've changed me as well. Each one picked away the ice of this cold, dead heart with their presence. All of them perfectly fit into my household as if they were made to be here.

"You've outdone yourself, Lorcan." Clouden says, around a mouthful of food. He fills up his glass from the decanter of freshly procured O negative.

Both Audelia and Virenda are shoveling bite after bite in, and the only noises coming from them are the scraping of forks against their plates.

Erasmus nods to show his agreement while adding, "Det er lækkert." Scooping up another bite, he offers his spoon to Seven to taste, and he gratefully accepts. If I'm to guess, Seven must enjoy the meal as well. While chewing, he's humming and dancing in his seat.

"I am so happy you're enjoying it," I reply.

And they *are* enjoying it, so much that there isn't much room for conversation until Clouden decides to push a few buttons. "You know, there's talk on the streets that LeBeaux's makes the best gumbo in the city."

I almost choke on the bite of food.

"Oh, yes!" Seven says. "I've heard of that place. It's in all the local magazines. I hear they make a pretty good Fish Creole dish too!" The two brothers share a cheeky little grin.

Erasmus adds his two cents in to Seven. "Sounds like somewhere you should take me on a date to."

They're doing this just to rile me up and it works. "I'll have you know"—I point my fork at each one of them— "Hunter LeBeaux stole that recipe from me and tampered with the ingredients!"

"Oh! Take us too!" Audelia says to Erasmus, and Virenda nods quickly along with her.

"No one is going to LeBeaux's without me!" I shout playfully. "Before we do venture there, you're each going to try *my* gumbo. Or perhaps I'll cook up a pot and we can bring it with us." I'm sure Hunter will be absolutely thrilled to see me anyway.

Glancing at us all, Seven replies, "It's a date!"

Happily, we all continue our feast. Until it hits me. No one's done a celebratory toast yet. I stand. Raising my glass, I salute them all. Each one pauses their meal to join in lifting their cups.

"We are not bonded by the blood that runs in our veins," I begin, "but by the blood that runs through the body of this dinner and all others we enjoy together." With my wine glass in hand, I gesture to the feast laid before us. "It's been a pleasure opening my home to you. It's also been an honor that you've accepted to live here with me. Fate has a wonderful way of placing us all exactly where we need to be."

Just for fun I raise my glass to the newest jar on my shelf as well. A nice little label card with my cursive handwriting says 'Callinicus' on it.

Since the stalker and Cal are gone, I have felt the return of ease slip back into place. This instant, as my wine glass presses to my lips, a new prickling sensation forms at the base of my skull just above my spine. It can only mean one thing: someone is watching me. While all eyes at the dinner table, including the dinner, are on me, this tingle of awareness is not from any of them. Whenever this happens, danger is typically not far from my doorstep. The window leading out to the vast gardens of my backyard is where my eyes land.

Danger is outside of these household walls. How utterly romantic. Danger is inside them as well. Whatever it may be, whoever it may be, I raise my glass to the window in salute. No one at the table pays any mind to this little gesture. They all are aware that the inner workings of my mind are far from being understood, thus, any little notion that I am mentally unstable goes without notice.

Until this danger reveals itself, I will wait patiently… and enjoy my dinner.

The End
For now.

LORCAN'S GUMBO RECIPE

AKA: The Best Gumbo
(Not LeBeaux's)

All human meat has been substituted.

INGREDIENTS:

1 large pot

1 and ½ cup of oil

1 and ½ cup flour (have more on hand to add to the roux later if not desired thickness)

4-6 Lbs Of chicken (on the bone is best for added flavor)

2 Lbs smoked (or andouille) sausage (can be pork, beed, etc.)

Creole Seasoning

½ tsp cayenne pepper

½ tsp garlic powder

½ tsp onion powder

(add more of these seasonings if needed)

1-2 bay leaves

Salt and pepper to taste

1 tsp thyme, dried

1 tsp basil, dried

3-4 medium onions

2 large bell peppers

½ bunch of parsley without the stems

5-6 celery stalks

Chicken bouillon to taste

DIRECTIONS:

Chop all vegetables.

Fill a 12 quart pot ½ of the way full with water. Put the water to boil.

Heat up oil in a cast iron skillet (medium high).

When the oil is hot, add the flour. Turn the burner down to medium. Stir constantly (with a wooden spoon for best results). Keep on medium. This process can take quite a long time. It can take 45 minutes to make a roux. The time can vary depending on your stove. Make sure to stir constantly so you don't burn your roux!

When the roux is dark enough (the color of chocolate), add in some of the chopped onions and bell peppers. Keep stirring. When roux is the desired color (dark chocolate, almost black), add to boiling water (Make sure the water is boiling or the roux will separate!). If you see a lot of little black specks, that means you burned your roux, and you must start over. (A few specks is normal... a lot is not!)

Also, if you decide to "taste test" at this point, just know that it will not taste good at all! It will taste very bitter (and sort of like burned coffee), but don't worry... nothing is wrong. It doesn't get flavor until you add in all the other ingredients.

Add in the rest of the vegetables.

While that cooks, chop and then brown sausage in a pan. Once sausage is brown, add to the pot.

While that cooks, cut up chicken breasts into cubes and season with Tony's seasoning and the rest of the seasonings. (If using chicken legs on the bone, remove the skin before seasoning.) Add to the pot.

Cook for another 30 minutes – 1 hour (make sure chicken is done).

Season with chicken bouillon (about ¼ or 1/3 cup of chicken bouillon, depending on how salty you like it... with 15 minutes of cooking time left.

Serve over rice.

This recipe can be halved. It makes about 20 servings.

COMING SOON

The House of Death
The Darkness

S.B. De'Vile

ACKNOWLEDGMENTS

Everyone wants a hero but without a good villain, what's the point?. What started out as just an idea for a morally gray character, turned into something so much more. Lorcan popped into my head one day and threatened to turn me into dinner if I didn't tell his tale. So, here we are.

To my husband who listened to every gross and disturbing idea that Lorcan and crew came up with, I love you. Thank you for believing in De'Vile and everything I write. Thank you for the many years of putting up with my chaos.

Ashley. I cannot begin to thank you enough. Thank you so much for allowing your Divine crew to be a part of Lorcan's story and thank you for being the very best friend. The Justice to my Lorcan.

To my wonderful editors William Tate and Tylee. Both of you have helped tremendously to polish up this story. Your keen sense of detail is certainly unmatched. William Tate the talent you have for spotting errors is absolutely unfathomable.

My amazing beta readers Amanda and Ann. Thank you for making sure everything made sense and for catching the things that didn't. Your feedback has really helped this book become reality.

To my cover artist. Thank you for coming along with me on this journey. Your graphics inspired me to make sure my story lived up to the beauty of them.

A special shout out to J.Z. Stone and William Tate for all the advice and help. Just being there for me and being you. It's been a privilege to call you my friends. And also to Crystal and Rose for all the help you've given me throughout this madness.

Many times I abandoned the word document for this story, only to be reeled right back in by some amazing people. This book would not be finished if it wasn't for the unwavering support of my writing community. There's too many people to name within it who inspired and motivated me to keep going, but you know who you are. If you don't think this means you, it probably does. When all seemed lost, you helped me find the way again. I can never thank you all enough.

S.B. De'Vile
September 2024